What Lies Beyond?

What Lies Beyond?

A Collection of True Supernatural Stories

Dr. Brij Mohan

Nine BOOKS

वाणी प्रकाशन

Presents

Nine BOOKS

4695, 21-A, Daryaganj, New Delhi 110 002

— Branch —

Ashok Rajpath, Patna 800 004

Phone : +91 11 23273167 Fax : +91 11 23275710

www.vaniprakashan.in
sales@vaniprakashan.in
vaniprakashan@gmail.com

WHAT LIES BEYOND?

(A Collection of True Supernatural Stories)

by Dr. Brij Mohan

ISBN : 978-93-5229-443-5
Gothic Stories/Stories

First Edition

Price : ₹ 350

Printed at Om Affset, Delhi 110 093

Vani Prakashan's signature motif is created by Artist Maqbool Fida Husain

PREFACE

Does life exist beyond death? If so, what kind of life is it? In what way does it differ from our physical existence here? Such questions had been troubling me since childhood. In order to quench my thirst I studied as many books on the subject as I could lay my hands on, at the library of the Banaras Hindu University. Then I was tempted to write a book on the topic and incorporate my own ideas and experience connected therewith.

Most thinking men realise that the real Ego, the real man, is not the physical body and that there is something within him of a spiritual nature, something in control, something that has character. No one attributes character to the physical body. In other words, the real "I" is the Soul within us. This Soul is clothed with a Body, a spiritual body, a replica of the human body, and that this Soul Body, and the Soul within it, live on after the death of the human body. Persons endowed with the gift of discerning Spirits, usually called mediums, can see these Soul Bodies and be the means of conversation between the living and the so-called dead. Some mediums are so gifted that they can give solidity to the Soul Body so that it can be seen and felt by all. There is a mass of evidence to prove that the Soul and its Body can leave the human body temporarily during life, and can be seen and recognised in the same way as the Spirits of the dead. There are a number of interesting cases in which people have seen their own doubles, that is, seen their Soul Bodies, while out of their human body. During these excursions, the Soul Body remains attached to the physical body through a Cord. The breaking of this cord results in death.

The chief "direct" evidence for survival consists of (1) earth-memories that have been transmitted, via mediums, from surviving souls; (2) cases in which there is purpose beyond death and (3) cases in which personal characteristics were correctly described through mediums. They do give an inkling that the Soul Body is an objective reality. It is primary, more "real" and enduring than the physical body; the latter is merely its temporary "condensation" the means by which it interacts with the physical world. If a man can leave his physical body temporarily and continue to exist as a self-conscious being, the fact would provide a strong presumption that eventually, when he comes to leave his physical body permanently, i.e., to die, he will then also continue to exist as a self-conscious being in that second body. A number of experiments indicate, that, in addition to our physical body, we possess another body of the same shape, composed of a sort of etheric or semi-fluid substance-which has given rise to the supposition that it is composed of matter of a different degree of density, or solidity, than the matter we know. The nature of this 'etheric' body is now known; and many experiments have been conducted in an attempt to detach it from the physical body, and with some success. It is presumed that this body survives the shock of death and that it is the seat of consciousness.

It is probably no exaggeration to say that we know less about the nature of man than about the solar system. The primary need is for an intensification and extension of research into the nature of man himself, and all other branches of research should stem only from within the limits of knowledge thus acquired. It throws valuable light on what we really are, in contra-distinction to what common-sense urges us to believe that we are. It also clarifies our situation in the Universe by showing that selfhood is not an ephemeral product of the brain but is linked with the core of Reality. To realise these things is the first step towards bringing life and immortality to light. A careful and honest enquiry into psychic phenomena will yield often richer treasures for the well-being of man than physics, chemistry and biology have given them, vast though those treasures are.

Dr. Brij Mohan

The contribution of Sh. Rajnish Kumar, working as Copy Writer in Information & Public Relation Department, Haryana and Sh. Mukesh Mehta, working as Junior Scale Stenographer in Haryana Civil Secretariat in publication of this book is praiseworthy.

Krishna Mohan

CONTENTS

PART-I : Direct Phenomena

PART-IV : Epilogue

PART–I
Direct Phenomena

INTRODUCTION

Two currents of ideas are running in our society these days. If you were to say that (in the epic Ramayan), Ravan took Sita by the air-route, the conservative would at once corroborate your statement as cent per cent truth. They would say, "after all, there used to be airplanes and flying cots during those days as well. Otherwise, how could such things be mentioned in our ancient books?" On the other hand, the newly educated men would at once remark, "This is all fantasy. There were no machines during those days. The machine is a gift of modern science."

But there is a via media between these two extreme courses. We do not say all that is mentioned in our old book is gospel truth. At the same time it would be foolish to under rate all that is given therein as errant nonsense. When people told us that the ancient sages (called rishis) in India, could communicate with each other, thousands of kilometres apart, the younger generation would make fun of it. But today, we find the phenomena of telepathy and television as realities before our eyes. Science is advancing rapidly. The day-dreams of yesterday become realities today. Could anybody think of the talkie and radio about a century back? When we read in old novels about buildings which could open only on subtle devices being applied, we would laugh them away. But today we find in garrages which open automatically when the motor-car approaches near them. Taps have been established at many places which are such that if you take a glass near them they would eject water or some other liquid.

We are intelligent and rational beings. We can test almost everything on the touchstone of our rational faculty. We should consider only those things impossible which are ostensibly proved as such. It is not wise to declare that everything contained in our ancient books is fantastic and impossible.

Gather together a few young boys and begin narrating ghost stories. You will find that at least one or two of them would unhesitatingly declare that all talk of ghosts can't be hypocrisy or sheer nonsense. There may be one or two who will say that something ominous is going to follow.

But if you were to tell the same set of youth that you are going to tell them tales concerning spirits and the reincarnation, they will begin to listen with great credibility. The mere substitution of the word, 'spirit' for 'ghosts' will enhance the respectability of a story.

And there is a reason for it. There is definite fraud in many ghost stories. Besides, quite a few events of this kind are a result of hallucination. If you were to collect ten ghost stories, it is possible that a majority of them may be based either on fraud or on delusion. There will be just one or two which may be called genuine events. That is why the more careful set of people observe extraordinary precaution in dealing with such stories. Hence, it becomes difficult to give credence even to true stories.

Once the following advertisement appeared in newspapers:

'I have a cottage at a distance of about 10 kilometres from Lahore city. It has been lying vacant for years. Nobody buys or takes it on rent. Once or twice it was taken on rent by certain persons. They slept in it for the night. But the next morning they were found lying unconscious on some road or in some turret nearby. It is said, that the cottage is haunted.

'Whoever solves this mystery, will be given a cash reward of Rs. 5,000/-'

Shri Villa.

The advertiser was a wealthy Marwari of Lahore.

The advertisement was read by many people. A certain youth was unemployed. He had only one sister who was a patient of tuberculosis. His parents were dead and he had no brother. And he had no money to get his sister treated. He began to think on the following lines :

"Let me try my luck. If I win, I will get Rs. 5,000 and with the amount I could get my sister treated. And if I die in the venture, there is nobody to bemoan my loss. My only sister is on the threshold of death. Who else is there to weep for me?"

The youngman met the Marwari and told him of his decision. The latter took him in his car to the cottage. It was a very big cottage with a central hall and big rooms all around. There was a lawn before the cottage and a huge garden behind. There was a hut at the end of the garden and a road beyond. A gardener lived in the hut and looked after the cottage and the garden.

The Marwari called the gardener and told him that the youngman would stay in the cottage that night. The youngman put several searching questions to the gardener. The information that he gathered therefrom was that the gardener worked in the garden during the day. Sometimes he cleaned the cottage. But at night he dare not to go near the cottage. If ever he had to go out during the night, he would use the hind road.

The youngman took a round of the garden. At one place he found something glittering on the ground. He picked it up and it was a needle of a gramophone record. He did not pay much attention to it.

The Marwari brought the young man to his home. The two ate together and then took rest. At night, before starting for his errant, he took a pistol from the Marwari and loaded it with three cartridges. He took three more cartridges with him and put them in his pocket. And then the two started. The Marwari took him to the cottage and left him there. The youngman placed a chair in the hall and sat in it. He had already closed the doors of all the rooms around. A lamp was glowing in the hall. He decided to pass the entire night that way.

The clock struck one. All of a sudden, the young man began to hear somebody laughing boisterously below the floor of the hall. The laughter was diabolical, as if some demon was laughing. The young man went on listening without moving from his seat.

In a couple of minutes the laughter subsided and silence began to reign supreme. Hardly had a few more minutes elapsed, when he heard somebody crying loudly from over the roof of the hall. It appeared as if somebody was torturing a woman and the latter was crying out of helplessness.

The young man did not lose courage. Nor did he budge from his chair. There was silence for a few minutes. And then. lo! A drop of some liquid fell from a girder of the ceiling. He looked at it intently. The drop had fallen very near the chair and appeared to be that of blood. The youngman shifted his chair a few inches. A few more drops fell near each other within the next few minutes.

The young man was of undaunted courage. He sat motionless. And lo! He found a human skull entering the room through the aperture of the drain in a corner of the hall. The skull went on crawling. When it reached his chair, he took courage and gave it a hit with his leg. The skull was thrown away several feet and from underneath it emerged a rat!

This incidence gave the youth fresh courage for it gave him an inkling that the whole affair was man-managed and by no means supernatural.

He again sat in the chair. A few minutes later a roll of paper fell down near his chair. He did not touch it, for, who knows, there might be a bomb in it! Some kind of smoke was coming out of the roll of paper. When the smoke entered the nose and ears of the man, he became unconscious. He could not say how long he remained in that condition. When he came to, he was still sitting in the chair.

A few minutes elapsed. A bolt of one of the doors opened automatically, and a black figure entered the hall. The figure that entered, had wrapped itself all around with a black covering. Only there was a screen before the two eyes.

The figure began to advance towards the young man. The latter took courage to bring out his pistol and shot at the figure. It touched his body, but to no purpose. The figure laughed with comtempt and again stepped towards the young man. The latter left the chair and began moving away from the black figure. The figure was moving towards the young man, but in such a way as to allow him a passage out through the open door. It was evident that the black figure did not want to hurt him, but wanted him to go out of the hall in sheer terror. The young man fired the remaining two bullets on the figure but still there was no result.

Even then the young man did not lose heart. He took out an extra bullet from his pocket, loaded the pistol and aimed it at the figure. He was on the point of firing when the black figure raised his hands and cried out,'For heaven's sake, do not fire.'

The young man got back his lost courage. He stepped forward, knocked down the black figure on the ground and sat down on his chest. He lifted the black veil from his face and to his bewilderment, recognised the gardener behind the black covering.

The young man released the gardener and asked him what the matter was. The gardener said he would tell him the whole truth on a definite promise that lie would not be fired from the job. On getting the assurance, he narrated the entire story.

There was another cottage near this cottage, owned by another wealthy man, Ram Prakash. The latter wanted to buy the cottage. He thought that if it could somehow be proved that the cottage was haunted, he could purchase it at a throw-away price. So, he bribed the gardener into his confidence, and the two planned together.

When the gardener was told that someone was expected to pass the night in the cottage, he would get things ready. Ram Prakash had given him his gramophone. Along with it, lie gave him two records: one of laughter, the other of sobs and cries. There was a basement in the cottage, with a trap door. First of all, the gardener would take his gramophone to the basement and play the record of laughter. If this failed, he would take it to the roof of the building and play on the other record.

There were iron girders in the ceiling of the hall. The ceiling of the hall was a few feet higher than that of the rooms. There were several ventilators in the walls of the hall, of which one was just in front of a girder. Edges protruded on both sides of girders. The gardener took a glass tube and closed one end of it with cotton. He filled the tube with red water and placed a big piece of straw in it. The other end of the straw came out of the ventilator on the roof of one of the rooms. The gardener would push the straw into the tube. This would push the red water and drops would fall inside the hall from behind the edge of the girder. This was the strategy.

The gardener had several lines of attack. He had preserved a human skull. He would place a rat at the opening of the aperture of the drain outside the hall, cover it with the skull and give it a push. Naturally, when the rat would move, the skull moved along with it.

The gardener made a very small aperture in the door leading to one of the rooms and pushed a wire into it. He tied the wire to the bolt of the door. Thus, he could open the door from the room simply by pulling the wire, without entering the hall. First, he would put some strong intoxicating powder in a roll of paper and throw it into the hall from one of the ventilators. When the young man became unconscious through the influence of the powder he entered the hall, took out the pistol from his pocket and replaced the cartridges by fake ones. Had he known that he had more cartridges in the pocket, he would replace them too. So, he remained unaffected by the fake cartridges. Had the young man fired from the extra cartridges, it would be enough to kill the gardener.

The rest of the matter was clear.

Next morning the young man took the gardener to the Marwari. He said to him, 'This gardener is a fake ghost'. The real ghost is Ram Prakash, the owner of the neighbouring cottage. The Marwari heard the entire story, gave a handsome reward to the young man and employed him in his business.

This event is purely based on fraud. Now we shall take up a case of fear produced by hallucination. This incident is proof positive of the fact that, there is no ghost as powerful as our own mind, and no hobgoblin more dangerous than our own imagination.

This too is a true fact, though the names have been changed as in the above mentioned incident.

This happened in the town of Kushalpur. It was a very big town. It was built in the old style and contained many ruins. Manohar Lal was transferred to this town as Kotwal (The highest Police Officer of the city). Many years back Manohar Lal had come to the town and familiarised himself with its streets and lanes. The day he took over charge, lie mounted a horse and started for a round of the town. Night was falling. The constable in attendance said to him, 'You may survey the entire town, but please do not go to Shyam Lane during the night. It is full of ruins. For a long distance, the lane is lonely and deserted and known to be haunted.'

Manohar Lal was a very undaunted man. He said. "Why behave like cowards. A policemen should not talk like this."

The constable said, "Please do not go into the lane today. First you visit it during the day two or three times, and then you may venture through it during the night."

Manohar Lal said "I am familiar with the lane. On one end of it, lives an old friend of mine, Ram Das. If you are so much afraid, you may reach the other end of the street by the other way and meet me. I am going through the street."

The constable felt helpless. The Kotwal st.rted on horse-back. He entered the Shyam Lane. It was really desolate. There were only one or two houses in the very beginning. The rest were all in the ruins. He crossed the entire lane and reached the end, where he met the constable. He said to the latter, "Why are you so afraid? There is nothing the matter with the lane. Take this horse. I will go back on foot."

The constable entreated him not to go through the lane again that night. He said the Kotwal could come to the street in daylight the next day. But the Kotwal did not pay any attention to it. He started back on foot. He held a sword in the scabbard.

The Kotwal had hardly crossed one fourth of the lane when it appeared to him that a white sheet was lying on the ground. He did not see any sheet on his way when he was crossing the lane for the first time. So, he became to feel embarrassed. He bent down to pick up the sheet. His hand touched the ground. There was no sheet.

The Kotwal was flabbergasted. He thought it was just a delusion. The lane was very narrow and was pitched dark all around. He advanced a few more paces forward when he found a woman with white clothes on, standing in the middle of the street. He was amazed at the presence of the woman. He asked her who she was. There was no answer. He repeated his query but again there was no reply. He half suspected, this too may be a hallucination. He stretched his hand to touch the woman. His hand touched a heap of leaves which made rattling sound. There was no woman!

The Kotwal found out that he had got back his lost courage. He proceeded a little further when he found an ox standing in the middle of the lane. This was the first time when he really began to half-believe in the existence of the ghosts. He took out his sword and attacked the ox. The sword moved in the air, as there was no ox nearby. The Kotwal had heard it and said that ghosts were afraid of the iron. He found this superstition confirmed as the ox had vanished at the sight of the sword.

The Kotwal was losing courage. He had crossed almost half the street. So, there was not going back. His mind began to ramble. He thought, "If somehow I could call at the house of my old friend, Ram Das. He proceeded very cautiously, measuring each step. He found that he was just in front of the house. He knocked at the door . Somebody answered from the window and questioned him who he was. He replied and gave his name.

Ram Das : Hello, Manohar Lal! When did you arrive, and how do I find you here at dead of night?

Manohar Lal : I have taken over the charge of the town today as Kotwal. Open the door I will tell you all of the story.

Ram Das came down, opened the door, let the Kotwal in and seated him in his sitting room. The Kotwal narrated to him the whole episode and concluded saying " After seeing the ox, I began to see ghost all around. Somehow I have escaped death and came to you."

Ram Das said to him, "Manohar Lal. You might have seen many types of ghosts, but not like this type."

So saying, Ram Das changed his appearance. His body expended by 14m and ultimately it filled the entire room. From his mouth came out ferocious teeth. His hands were replaced by claws. His feet were turned towards the back. His face became so I terrible as to outbeat the face of demons.

On seeing this sight, Manohar Lal went into a swoon. When lie came to his senses, he found himself lying in the same street! He had not crossed the lane, nor did he go to the house of Ram Das. It was all his imagination!

The Kotwal was in a pitiable state of mind. He would stand up and again fall down. Dreadful figures appeared on all sides. He fought to himself, 'Let me take up courage once and cross the entire street.'

He stood up and ran hard. He found himself at the outer end of the street. There was a betel seller's shop just in front of the street. He reached the shop and paused to take some rest. The shop-keeper gave him a seat. Manohar Lal narrated to him the entire story: white sheet, woman in white, ox and the imaginary conversations with Ram Das etc.

On hearing the narration, the shopkeeper said, "Mr Kotwal, you might have seen many ghosts, but not the one I can show you." So saying he enlarged his body. In a moment it became even more terrible than the body of Ram Das had been. The Kotwal again fell down unconscious. When he awoke, he was lying in the same street.

The Kotwal was thinking on the following lines, "Am I destined to die like this? A fearless man like me, to be afraid of ghosts. It is absurd!

No, I will make one more attempt and stop only at my house.'

He stood up, ran hard and reached his house. He knocked at the door. All the inmates were asleep except the maid. She served food to him. The Kotwal began taking food. At the same time he began narrating the entire story to the maid. He talked of everything including the sheet, the woman, the ox, the imaginary meeting with Ram Das, and in the end, the incident with the shopkeeper.

Hearing the story, the maid said. "Sir, You may have seen ghosts and ghosts, but you could not have seen a witch like this.

So saying, the maid loosened her hair, and transformed herself into such a hideous shape that she became almost a hobgoblin. Her body became enormous, big front teeth bulged out and her hands touched the ceiling. The Kotwal again went into a swoon, When he opened his eyes, he was lying in the same street.

The Kotwal passed the night in the lane. Next morning, search parties were sent to find him. His kinsmen went into the same street with his family men. They found him lying in the middle of the street. They called aloud to him. The Kotwal did not open his eyes, but said, "I understand, you are the same fellow again. I will not open my eyes now."

People tried to explain to him that they were his near and dear ones. But the Kotwal did not open his eyes. He was taken to the hospital. There he went on talking in meaningless jargon. He had sometimes lucid intervals when he would talk of the white sheet, the woman in white, the ox etc. People reconstructed the story with such loose joints as these. He could not give any connected account of the whole incident, because within a few days he died, such is the power of delusion!

Neither of the above mentioned incidents is a psychic story. But it does not follow that all such psychic stories are false. In every household you will find a few ghost stories connected otherewith. And almost every one of us has a stock of such incidents in his equipment. Even if we suppose that ninety per cent of such stories are either false or unreal, what about the remaining ten per cent? How does science explain them? Thousands of people in the world have had psychic experiences, if not hundreds of thousands. And these persons do not include among them only illiterate rustics, but many highly educated people. And a large percentage of them consist of people who would test each and every incident before giving it credibility. Can we say that all of them are liars, or suffering from some mental derangement, or under the spell of some severe delusion? Here we shall mention only two short incidents of the kind :

(1) This was reported in 'The Northern India Patrika,' Allahabad, India, on Sept. 5, 1954; the writer is a lady:

During the summer of 1951 we went to Jhansi. A newly married aunt of mine died in the house that we had occupied, only a few months back. The death was due to heart failure. She was very fond of me. As we were almost equal in age, we were more friends than relatives. So, I used to think a good deal about her.

I used to sleep in front of the room in which she breathed her last. The cot of my mother was very near to that of mine. The other inmates of the house slept elsewhere.

Jhansi was pretty cold during those days. Therefore, we kept blankets with us. One night I forgot to keep a blanket on my cot. It was about 2 in the morning that I woke up and began to shiver. I was on the point of asking my mother to give me a blanket. And lo! I found a human figure standing near my bed. I recognised her at once. She was none other than my old familiar aunt. The same smiling face, the same attractive features. Finding me shivering, she said' 'My sister (that is, my mother) has gone down. I am giving you a blanket'. I had not spoken a word, when she gave me a blanket. I stared at her, but immediately she vanished. I looked at the bed of my mother which was vacant. My mother was not there. Later on, I came to know that she had gone down, on hearing my young sister cry, who was sleeping with my grand-mother.

I began to reflect. I was not at all afraid, for I loved my aunt dearly. But I could not make out how it all happened. It cannot be called a hallucination, because I did not know that she had gone down. Besides, the blanket was still there on my bed. I went on cogitating for half an hour and then went to bed.

Since that day I have been convinced that there are certain spirits who are good enough to help those whom they loved in the life gone by.

(2) This incident too is from the same paper. The date has gone into oblivion :

Mr Mukherji was the headmaster of a Government High School.

His only son was very well-behaved and sweet-tongued, but a little morose. He was about 17. He lost his mother during childhood. His father was a deeply religious man. He did not marry again. The boy passed the High School examination with great distinction, but he fell ill soon after.

One night Mr Mukherji was sitting near the cot of his ailing son. There was no lady in the house. Therefore, several of his students used to nurse the boy. They were sitting together. As soon as the clock struck eight, a lady entered the room. She was in saffron. She wore a rosary of beads in her neck and she had mendicant's pair of tongs in her hand. Mr Mukherji and all the boys stood up out of respect for her, but none of them spoke a word. So long as the lady was there everyone remained standing, almost cut in alabaster. Mr Mukherji recognised her as his late wife. She went to the ailing son, touched his forehead with her hand and disappeared. The whole thing hardly took a minute or two. When they came back to their own, they found that the boy had left this ephemeral world and gone to join the greater number. The spirit of the mother had come only to fetch him!

Had Mr. Mukherji alone seen the lady, we could say that this was his delusion. But will it make sense to say that all of his students also suffered from the same hallucination? And a hallucination exactly of the same type for all!

We have given two incidents only by way of illustration.

The remaining stories that we are giving in this book have been taken from newspaper and periodicals. The number of such stories would be legion, but we have collected only those of them that have appeared to us credible. Quite a few of them are such that the spirits that have appeared have left some insignia of theirs as a memento.

In 1966-67 I was in California, with my family. Watching the television set was a daily routine with us. There used to be a weekly programme called 'One Step Beyond.' Such supernatural incidents were televised beautifully in that programme. In the beginning, announcer would say, 'We can tell you when and where these incidents occurred. But how they occurred, we cannot answer. But the incidents are true, there can be no doubt about it.' We have taken few stories therefrom.

We have given the source of the incidents wherever we could. We have given the names and dates of newspapers and periodicals in case of those we have been able to preserve. Whenever we came across the report of such an incident, we could take of a clipping and stitch it in our file. But sometimes we forgot. In such cases we have referred only to the name of the periodical. There are only a few in the case of which we are unable to give even the name of the source.

CHANGED THE ROUTE OF THE SHIP

(Courtesy : One Step Beyond)

A ship was sailing on the sea. Suddenly, the captain observed that she had changed her course. She was drifting several kilometres away from her assigned course. He went to the sailors and asked them under whose order they had changed the course of the ship. The sailors replied that there was an order to that affect on the usual notice-board. The Assistant Captain used to write day-to-day orders with a piece of a chalk on the requisite board. The captain went up to the board to find out what the matter was. There was actually an order to that effect written with the same kind of chalk!

The Captain called the Assistant Captain. The latter denied having written such an order. Even the piece of chalk was missing from his pocket. The Captain sent him back to work, saying that he would deal with him later on. Then he called all the sailors and asked them to stand in a row. He examined the pocket of each one of them. No chalk was found with any of them.

The Captain went to each and every room and closet of the ship to find out if there was someone lurking somewhere. He heard a sound in one of the rooms. He ran towards it. He saw a very lean and thin man running out from a room. He was wearing white clothes. The Captain searched his locker and found the piece of the chalk which was used by the Assistant Captain for writing order. The Captain caught hold of him and asked him, "Who are you and how have you come here?" The man did not give him any answer. The Captain repeated the question again and again, but the man remained silent. The Captain tied him in chains and went to the deck.

The ship had deflected very far from the prescribed course. It reached a place which was excessively cold. Snow-storms used to frequent the place. All of a sudden they heard voices of several people. The Captain saw from the deck that a small boat was sailing at a little distance. It had several people on board. The Captain ordered that a life-boat be hauled. A few sailors rowed the life-boat so that a life-boat be hauled. A few sailors rowed the life-boat to that boat. They saw that the boat was damaged and was unfit for sailing. It was oscillating on the waves.

There were five men on board the boat. They told the captain, when they were brought to the ship, that their boat was damaged in a storm. They had been lying in the boat for several days, hungry and thirsty. One of their companions was dead. All of them were presented before the captain. And lo! The dead man was no other than the one captain had chained below in the ship!

The captain went down and found that the chain was there but the man had gone. There was no doubt, it was the spirit of the dead man that changed the course of the ship, so that his companions may be lifted on board the ship whereby their lives may be saved.

UNCLE'S SPIRIT

(This item appeared in the Daily Leader between 1935 and 1940)

Ram Kishore was a resident of Aligarh, a small town between Delhi and Kanpur in India. An uncle of his lived in the street Bagh Mazaffar Khan Agra.

Once Ram Kishore went to Agra and knocked at the house of his uncle. There was an outer sitting room in the house though it was connected with the main building on the inside. The uncle, who was in the sitting room, opened the door and let him in. There were a table and a few chairs. The following conversation ensued :

Uncle	You have visited us after a very long time today.
Ram	Yes, uncle, I was involved in some kind of botheration.
Uncle	Is everything all right at home?
Ram	By your grace, it is O.K. I would like to consult you on a very important matter.
Uncle	Certainly. What is it about?
Ram	I have been told about certain plot of land situated very near this house, is on sale. I would like to see it.
Uncle	Yes, I know the plot very well. The owner is an acquaintance of mine. If you are keen on it, the deal can be affected.
Ram	If you are free, I would like to have a look at it just now.
Uncle	I am quite free. Let us start.

They both started. The plot was not far from the street. There was a terrace in the middle of the plot. Both of them sat down on it. The uncle told Ram Kishore whose plot it was, how much it would cost approximately etc. They went on talking for a long time. Then they came to the street. When Ram wanted to depart, his uncle asked him if he would not like to see his aunt. Ram said he was in a hurry at the moment. He would come again in the afternoon and then he would meet her, he added.

And so Ram departed. In the afternoon he again went to the house and knocked at the door. His aunt opened the door and led him inside the house. After a little conversation Ram asked her where uncle was.

Aunt : Don't you know it? Your uncle expired a month back.

Ram : was flabbergasted. He said to her, 'What are you talking about? This morning I met him at this very house'.

Aunt : Have you gone crazy? Do you think I would tell lie of this magnitude?

Ram did not know what to say. He went to several neighbours and enquired of them. It was a bitter truth. His uncle was no more. It was about a month back that he breathed his last! All the neighbours had accompanied the pier to the cremation ground. The obsequies were all over.

This event was narrated by Ram Kishore himself in the letter. In the end he wrote thus :

'I am a perfectly normal person. I am fully in my senses. Neither there is a loose screw in my brain, nor do I suffer from hallucinations. There can be absolutely no doubt that I did meet my uncle in flesh and blood. And he was with me for hours. I am under no delusions about it.

THE LATE CALLER
(Courtesy : Northern India Patrika)

S. Roy Chowdhury

It was in 1944. I came home on leave from the battle of Burma. It was nightfall and we just had our dinner. It was unbearable hot. So, I sat in the verandah to see if I could get some random breeze of air.

The clock in the sitting room struck twelve. I saw a dim shadow standing against the gate of the bungalow. As it was dark, it took me some time to recognise the figure. He was my very dear friend Pratap. He and I used to play together in childhood. Also, we studied together and also joined the forces together. It so chanced that we were attached to the same battalion. His house was a short distance from mine. I thought perhaps he had also taken leave and came home. This gave me comfort.

I called aloud, 'Come along, Pratap. Why are you standing there?' But he did not come in. He put his hand on the gate. His lips opened as if he wanted to speak. But it appeared he had lost his power of speech because of something that choked his throat.

In a very faint voice he said, "Sachin, I have to go. Only I had intense longing to see you." It seemed as if his voice was coming from far off. I was astounded as well as annoyed.

I said, 'Hang it all. At least take a cigarette and have a puff. Where is the desperate hurry about going back?'

But Pratap shook his head. In still fainter voice he said, 'No, I have to go.' And then he disappears in the darkness.

I was flabbergasted at the behaviour of Pratap. And then I recollected that he was in full military uniform. He had even a thin helmet on his head. I thought to myself, 'Now I understand. He must have been tired.

Perhaps he came straight from the airport. He could not even change his clothes. So, he came only to give me a glimpse. Even that was enough under the circumstances.'

Next day, I had to go to my village rather early. I came back from there after two days. In the afternoon I thought of spending the evening with Pratap. So I rang him up.

On the phone I, asked for Captain Bose (that is Pratap)

The answer was in a choked voice. 'Pratap Bose, you mean' his elder brother was speaking.

There was silence for a few movements. And then his brother again spoke.

'Captain Roy Chowdhury. Only today we have received the heart-rending news that Pratap expired four days back at eleven at night. Again, a dead silence. And then he put off the speaker.

The day Pratap died, that was the night I had seen the shadow-figure of Pratap.

IN THE JUNGLE OF CHAKIA

(Courtesy : Daily Aaj, 21st March, 1964)

Narayan Dutt Sharma

On the 10th of February, 1964, six friends started on cycles from Varanasi and reached Chakia, a township about 50 kilometres to the south-east. Next day, after seeing the dam of Karmnasa, they started to see the fair at Jagesar. At about 1 'O'clock they started back for Chakia. It was decided to leave the main road, take the route to Am Chua through the forest and return from there to Chakia. (These are all small places nearabout the same locality.)

Two of the party, Ram Lakhan Triphathi and Ram Harsh Pandey, had seen the jungle and were familiar with its dangers. So, naturally the two led the rest on the way. On traversing about a dozen kms., they found they had lost the way.

Tripathi recollected that somewhere in the locality there was a temple of God Hanuman. A red flag used to hang from a tree near that temple. If he could find the flag, he could perhaps hunt out the right track. After roaming about for a long time in the hilly tract, they succeeded in spotting the flag. Reaching the temple, he remembered the way. They all started for Am Chua, but it was dusk before they reached the place.

On the way they did not meet anybody. Tripathi made some sound resembling "Koo-koo." There was a response in similar vein from somewhere near. They all started towards the source of the sound. About 3 kms from Am Chua to the south-west there is a colony of the name Dakhee. It contains just three or four families of cowherds, who live in huts. A little outside the colony they were met by one of the cowherds, Baij Nath by name. It was he who had responded the sound of koo-koo.

Baij Nath took them to his hut, spread some straw on the ground and got some milk. These people were very tired. They took the milk and went into deep slumber.

The weather was cold. One of the six namely, Narayan Putt, got awake. He saw that all the inhabitants of the colony were asleep. He found that besides him, there was just one man who was awake, the guard of the night.

There was a dreadful silence in the atmosphere. All of a sudden, the silence was broken by the groan of someone from not far off. He almost missed a beat. The groan was so painful that he could hardly bear it. And then one more groan, and again one more. We went on hearing one groan after another with intervals of silence.

One of the other friends, Bhajrang Dwivedi, was sleeping near Sharma. He awakened him. On hearing the groan sound, Dwivedi's plight became even worse. But both pretended to be brave for each other. Therefore, without awakening the others and taking a spear, a stick and a dagger, they started towards the sound. They had picked there weapons from a village on the way. They had hardly walked half a kilometre when they found a very pretty damsel lying, face downwards, on the ground and groaning pitiably. She must have been between 18 and 24 in age. They helped her to get up. Her body was badly bruised and wounded and her garments - a cotton saree and a silk blouse-were besmeared with blood.

The girl had not enough strength to talk. Through signs she could explain to them with difficulty that her husband was sleeping in their hut nearby. So, they helped her to move her towards the hut. In a short while they reached the spot. Probably her husband had heard them talking. Therefore, he was awake and standing at the door of the hut when they reached. Seeing his wife in such a plight he was visibly moved. He exclaimed, 'Oh' Kalpana (that was her name)!

All of a sudden, the young man went inside the hut and Baij Nath brought a gun. He put the nozzle of the gun on the breast of Ang Dev, and was on the point of shooting when the lady snatched the gun and threw it away. The next moment she fell down and swooned. They wanted to lift her up, but her husband forbade them to do so. Observing the demeanour of the husband they both thought the safest thing is to slip away from there.

They came back to the hut of Baij Nath, but they could not get another wink of sleep that night.

As soon as the day broke, both of them started to find out the welfare of the damsel. But strange to say, they spent three hours in the forest, searching for the hut, the husband and the wife, and could not find any of them. Frustrated, they came back to Am Chua. Pandey was the only one of their friends there. They narrated the entire story to him. On hearing the account he gave a loud laugh.

People may believe it or not. Still, the episode of the previous night was no dream or illusion. It was a reality. When they were returning from the hut of the lady during the night, the coat of Dev got stuck in the shrubbery and it was torn at places. As Dev did not get it mended, it was still there to bear witness to the facts.

One thing more. It had rained two days previously. Water had collected at several places. On the way back the previous night, a foot of Sharma dropped in such a pool and his trousers got drenched. The torn coat of one and the drenched trousers of the other were stark realities for which Ram Chandra had no answer. Still, he continued making fun of the two. So, they had the guts to narrate the story to the other three friends.

When the two could narrat the event to Baij Nath, he narrated exactly the same incident to others several times before. But now, when he hears the groans, he takes no notice of them. Two aged persons, Saryu and Matru, corroborated the story. Matru showed them his own son who had gone after the groaning sound, and lost his head the same night. He had not become normal to this day.

There is a village Jamsotte about 18 kms from Chakia on the road Chakia-Naugarh and about one km. to the east off the road. When they reached that village some inhabitants of locality were collected and told about the incident. Several of them told them the similar thing had occurred to them too. One of the aged persons also told them that similar groans are heard on the 13th night after the full moon every month. Nothing more could be gathered about the episode.

MYSTERY : THAT COULD NOT BE SOLVED

(Courtesy : Northern India Patrika)

T.S. Luthra

They were the last days of September 1947. The repercussions of the partition in the country had yet not subsided when a fresh calamity befell on Ferozepur, border town of Punjab. The rivers Satluj and Beas were in unprecedented spate and the city authorities found the job beyond them. The flood water entered the main part of the town. When the local authorities could not cope with the problem. they ordered the town to be vacated. The inhabitants too did their utmost but when they found the matter beyond their control, they decided to quit the city. There were just three or four families which were too stubborn to leave. One out of these families was the target of the incident we are going to narrate.

Taking provisions and few odds and ends the family went up to the roof of the house. For three days, the level of the water kept on rising, and in some parts of the town, water stood 2 metres high. The day after, the house began to crumble. There were no provisions left and the next day, all of them began to feel unbearably hungry. Mr. Luther, the head of the family, decided to descend in search of food.

Water had began to subside. Still, it was knee-deep for Mr. Luther on the ground floor. The road was under water. Still, an officer helped him to reach the road. He came across bodies of two young men who had lost their lives in the flood. They were emitting a foul smell. Luther forgot that he too was standing on the death's door and he closed his eyes. He did not know how to swim. But he could cry aloud.

Suddenly, Luther's foot slipped and he lost his balance. He cried but he found as if someone was lifting him from below. He somehow held his own and set his foot on rough ground. He found that his intimate college friend, Satish, had saved his life. Luther looked at him gratefully and in response Satish smiled. Luther asked him about the welfare of his family. Satish told all was well with them. Luther was very pleased and he asked him to accompany home. Satish declined the offer, saying that he would be late, his kinsmen would get worried. So; he had to go immediately. Therefore, Luther went his way and so did Satish. In this turmoil Luther forgot all about the problem of food and he reached the roof of the house where he had left his fımily. He narrated the entire incident to them.

On the seventh day the fury of the Nature ıbated. Luther's family came to the ground floor of the house, and began to think 'What next' They were discussing the matter when the elder brother of Satish reached there. He was terribly upset and almost in tears. On being questioned, he wept and told them that six days ago his brother Satish died of a heart disease. Luther was flabbergasted. He said 'How is it possible? Satish's brother went on saying'How young, how noble, how kind-hearted Satish was! Where will I find such a brother again? He has left his deceitful, emphemeral world for good. The Luther family tried hard to console him.

When he went away the family pestered Luther with questions and counter-questions saying. 'You said, you met him only three days back,' and he saved your life in your presence his brother has told us that he expired six days back. What have you to say to that? Luther said, 'Whatever he might say; this is an absolute truth, that Satish saved my life three days back. Do not doubt either my veracity or my senses. We talked to each other. I was perfectly in my senses when he met me.'

Then Luther went to cogitate, 'How did it all happen? Did his ghost save my life? If that is so, how could he speak? And then, how did he catch hold of me? How is it that he appeared to be a man of flesh and blood?'

For Luther the mystery remained a mystery. He could not find only one answer to it : A friend in need is a friend indeed. Satish did his duty after death.' He could not think of any other solution to the problem.

FATHER SAVES THE SON

(Courtesy : One Step Beyond)

The father and son used to perform in the circus. Both would hang down from a swing. First of all, both of them would show feats on the swings. Then one of them would hang down, head downwards on his swings. The other would hang down, head up, on his swing. Then the latter would take a swing or two, turn somersault and jump to a place directly below the other. The former would catch hold of him with his hands. Even the slightest error would result in the latters' hurling down below and breaking his ribs. It could even end in his death.

One day, the father and the son fell down. The father slapped the son. It hurt the boy. He began bleeding through the mouth. He wiped out the blood, but said, in a voice of anger, 'Papa, today my hands are besmeared with blood. Remember, your hands may slip out of my hands while giving the performance this evening.

Hearing this, the father became mortally afraid. His wife was nearby. She tried to pacify him by saying, 'He is a child, after all. He has said it in a moment of excitement. You know he cannot do such a thing. By the time he goes to the circus, he will forget the whole affair.'

The two reached the circus pavilion. The manager of the circus said, 'Ladies and gentlemen, now, you will witness the most risky game in the world. Two persons, father and son, are co-partners in this game. There is no screen on the ground which can save the falling acrobat. So, please hold your breath while witnessing the game.

Father and son went up to their swings. First, the son took the somersault, after the usual feats, and reached immediately below the father. The father caught hold of his hands. The event was cheered by the audience.

Then the father took the somersault, and reached below the son. The son stretch out his hands to catch hold of the father, but lo! the Father's hands slipped from those of the son, and he fell down about 15 metres below on the ground. He swooned and broke the bones of his hands and feet. At once he was removed to the hospital.

The son saw the horrifying event with bewildered eyes and came down. He thought the blame was entirely his. He left the circus the very next day. The proprietor of the circus came to him personally and tried hard to dissuade him from the idea, but he refused point blank to serve in the circus any more.

Weeks passed by. The father was in the hospital and he was given the best possible treatment. He hovered between life and death. The son used to loiter like a man off his head. But now he found financial stringency staring him in the face. The income was dwindling, but the expenses increased with the treatment of his father. He was thinking as to how to find a way out of the difficulty. His friends advised him to join the circus again. They were sure the proprietor there would welcome him back. But now there was another difficulty in his way, he had lost practice and so was out of form. He doubted if he would ever again be able to show the game.

The son wanted to test his capability. One day he went to the circus with a friend of his during the day. The hall was vacant. He left his friend outside. He entered the hall and went up the swing. He took a few swings and then muttered to himself, Father. Today, it is your turn, you can take revenge if you like, by slipping off my hands. Saying this, he turned a somersault and jumped to the other swing, as he used to do. And then, to his amazement he found that the two hands stretched down from the other swing and caught hold of him. He was saved from falling down.

On hearing the boy talk to somebody, the friend who was outside, came inside the hall and asked him whom he was talking to. The son replied, 'Didn't you see? Papa came here just now. He caught hold of me and saved me from falling down.' His friend said, 'It seems you are drunk. The boy said, 'I am not. What I have told you is true, cent per cent., The friend observed that the other swing was still moving to and fro. So, he had to believe that the boy had been swinging at it. Thereafter he must had jumped to the other swing from which he was hanging now. Still, he could hardly admit that his father, who could not move from the bed, would be able to come and help the son in the circus hall!

The boy came down from the swing and the two reached the hospital. They found the bed of the father vacant. The son apprehended that the worst had happened. He asked a nurse where his father was. She told him that he has gone below for a check-up.

Son : How is he now?

Nurse : His brain is now all right. But he cannot move his hands and feet. Still, something miraculous happened a short time back. He lifted his hands as if to help someone, though for the last several weeks he has not been able to move them at all.

The father was brought back to the bed. The son clunged to him and said, 'Papa! His voice was choked with emotion. The eyes of the father were too full of tears to be able to speak!

A HEADLESS GHOST

(Courtesy : Northern India Patrika)

R.M.B.

I had to go to the house of Uncle Elwin, for which there were two routes. The longer route took only a few minutes more, but it was a beautiful way. But my grandmother insisted that I must take the shorter course. Perhaps she had heard about the headless ghost and she also knew that the way passed through the crossing of illusions.

I could not imagine that by taking the shorter route, I was inviting trouble. I was going to Uncle Elwin's house for the first time. My grandmother drew a chart on paper and explained the entire route to me. She had also told me of the sign-boards I would cross. She positively asked me not to follow the broad road near the new colony. She also told me that at one end of the road there was a crossing where almost everybody lost the way. But she did not tell me that there was an inexplicable mystery behind the crossing. She thought I was just an urchin and forgot that I was now crossing fifteen.

Hardly ten minutes had elapsed after the last train left the station. Still, the big expanses in front of the station presented a desolate appearance. Not to speak of human beings, even a bird did not chirp at that time. Ordinarily, it is full of porters, carriages and tourists. I slowly came out of the railway station and began to ponder as to which of the two routes ahead to follow. A porter came running to tell me there would be no train for four hours, there was no likelihood of getting a conveyance. I did not care for conveyance either, as I had only a light case with me which I could carry easily upto the house of my uncle. The sky was clear and the full moon shown in her brilliance. The marble mansions on the road looked simply splendid on this background. I could not resist the temptation of going by the shorter route because of such a beautiful spectacle. But little could I imagine that I would have the most dreadful experience of my life on that route something which would make my hair stand on end. And not unlikely that I may receive a thrashing too!

The forecast of my grandmother was quite correct. I did not notice the first turning on the right and being taken in by the splendour of the magnificent buildings. I reached the crossing of illusions. I looked at the watch. It was half past ten. I realised that I had lost the way. Otherwise, I should have reached the house of my uncle twenty minutes earlier. Had I turned right, on the very first turning, I would arrive just in front of my uncle's house. From the broad road I turned to the left but that led me to a blind alley. I was anxious to reach my uncle's house by 11, otherwise, he would get worried and send out servants to hunt me out. And I did not want such a furore should be created for me. Luckily for me, a vacant tonga (horse carriage) was coming from the opposite direction. I engaged it and explained my place of destination to him in as clear language as possible. He was familiar with every inch of ground in that locality. So, he said he would take the shortest route to my uncle's house.

At the next crossing, the driver stopped and began to think. I asked him why he was wasting time. He admitted, he too had lost the way. He came back to the same deceitful crossing. He thought he would meet somebody on the road who would be able to direct him.

At once his face brightened as if he remembered something wonderful. He ran towards the first building on the turning on the right. The house was about 8 or 10 metres from the main road. There was no light on either the ground floor of the building or on the first. And no human or animal was anywhere visible inside the compound. I wondered from whom he would ask the way. He went up the staircase, had a look at the verandah and came back smiling and said to me, "There is some indistinct figure in the verandah upstairs, Sir, This was very likely as the mansion nearby was fully lit and everything in the vicinity was perfectly visible. The driver said to me, "When I reached the verandah, I found a person walking up and down in the verandah with a military gait. He might be waiting for the 'daily messenger.'

Come, let us ask him the way, lest he goes away on duty. I am not sure if he can follow Hindi very well. So, you better talk to him in English.'

Not a bad idea! I thought the gentleman was a God-sent. But even then something stopped me from going upstairs. I was hearing the heavy footsteps of the man. He was not quite visible from the place from where I was standing. So, I descended a couple of steps below. Now I could easily see the shadow figure walking to and fro in the verandah. I was standing in moonlight. So, anybody who was in the verandah could see me easily. Hence, I thought he would himself talk to me when he would observe me. But he paid absolutely no heed to me. Then I called aloud to the driver to tell the gentleman that I wanted to talk to him. I thought now lie would surely take notice of me, but he remained as indifferent to me as before. He was walking very near the wall. So, I could see his body only from the shoulder to the knees. His head was hidden behind the arches of the verandah. Therefore, I could not see it.

Having failed to attract the attention of the gentleman, I asked the driver to ascend up to the uppermost stair and talk to the man. He went to the uppermost stair and told the person walking that a certain gentleman who was down below, wanted to talk to him. And then he waited for the answer. When he addressed the gentleman, the latter was at the other end of the verandah. He did not say a word and came back to the driver. When he had crossed half the verandah, the driver ran back and with panting breath, told me that the gentleman was headless. On hearing this, I began to tremble for I too had not seen his head. I covered my fear and said to the driver, 'His head is not visible because of the dense shadow of the arches of the verandah. That is all. He was terribly afraid. Still, my words put some courage in him and he became willing to take another chance. I went behind him to give him moral support. This time, he stood several stairs below the verandah. Only his head was above the level of the floor of the verandah.

The driver cast a glance at the person and then beckoned to me. I went near him. When that headless man approached us, my heart almost missed a beat. He was really headless. When he was several paces away from us, the driver repeated his words. He was far to much afraid to look at him. On the other hand he, was intently looking at me, lest I may run down the staircase. I was standing like a statue and reflecting over the words of my grandmother as well as the deceitful crossing. It appeared as if my feet were glued to the ground. That fellow came straight to the driver, and without saying a word, gave him a kick. The driver raised his hand in self-defence and fell down on the stair. The kick hurt him on the left palm. He came hurtling into my arms. We ran in terror. When we reached the street, in the light I saw a red sign on his left palm as a result of the kick.

This time I could have a close look at the shadow figure. There was absolutely no doubt that he had no head I helped the driver to the carriage. I too had received a terrific shock that I did not talk to him on the way or, nor even glanced at him. We sat down on the tonga, stupefied and stunned. Our hearts were palpitating heavily

How fortunate ! As soon as we sat down on the tonga, we saw the daily messenger on his beat. We seated him on the tonga and he showed the way. He told us that the headless man walked from 10.30 to midnight every day, in the verandah like this. He mentioned to us that about half a dozen persons have received his kick so far in the same fashion. He was surprised at our ignorance as the phenomena was well known in that neighbourhood. Now I understood why my grandmother forbade me to take the route.

THE LADY-LOVER OF A BOY

(Courtesy, Northern India Patrika)

Narendra N. Banerji

This happened 20 years ago. Mr. Sudershan Banerji worked with a landlord of Rajshahi. He used to live in a rented house with his wife and eight years old younger son Vibhu. Vibhu was a very handsome and healthy boy. He was studying at local school. His elder brother Shameer was a judicial officer at Calcutta.

Vibhu used to sleep alone in a room. One night, when all were asleep, Vibhu heard the tinkling sound of some silver coins falling on the ground. This awakened him. It was midnight. He did not pay much attention to it and went to sleep again. Next morning, when his mother swept the floor of the room, she found several silver rupees on the ground. He called her husband, Sudershan showed him the coins. The latter could not make out as to where the coins came from. He asked Vibhu, the latter could only tell him that during the night, he once heard the tinkling sound of coins.

Since that day, this became a frequent occurrence. The inmates of the house tried their utmost to find out the source of the coins, but failed.

Sudarshan kept the secret to himself. Nevertheless, after a short while, it became a common topic in the neighbourhood. A stream of curious visitors poured in to find out the truth. But as the number of visitors increased, the shower of the coins decreased.

Sudarshan gave a detailed description of the event in a letter to his elder son, Shameer, who was called to Raj Shahi. A week later Shameer reached Raj Shahi in the afternoon. His mother took him to the room of Vibhu immediately. Shameer listened to the story patiently and then gave a loud laugh. He said all this talk was bunkum. Hardly had he uttered these words, when the table on which his watch was lying, turned turtle, as if overturned by some invisible power. The watch was broken to pieces.

All the inmates of the house were stunned. Shameer left the room and searched every nook and comer of the house to find out as to who was behind the mischief. But to no purpose. The incident occurred in his presence. Still, he was unwilling to admit that there was any supernatural hand behind it.

That night, Shameer slept in the same room with Vibhu. Till late they went on talking about the mysterious coins. But Vibhu could not add anything to the, information he had already given. No coin fell that night. Next day Shameer started for Calcutta.

Nothing happened for about a fortnight. Vibhu used to get up late. But one day he got up early. He went straight to his father and told him that he had witnessed a strange scene during the night.

Father : What is it?

Son : Something very strange!

Vibhu was hesitating to tell him the truth. The father got annoyed. He said, 'How silly! Don't tease me in the morning. Go and do your work.'

Vibhu : Last night, at what time I cannot say, I saw a very pretty and gaily dressed damsel sitting on my cot and staring at me. First of all, I got scared. But as long as she remained, she did not utter a word, nor did me any harm.'

Sudarshan thought the boy had seen something in his dream. So he did not attach any importance to the matter. But since then Vibhu began to see the same lady every night.

A few days latter the parents of the boy began to realise that he was languishing, thought apparently he was suffering from any ailment. They consulted a physician. The latter gave him a thorough check-up but could not find any trace of a disease. Even then he prescribed some medicines. The boy took the medicines as directed for about a month. But still, his health went on falling. Alarmed, the parents consulted a doctor of a repute. For five weeks the boy was under the treatment of the doctor. But still, no result. He went on losing health, till he was reduced to a skeleton.

The parents were at their wit's end and did not know what to do. The mother of the boy suggested that probably the boy was suffering from some supernatural malady, and had absolutely no physical ailment. The boy was perhaps under the influence of some evil spirit. The doctor would be of no avail in such case. She suggested that some astrologer be consulted.

Sudarshan had no faith in astrologers. Still, he went to an old astrologer and narrated the entire story to him. The astrologer thought over the matter and said, "The damsel that comes to your boy is a fairy. Your boy is extremely handsome."

The fairy had taken a fancy for him. Since she cannot satisfy her desire, she is determined to take his life. I have cured several victims of this type. But the condition of your son has become serious. You are rather late. Now your son is completely under the clutches of the fairy and it is extremely difficult to extricate him. Why did you not come to me before? Try not to lose heart. I will do my best.

The astrologer told Sudarshan that he would come to his house next Saturday. After certain rituals he would prepare a talisman which should be tied to the right arm of the boy with a red piece of thread.

The fairy came to Vibhu every night as usual. But now her stay on the bed of the boy was prolonged and she would go on sobbing all the time.

The astrologer came to the house on the appointed day. He sent Vibhu to take a bath in the river. He went on performing rituals in meantime. No one but Vibhu was allowed inside the room. After some time, the astrologer came out of the room and said, I have found out the whole truth from the fairy on the night of 'full moon, this boy was dressed in very fine attire and he was taking walk in the garden with his father under the pium tree. His face was shining in the moonlight and he appeared very attractive. The fairy was on the tree. She fell in love with the boy. She is not prepared to part with him. Still, I will try'.

Sudarshan believed in each and every word of what the astrologer said. He remembered that he had an invitation to attend a marriage ceremony which was to be held on the night of the full moon. The bridegroom's party told him that they would take him along from his house. For some reason they were delayed. And the father and son were passing the time in the garden.

Then the astrologer went on with another round of sacrifice and oblations. In the end, he came out and said,'After all, I have succeeded in satisfying the damsel. She has agreed to leave him alone, on condition that he would never again go under that plum tree'.

The father and son gave their assent. The astrologer put a talisman on the right arm of the boy. Since that day he was never again visited by the fairy. Needless to say, the boy never again went under the plum tree.

RECONSTRUCTION OF A BODY WITH BONES

Ascetic Vigyanashram was born in a Brahmin family of Rai Bareli, a district of Uttar Pradesh in India. He left the household at the early age of 16. For some time he served the Army. Then he became a mendicant. In Uttarakhand, the northernmost region of the province, he met a hermit who introduced him to Yoga.

The ascetic gave the first demonstration of putting life into a skeleton in 1960, in the Agrasen Gymnasium of Kanpur. The performance was witnessed by Director of the gymnasium and a huge mass of the population of the city. The event was reported in newspapers. The person who was rejuvenated from the skeleton, happened to be an inhabitant of Bithoor, a township near Kanpur. He was a Brahmin who was a little off his head. According to swamiji (the ascetic) the cause of his mental derangement was the blazes. What happened to him later on, swamiji did not tell us.

The second demonstration was also held at Kanpur in the presence of local authorities and several doctors. Mr.Kedia was anxious that his son-in-law, who had died recently at Jaipur, should be rejuvenated. But very few of his bones could be procured. Therefore, swamiji was dubious of his success in the matter. Consequently, he sent for another skeleton as well. He thought that if the entire body could not be reconstructed and the soul entered the partial body, it would be an embarrassing position for him. Under such circumstances, he thought, he would put life into the other body. And things happened as he apprehended. The entire body could not be constructed with the first set of bones but the soul entered the partially constructed body. So, swamiji introduced the soul into the other skeleton. The result was that the new man thus evolved lived the life of the son-in-law of Mr.Kedia, but his body as different from that of his former life. That person still lives with the preceptor of swamiji.

Nau Gaon is a village about 32 kms. from Mirzapur. The village is situated on one side of the Ganga, whereas on the other side is the district of Gopigunj in which there is a village Barhinpur. The third demonstration of swamiji took place in that village which was witnessed by the magistrate of the district as well as thousands of inhabitants of the locality.

Swamiji used to frequent the house of Mr. Dularay Lal Pathak who lived in Nau Gaon. Once he came and started usual satsang (mass chanting of hymns). Some youths who were present on the occasion criticised such prayers and rituals cathingly.

Provoked by their remarks swamiji offered to perform his fourth demonstration there and then in order to rehabilitate the powers of Hindu Philosophy. Therefore, he sent for a skeleton. First of all, Mr. Pathak brought just one bone. Swamiji rejected it. Then a skeleton was brought from the cremation ground of Rampur. Swamiji bathed the body and kept it for a day. But the next day, he said that it belonged to a woman. Where would he keep her after rejuvenating the body?

So, a search began for another dead body. Jattoo Lal, an inhabitant of the village, succeeded in bringing the shattered bones of a person who died in Gaura, a village nearby. The swami examined the remains of the body and accepted them. This happened on April 26. It was decided to hold the demonstration between 7 a.m. and 8 a.m. on the 29th April. And swamiji began his ablutions. He went on with his yogic practices throughout the night of the 27th and 28th. On the 29th at dawn, the bones were placed on the sands of the Ganga where swamiji was performing his exercises. Swamiji arranged the bones into shape and covered them with a cloth. Later on, he surrounded the place with thick canvas.

Somehow people began to suspect foul play and began whispering. They thought there was some mystery about the spot. When the matter reached the ears of swamiji he asked them to choose some other place. The body was taken to a spot of their choice and it was again put to shape and covered. For a few minutes swamiji stayed inside the canvas and performed certain rituals. He cut a lemon into two and placed it on the bones. At the same time a cracking sound was issued from the bones. The swami came out, uncovered the curtain, took some rice, chanted some incantations and threw it on the bones. The bones began to show signs of vibrations. And then breathing began, and in a few moments, the body stood up like a perfect human being. He was given a tangerine which he ate. A doctor felt his pulse and said he had high fever. Also, that he would be all right in a couple of days.

The next day, the journalists found that man was perfectly hale and hearty. People who saw the event before their own eyes, refuse to believe it even now. They are anxious to know, what next? Swamiji has put certain restrictions on his interviews with people.

He says for the present he would keep him with himself. Then he would send him to his preceptor in Uttarakhand.

THE ILLUSION OF A DARK NIGHT

It was 1935. Some youths of Rajkot established an institution known as, 'The Theater Reform Union'. They decided first of all to enact the play Poisonous Snake'. They began their rehearsal in an old house near Sanghavi circus. All the artists were honorary. They would meet even their refreshment expenses from their own pockets. Those were the days of the Ramzan festival of muslims. So, muslim hotels were kept open all night. After rehearsal these young men would return on their cycles and take some refreshment on the way at some hotel. Some times they would finish their rehearsal very late in the night. Even then they would not change their routine.

It was such a night as this. The time was about 1.30 a.m. or so. Three of the young men were returning on their bicycles after taking some snacks at a restaurant. They were Bulabhai, Umarbhai and Hakoobhai. There was a bridge on the way which connected the two parts of the city. They had hardly reached the place when they found a woman wailing at the entrance of house. They were very surprised, and got down from their cycles. The woman spoke to them in a heart-rending voice:

'My only son is ill. There is no male in the house. Can you do me the favour of calling a doctor?

Umarbhai at once started to call a doctor. The other two stayed with the woman. A couple of minutes later, the lady said to them;

'It was long back that I came down. The baby must be crying in the cradle. It would be kind of you if you come with me upstairs as there is nobody near the baby.'

Bulabhai accompanied the lady upstairs whereas Hakoobhai stayed behind to guard the cycles. The lady and Bulabhai went into the house through the door. They crossed the staircase and reached the upper storey. There was a cradle inside a room in which a baby was sleeping.

The lady asked Bulabhai to see if the baby', fever had subsided.

Bulabhai proceeded cautiously towards the baby so as not to disturb him in his sleep. He stretched his hand to feel the pulse of the baby.

But, what a miracle! He did not touch any body! His fingers were simply groping in the air. There was no human body around. Bulabhai's palpitation increased. He turned back to see that the lady was standing in the middle of the door. He was at his wit's end. Trembling he said to the lady; 'Why is the body of the baby like this?

The lady replied,'It is bound to be like this, for the baby has been dead these ten years.'

Bulabhai's heart missed a beat. He was stupefied and stunned. He had not the courage to say one word more. He pushed the lady aside and ran down. He did not stop even on reaching the ground floor. Seeing him in this plight, Hakoobhjai asked him what the matter was. But Bulabhai had no time to lose. He went on running until he reached Dharmendra Road. He collided against the lamp-post on the corner and fell unconscious.

Hakoobhai ran after Bulabhai. At the same time Umarbhai reached the spot with a Doctor. The Doctor brought Bulabhai to his senses. The latter opened his eyes. Seeing a small crowd around him he felt reassured.

Bulabhai narrated the story to the doctor. The latter did not give the tale any credence. Almost all of them were of the opinion that they should all go to the house and find out the truth behind the story themselves. On reaching the house they found that there was a big lock on the door of the house through which Bulabhai had entered a short time back with the lady! And what was more, the lock was rusted as if it had not been opened for years.

The Doctor refused to believe that Bulabhai could have entered through the door. He thought the latter was under some delusion, but Hakoobhai bore witness to the fact that it was through that very door that he had entered.

In the mean time hearing the altercation, several neighbours gathered outside the house. They all planned to go to the owner of the house and ask him since when the house had not been opened.

The owner's house stood in a lane nearby. Mr Nagar, the neighbour was awakened and apprised of the situation. He attested to the fact that the house had not been opened for the last ten years. And then he narrated the following story connected with the house :

This happened about ten years back. A widow used to live in the house with her infant as a tenant. All of a sudden, the baby got ill and expired during the course of a single day. This was too much for the lady to bear. She lost her head and one day, she committed suicide.

The widow was seen several times after this tragedy. For the same reason, other tenants of the house vacated it. Since then I have kept the house locked and never opened it again. How, on earth, it is possible, that someone could have entered it?

Bulabhai insisted that he did go inside the house through that very door. Not only that. He left his sandels outside the room in which he saw the baby sleeping in the cradle.

All of them decided to enter the house. Mr Nagar had brought a bunch of keys with him. The specific key was hunted out. It was a job to open that rusted lock; but somehow it was opened. All the persons went into the door and began ascending the staircase. There was dust all round the staircase, but on every step there was a clear imprint of a foot as if someone had very recently trodden thereon. All of them were flabbergasted to see this and had to admit that Bulabhai had actually entered the house through the door and the staircase.

They reached the room in which Bulabhai had seen the baby in the cradle. The pair of sandels were there outside the room all right, but the room was locked from outside! That lock too was opened after some difficulty. Inside the room there were clear imprints of the same foot as the one on the staircase. But the cradle was empty. Nor was there any trace of the woman!

THE GIRL NAMED LAVENDER

There is a hilly wilderness a few kilometres to the north-west of New York through which flows river Ramboo. A pcstmaster used to live in a village on the bank thereof. He was a religious man. On Sunday, he took a class of school children in a church. This is a story about one of the girls who used to come to the class.

On a certain Wednesday, a few clothes were received in the village from a church of New York for distribution among the poor children. As soon as the Post Master rang the bell for the distribution of the clothes, the girl was seen on the premises. She was bare-footed and was wearing clothes which were visibly too short for her body. Clothes were being distributed, but she did not seem to be interested in them.

A shining cloth of the colour lavender came out of bundle. No other child showed any interest in the cloth, but the girl jumped at it and snatched it from the hands of the functionary incharge, and immediately she ran off from the compound.

Since that day the girl did not put on any dress but that. Whether it was morning, noon or evening, whether she was at school, on the plain or on the hills, she was always seen in the same dress. It was the middle of December and the weather was bitingly cold. The Postmaster opened the window for starting his daily routine. The customer who had arrived at the window, were not so anxious to collect their mail as to deliver a sad news to him. They told him that a corpse of a girl who died of cold was found on the road a few kilometres away. The lavender dress she was wearing did not suffice for the shivering cold which had blown that day.

This happened in 1939. About ten years passed. Around 1949 the stories began to circulate about the same girl. And there was no end to them. Strange to say, all these stories originated from the universities of New York and no way were connected with the village where the girl lived.

On a Saturday evening two students of the Hamilton College were going in a car to join a dance in Toksedo Park. They found a girl standing on the road in the valley of River Ramopo. They wanted to give her lift in case she wanted to go in the same direction. The girl assented and sat down in the car. The two boys were fascinated by the simplicity and sweetness of the girl. They asked her to accompany them to the dance. The girl agreed. On reaching the dancing hall, they introduced her to their hosts. The girl told them they could call her Lavender.

After the dance was over, they all returned together. It was exceptionally cold. So, one of the boys gave his overcoat to the girl. The girl led the way to her house. They all reached a delapidated hut. The girl bid them good bye, said they would meet again soon, and entered the hut. When the boys had not gone, the one who had lent her his overcoat, was reminded of it. He thought he could collect it the next day while on his way to university.

The next day the boys reached the hut. An old woman answered their call. When they enquired about the girl Lavender, she said, It seems you are very old friends of hers, for she has been dead ten years now.

The boys protested if, 'We are not enquiring about any such girl. We are enquiring about the girl who met us last evening. We lent her an overcoat which we have come to collect.'

Then the two boys narrated the entire story to the old woman. In the end they added, 'Lavender brought us to this very hut and entered it. She bade us good-bye told us we would meet again soon.'

The woman said, 'This beats me. There is no other girl with the name Lavender in the vicinity. And the girl who lived with me in this hut, died ten years back. Come, I will show you her grave."

The woman took the boys to the graveyard which was not far. She showed them the grave in which the girl was buried.

On the grave was engraved the name of the girl. Also, the overcoat of the boy was lying on the grave, really folded.

THE HAUNTED PLAIN

My uncle invited me to spend the vacation in the hills with him. The journey was long and boring and it took me twenty-four hours. We reached Dehra Doon and in another hop we would be at Mussourie. This part of the journey was so breath taking that we did not notice the passage of time.

The hill people are simple and truthful. They are not cheats like the people of the plains. There are only two things in the hills about which one has to be conscious, one may slip in a waterfall, or, lose the way in a valley. My uncle forewarned me regarding these two things in the very beginning.

There was a panoramic plain near our dwelling. It was so big that it could accommodate two football fields. It was about 35 metres from the highway but there was a valley in between. One look at the plain would assure anybody that it had been cut and trimmed almost immediately before. Its verdure was so fascinating that I could not recall its equal anywhere on the plains. At the first sight we thought the ground had been prepared for some game of the Europeans. We spotted a footway which led from the high road to that lawn. The footway branched off from the road about half a kilometre from our house, and was not in a well-maintaied condition. Still, we thought it would do.

We reached the plains and began taking rounds around it for, we were afraid, it would be forbidden to tread over it.

In the afternoon we had a good look at the lawn. There was not a single stone, brick or even a plant there. The ground was a velvety soft and we conjectured it belonged to some club which was spending a good bit on its maintenance. We could also see that the shade of the lawn was not same throughout. Several shades of the green colour were blended together to give a wonderfully artistic appearance to the plain. We felt like sitting there and watching a beautiful spectacle of nature. We are taken in by the spot. There was a clear line demarcation around the boundary of the lawn. Outside the boundary there were many pebbles and blocks of bricks. Besides, there were a few tall hilly trees too. There were several spots where picnic parties could enjoy themselves.

We stayed on the lawn for about two hours but we did not see any gardener there. There was a stream nearby in which cool, clear water flowed from one part of the valley to the other. But it was not a fall, so there was nothing to be afraid of.

When the sun began to set, we returned home. We were very much satisfied with our achievement of the first day. Now, we became curious to know as to who owned the lawn and whether there was any keeper or guard of the place or not.

It was necessary for us to know all this with a view to ascertain as to what times we could use it uninterruptedly.

I was the only male member of the party. So, naturally, this investigation was entrusted to me. It was only ten minutes' walk from our house to the lawn. Besides, it was at a cosiderable height, compared with the place where I used to see the lawn. So, I could have a good look at the lawn even from my house. I made it a point to stir out every morning at about 6 and roam about the place till 8 a.m. By 8.30 a.m. I would be back and finish my breakfast. There was a church nearby, the bell of which helped me in timing my routine. Even then I did not succeed. This programme went on for one full week, but during this time I could not spot any guard or gardener of the plain. Between breakfast and lunch we could have an outing on the lawn everyday without any hindrance. Between midday and afternoon we were sole monarchs of the plain. Strange as it would appear, the place being so beautiful, still no trotter or even an observer was ever seen on the plain. Even in the evening we could not find any soul stirring these.

We were observing the place from sunrise to sunset, but could not solve the mystery.

Now, when we taxied our brain, a new idea stuck us. We felt sure this lawn was being used as an open dancing hall. The idea took shape in our minds so we decided to stay out till 10 p.m. When we would return at about ten in the evening, we would surely find people gathering on the lawn. We tried this new experiment for another week, still nothing came out but I trained at school never to loose heart. This training had become a part and parcel of my life.

And then came the unforgettable night of the full moon. The moonlight and a cool breeze had added to the charm of the lawn. That night I decided to keep a watch till 11 p.m. but a little after ten a few shadows began moving on the plain. For sometime. I saw nothing but shadows and I could not make out whose shadows they were. I began it shudder at the sight. I was in a dilemma as to whether I should run back home or witness the next scene coming after. In the end I decided to stay on.

Every day added to our courage. We played all our games on the plain. That very afternoon we constructed several miniature houses with blocks of stones, which were intact till then. And now was going to be enacted the last and the most interesting scene of the show.

After shadows I began to see several peculiar figures on the lawn and their numbers went on increasing. They were searching something on the plain. Soon they reached the spot where we constructed miniature houses the same afternoon. And what did I behold? The blocks of stones began jumping in the air of their own accord and falling down outside the boundary of the lawn. Who would believe me? I was wondering whether it was black magic or the miracle of some super natural agency? I thanked God I was too near the lawn.

Otherwise, I do not know what would happen to me. Stones were flying like bits of paper. Those figures stood still with anger in their countenances until the entire lawn was cleared of all odds and ends. And then the figures began to move again. Some of them appeared to be male, others female, but all of them bearing peculiar shapes. Some of them were unusually tall. The mien of such figures was totally different from that of the others. It seemed it was a display of ghosts. I felt like moving towards home, but before starting I had another look at the scene.

Now, they were moving about very swiftly. All of them seemed entangled in something which was not visible to me.

A shiver ran through my body at this last sight. I took the short cut to my house, which was surrounded by tall, shade trees. I looked back and was flabbergasted. Skeletons had taken the place of those figures. And these skeletons were also moving about. I ran fast and stopped only on reaching my bed in the house. I did not have a wink of sleep, but pretended to snore all through lest someone may put me some uncomfortable questions.

The next day I put very searching question to my uncle regarding the lawn. He told me the plain was haunted and carried several tales about it. But one thing was sure. No building could be constructed on the spot so far. Whenever anybody attempted to build something on it, the walls would all be laid flat during the night and the bricks, lime - the entire building material, would be thrown off beyond the boundary line of the lawn, and in the morning the lawn would appear cleared of all such debris. I had to accept these facts because it tallied with my own experience.

THE SHADOW FIGURE

A very liberal-minded man belonged to a wealthy family of Ireland. He had brought up a boy and girl since childhood. The boy was handsome and the girl delicate. They were not brother and sister. Still, due to such close association they loved each other as such. They used to be together almost always. They ate, sat and studied together. When they came of age, the boy was called Lord Tyron and the girl Lady Bresford. So, it would be proper to name them as such in this story.

The guardian of the children was theist only in name. He doubted the existence of God. And these ideas of his passed on to the two children. But hardly had they reached the impressionable age of fourteen, when their guardian died. The charge of the children fell upon a deeply religious man. Because of contact with him the children turned theists. But the germ of agnosticism which had taken root in their hearts did not completely die out.

Several years passed. Both the children were now married. The girl had now adopted the name of Lady Bresford. She was very social and catholic in her views. Lord Tyron was a very liberal man. Both the families were very close.

They met each other frequently. Sometimes even now they talk of religious matters. They both had their doubts regarding the life beyond. One day they took a vow that the one who die first, would appear before the other in the form of a spirit and convince him in about the existence of spirits.

Lord Tyron had one daughter and Lady Bresford two. They were passing their time happily. For a long time they had not heard from each other.

One day something happened. The night was very gloomy. Lady Bresford was sleeping on a big cot in her bedroom, the room was feebly lighted. Suddenly she was awakened. And lo! she found Lord Tyron sitting on her bedside. She was flabbergasted. It was the middle of the night. Her husband was sleeping besides her. A gentleman entering the bedroom of a lady under such circumstances was totally unexpected and inexcusable. She did not exactly cry out, but a mild shriek did escape her mouth. But that did not awaken her husband. She picked up courage and said to the Lord, Brother Tyron. What kind of behaviour is this! Coming to my bedside at dead of night and so stealthily! This is shameful!

Lord Tyron said, 'Have you forgotten the vow we both took a long while back? I died last Tuesday in the evening. I have come to you only to fulfil my vow. I have come to tell you that the next world infact exist, and everybody gets what he deserves according to his deeds.'

After a pause, Lord Tyron began again 'You will soon beget a son who will marry my daughter. Now, that I have come, let me tell you certain things about your future, howsoever unpleasant they might be. Soon after you will become a widow. A short while after you will marry again. Your second husband will be a drunkard and a gambler. You will be very unhappy with him. You will get two daughters and in the end, a son. On your 47th birth year a son will be born and you will die within a month of his birth.

The lady began to shiver at such prospects. She asked the Lord, 'Is there any way to circumvent the mishaps?'

The spirit replied, 'There is just one way out. You should not marry again. But I do not think you will be able to exercise so much self-control. Marry you will. But let me tell you this much.
Never entertain any doubt regarding the existence of God. Otherwise you will suffer in the next world.'

Lady	:	Are you happy in the other world?
Spirit	:	I am. Were it not so, I would not come to you.
Lady	:	When I get up in the morning, how will I know that you came to me in the form of spirit? Why should I do not think this was all a dream?
Spirit	:	Tomorrow, you will get the news of my death through conventional channels.
Lady	:	What of that? I feel I saw you in a dream and in

my dream you gave the news of which, by coincidence, came out to be true. Dreams do sometimes come out to be true.

Spirit : All right. Then see this.

So saying, the spirit raised his hand, lifted up one end of the mosquito-curtain of her bed and hung it from the hook in the ceiling of the room. And then the Lord said,

'When you will see this in the morning, you will have to believe that I did come to you, as such a thing cannot be done by any human agency.'

Lady This is nothing. Sometimes one does things while sleeping which he cannot do while awake. In the morning when I get up, why should I not suppose that I had myself hung the mosquito-curtain? Such a thing can surely be done with the help of ladder.

Spirit You have your pocket-book and pencil nearby. I will put my signature on the pocket-book. You recognise my handwriting since childhood. In the morning you will have to admit the handwriting is mine.

The spirit took up the pocket-book and put his signature in it. But the lady was obstinate beyond a limit. She was not even satisfied even then. She said,

'I have been seeing your signs at hundreds of places since childhood. Is it impossible that I may imitate your handwriting?

The spirit was little annoyed. And then he said,

'I see that it is very difficult to convince you. If I like , I can touch you, but that will augur ill for you. In spirit world I have not reached that stage when our touch may be harmless to living persons. So, my touch will leave an indelible mark on your body.'

Lady I do not care, but I want conclusive proof.

Spirit All right, extend your hand towards me.

The the lady followed. The spirit caught hold of the tip of one of her fingers. A shiver ran through her body. She felt as if her finger was melting like ice. The nerves of her finger dried the same instant. The spirit said,

'Keep this a secret throughout your life. Otherwise, you will come to grief.'

So, saying, Lord Tyron vanished. For a long time, Lady Bresford was lost in thoughts. And then she went to sleep. As soon as she got up in the morning the mosquito-curtain caught her sight. She brought a ladder and brought it down. She had a look at her finger. She tied a black tape on it, when her husband questioned her about the tape. She asked him not to ask anything about it, otherwise some mishap may occur. The husband did not insist.

Lady Bresford was waiting for her mail impatiently. Her husband asked her, 'What is the matter? Why are you so impatient about the arrival of the mail today? Are you expecting any important letter today?

Lady : I am expecting the heart-rending news that Lord Tyron is no more.

Lord : Have you seen any terrible dream this night? Is that's why you are so much agitated? You know that dreams have hardly any substance in them.

In the meanwhile the mail arrived. It contained the sad news! The lady began to weep bitterly. The day, date and time of death of Lord Tyron was exactly in accordance with the tidings given by the spirit.

Time passed. Events happened as predicted. Lady Bresford became a widow. She had two daughters and a son. In respect to wealth too she was flourishing. She remembered everything that the spirit told her. In particular, the words:

'There is only one was of warding off trouble. Do not marry again. But you lack self-control. You are bound to marry again. Marry you will!'

In the western countries marriages are usually love affairs. Boys meet girls in cinema halls, picnic parties, dancing halls etc. Acquaintances are formed which develops into friendships. Love follows, culminating in marriage. Lady Bresford thought to herself, 'If I do not move in society, do not go to pictures or dances, do not partake at picnics etc., I will have no chance to meet boys. And thus, no affair will develop and no marriage will result. So, I can ward off trouble.'

So, she became practically a recluse. She would not only go to the houses of her immediate neighbour, who was a priest, and nowhere else. But inscrutable are the ways of destiny. The priest had a young son who was handsome and healthy. Lady Bresford had yet not crossed the threshold of youth and was even now quite attractive. The boy came back from his college after a few months. The acquaintance between the two gradually developed into mutual love.

The lady thought that the spirit told her, her future husband will be a gambler and a drunkard. But this boy had not yet developed any of these vices. No doubt, the spirit must be wrong in regard to this matter.

They say, love is blind. Marriage followed. Soon after the lady was disillusioned. The boy was a drunkard and a gambler. And worst still, he was hot-tempered! She began to repent.

In a course of time, the lady had two daughters and a son.

A few days later she began to calculate and found that she had already passed her 47th birthday. So, in regard to this matter as least, the forebodings of the spirit were wrong!

A month passed. The lady celebrated her birthday. By chance the preceptor-priest of the family arrived. He asked her of the welfare of her family. And she said,

'By the grace of God, I have passed my 47th birthday.

I happened to visit your birth-place. I had occasion to consult your birth register. You are beginning your 47th year and not 48th year today'.

The lady was stunned to hear this. Then she narrated the entire story to the priest and to a friend of hers Lady Cub who was also present. And then she said to her son whatever last words she had to say and asked him to sit outside as she was sleepy and needed some rest.

About one-and-a-half hours later, the priest and the son went into the room to see her. She was no more. They could have a glimpse only of her body. Lady Cub untied the black tape from her finger. The finger was exactly as they were told.

Following the advice of the mother which she had given before her death, her son married the daughter of Lord Tyron.

AN EYE-WITNESS'S ACCOUNT

Ghost! Don't be startled. But, come what may, you are bound to be startled. It is in the nature of things. There was a time when I too got startled at the broaching of the subject. But now I am a firm believer in such phenomena. I am narrating incidents that have occurred before my own eyes.

There was a cousin sister of mine at Bikaner. She was about 18 years. During those days it was a job to find a suitable match for girls. And my sister had not received much education. That made the problem more difficult. After a good deal of effort, she could be engaged to a boy in a village in Bengal. The boy's family ran a soap factory. There were two brothers and a mother in the family. The elder brother was already married. He had a few children.

The marriage party reached Bikaner. The bride's father was a man of status and she was his eldest daughter. So, naturally the whole gentry of the city was invited. The magnificent bungalow of the girl's father was situated at a rather secluded spot and the party was encamped at an equally lonely place. About three kilometres separated the two bungalows. There were several graveyards of Christians on the way which were lying in a dilapidated condition.

The auspicious moment of the marriage was past midnight. The moon was waning. The party started with the members almost dozing. As the night was dark, gas lamps were arranged in a good number. Men also partake in singing among the Punjabis. So, it was a boisterous procession. Even that lonely passage presented a gala appearance. The bridegroom was a handsome young man of 22. As a rule, Punjabis are healthy, but this boy was exceptionally so. He did not know any English. He was also joining in the merriment with his friends and speaking in Punjabi.

All of a sudden, all the gas lamps went out. It became pitch dark party was stunned. Particularly so, as robbers were rampant in the area those days. Panic took the place of joviality. About twenty minutes later, the lamps again lit up automatically. The party was astounded, and they proceeded but the hilarity previously there, had gone.

The marriage party reached the bungalow of the bride's father. As it was already getting late, the bridegroom was rushed to the marriage pandal. The entire assemblage was fascinated by the health and beauty of the bridegroom. There was all praise for the girl's good luck. After a few initial ceremonies, the bride and the bridegroom were brought out of the pandal and seated elsewhere. It is customary to cut jokes with the bridegroom. The boy was of an exceptionally hilarious temperament. He was retorting to every poser in his characteristic Punjabi. And lo! All of a sudden he went into a swoon. People around were flabbergasted!. It was not terribly hot. Nor was the bridegroom at all delicate. There were several doctors in the party, whose services were immediately requisitioned, they tried their level best, but could not bring the boy back to consciousness.

Some people suggested calling it exorcists. Men were rushed to call them. But, before any of them could arrive the boy began talking in Pure English an uncle of the Bride stepped forward. He was a modern, educated man and did not believe in ghosts. When he found the boy speaking in English fluently he was amazed as he knew the Boy did not know English at all. He asked the boy, 'Who are you?' The reply was in English, 'I am
Mr. Jackson.' And then questions and answers followed:

Q. What do you want?

A. For the moment, I want tea and toast, as I am hungry.

Q. If we provide you with these, will you go?

A. That depends upon my will.

Q. Where do you live?

A. I live on a peepal tree in the graveyard. Your procession made me feel uncomfortable. But as I could smell perfume, I was tempted to come here.

An old man in the party said that if he was to be given tea and toast, he would become still more powerful. Then it would be more difficult to out him. He suggested that hair of the bridegroom be cut off and buried on the other side of the river. And then this trouble would be over. Four persons came forward to catch hold of the boy. But they found to their amazement that there was so much physical strength in the boy that they all fell flat. The girl's father was at his wit's end. Several sturdy persons could somehow control the boy. And they said they were almost receiving electric shocks from the touch of the body.

The hair was cut, four persons ran with it to bury it. About ten minutes later, the bridegroom opened his eyes and asked the people around in Punjabi, 'What is the matter, and why are you crowding around me?'

They all relied, 'you had become unconscious.'

The boy gaped in wonder and said, 'What! Did I become unconscious? I had just a reeling sensation for a moment, and at the next instant, I see you crowding around me.'

They did not tell the boy the whole story as it might terrify him. Somehow, the marriage ceremony was gone through and the time came for the bride to take leave of her father's home. They were all terror-stricken, as the spirit of Mr. Jackson had said, while the hair were being taken, 'You may take me as far as you can, but I am not going to leave him.' The marriage party started back and nothing untoward happened.

The couple had a happy married life for some time. the husband took ample care to fulfil every desire of his wife. About a year elapsed. And then came the first Holi festival after marriage. This festival is celebrated among Hindus with great joviality. The husband bought many presents for his wife. In the evening he said to her, 'For the last so many days I have been trying to tell you something. But I hesitated as you would call it a weakness of my mind, and laugh at it.' The wife said, 'What is the big idea? Come out.' The husband replied, 'I feel sometimes that some invisible power is telling me that it is not going to leave me. I do not know if this is only an illusion of mine.' And then he added, 'There is no knowing what happens tomorrow. I have already got my life insured. If something happens to me, do not cry. The insurance money would stand you in good stead.'

The wife saw the scene of the marriage ceremony once more being enacted before her eyes. More significant were the words of Mr. Jackson, 'I will not leave him.' Apparently she said, 'Don't you worry. This is just a whim. Nothing is going to happen to you. Better carry this thing no further.'

The husband insisted,'Whatever you might say.This obsession does not leave me. There is some reality behind it.'

The wife said with tears,'Tomorrow we are to celebrate, and on the eve of it you are talking of such ominous things.'

Till that day the husband was hale and hearty. He had not even a slight temperature for a single day.

The next day some friends came and took the boy for celebrating the festival. He spent the entire day in merry-making with them. One of them invited the party to dinner. And he went to his place along with them. The food contained certain intoxicants as is customary on the occasion.

After dinner all the boys left for their homes. This boy reached his home where his wife was waiting. Soon after reaching he said he was feeling pain in the head. He asked her to apply some balm to his forehead. The wife thought this was due to the tension and strain of the day. She began applying balm. In the meanwhile the boy became unconscious. His eyes got perturbed. She called all the other inmates of the house. They all said it was the effect of the intoxicant and would soon be over. But the wife insisted on calling the doctor. A doctor came and examined him. He said, "The pulse and heart-beat are all right. I think he would be all right in half-an hour."

A little later, the boy opened his eyes. He beckoned to his wife and with tears in his eyes, he said that he was passing away. His wife began to sob bitterly. Several doctors were present throughout the night. But they could not explain as to what ailment the boy suffered from.

The wife immediately went to a nearby well and jumped into it. The members of the family were looking after the dead body when somebody told them that the wife of the dead man was nowhere to be seen. An urchin told them he heard somebody falling into the well. They all ran to the well and found that the girl was there. They all entreated her to come out. She agreed to come out only on condition that she would be allowed to perform 'sati', that is, burn herself on the pyre of her husband. Those were the days of the British and it was an offence to perform 'sati'. But they all apparently agreed to the condition and she consented to come out.

A big leather bucket was dropped into the well. The girl was half way up, when the rope of the bucket gave way. The girl again fell down. She was again hauled up. When she came up, they all found to their amazement that, in spite of two falls, she had not sustained even a slight bruise. Of course she was not allowed to perform sati.

The readers may now decide as to how it all happened. If you will not call it the activity of a spirit or ghost, what other name will you give it? You must admit that there was some power behind the event.

A SPOOK OF LAPLAND

Gottfrid was an inhabitant of Norbottern in Swedish Lapland. He had a hutment on the slope of a hill. He reared cows and sheep while his wife made boots in her spare time. Somebody asked him,'Any legends about this locality.' He replied,'Only the legend about the spook.'

Q. What is a spook?

A. He appears in diverse forms. Sometimes he is seen in woodlands, but I have never seen him myself.

Q. But, do you know anybody who has seen it himself?

This question made Gottfrid serious. After a pause he narrated the following episode:

'Once my father was carrying some bags of grain to the mill. He was accompanied by a friend of his, John. The night was dark and they had to cross a jungle.

'Suddenly the horse stopped with jerk. My father tried, but the horse would not move. He whipped him again and again, but the horse dug his feet in the ice and refused to budge. Once he did move a little, but it appeared as if he was trying to avoid one particular spot. But this was not possible in the forest. So, he stopped again.

My father thought there must be something mysterious regarding the spot. He came down, took up his axe, stepped to the front of the horse and moved the axe in the air several times. This had magical effect and the horse started.

John was so much terrified that no word escaped his mouth. When they reached the mill he opened his mouth and said that he had seen a corpse on the road at the spot where the horse had stood still.

And the wonder was that as soon as my father moved his axe, the corpse vanished. We had been hearing that spooks are afraid of only steel. This even confirmed the belief. Later on we were told that somebody was frozen to death and died in the ice at that very place the previous day.

'You know I do not believe in such phenomena. But the surprising thing was the horse too had seen something on the ground, to be sure. We can explain away the attitude of John as mere illusion, but the behaviour of the horse was not worth ignoring. Sure enough, there is something peculiar about the place. As to what it was I could not say.'

Now, Gottfrid was posed a pointed question,'Could you narrate some such incident which happened to yourself.? This question went home. Gottfied said.

'Yes, once I myself encountered the spook, and I was mortally afraid. I went to a field of mine on the hill. It was evening when we reached the place and my companions wished that we should pass the night there.

I was sleeping in the attic upstairs. I awoke a few hours later. I found a man bowing on my bed. He had his arms behind my back so that I could not move at all. The strangest thing was that though the room was amply lit, I could not see 'the man'. I was seeing only a shadow.

But little doubt, he was on my bed. I could even hear his breath. And lie was a man that too was certain. I could distinguish between the breath of a man and a woman.

I was indeed afraid at the moment. Just imagine, how dreadful the situation was I could see that somebody was trying to squeeze me to pain, but I found myself helpless. I was shuddering and perspiring. This predicament lasted quite some time. Every moment I felt he would thrust his knife into my throat. But nothing of the kind happened. He released me and went out through the closed door!

That was the movement when my agility was worth seeing. I jumped up and ran, but found the room vacant. It was evident that 'somebody' had entered the room, but that 'somebody' was 'nobody'. I cannot explain the phenomenon, try as I may. People can call it my illusion. This much is certain that I was not intoxicated, because I had not taken anything the previous night.'

THE BOY GHOST

This happened in 1942 when people were fleeing from Calcutta. I owned a press in the Gour Mohan Mukherjee Lane, Calcutta-6. The locality is very near the birth-place of Swami Vivekanand. There were three buildings inside the compound with a common gate. I lived in a ten-room house at the end of a narrow corridor. I had my office in the very first room on the right hand side of the building. There was a printing press in the adjoining room. I lived with my family on the ground floor of the building. There was another door in front of the office which was meant for only the members of my family.

It was about nine in the morning one day. I was chatting with some friends when I found a very handsome by swiftly entering through the door. I distinctly remember that he had curly hair, a round face and very fair complexion. He would be about 11 or 12 and he was wearing a Khaki Pair of trousers. I thought he might be someone connected with our neighbours. So I did not pay much heed to the matter. But when I went home for lunch I enquired about the boy. They all denied having seen such boy so I look the matter as closed, as I neither believed in spirits and ghosts, nor did the subject enter my mind at the moment.

Calcutta was being bombarded and I had to shift my family from the city. As a result I was alone in the house. One night, when I was asleep, I felt something cold touching my feet. I got up and saw the faint figure of a small boy. He had curly hair and he soon vanished. At once I recalled the incident of a few months back. I could notice a good deal of resemblance between that boy and this. Several times I uttered the name of my preceptor, Ramkrishna as an antidote against evil spirits and passed the night lying awake.

Strange as it may appear, I had similar experiences the next several nights every night I felt as if the boy was gently massaging my feet. I wondered as to what it all meant. Why does he after all, massage my feet? Was I in any way connected with him in my previous life? I could not make out anything.

There was a Brahmin astrologer who commanded great respect in our household. One day he was staying with me. We were sleeping on the same bed. At about midnight I was awakened by some sound. I found that the astrologer was crying aloud. I handled him roughly and somehow brought him to his senses.

I lighted the lamp and asked him what the matter was. He told me he found someone trying to strangle him. I said to him he had probably seen some terrifying dream. But he was still shuddering out of fear. He remained awake with eyes wide open and refused to go to bed again. Then I asked him to describe the man who, he thought, was trying to strangle him. He gave me a vivid description of the boy: 11 or 12 of age, very handsome, with curly hair. I understood the whole matter. But, for pacifying him I said,'But, why should he try to strangle you? On the contrary, he massages my feet every day, and has never hurt me at all'. For a long time I tried to calm him, but he could not get any sleep that night, but I slept soundly.

Several months passed. My financial position began to dwindle and I wound up my business. A year later a friend of mine got me a house on rent in the Mijhi Ram Majhi Street of Howrah. It was a two storeyed house with a big compound, but the rent was not much. I started my press again and my friend began assisting me in the job. Within a couple of months all the inmates of the house fell ill. I called my parents from Midnapur. My neighbour of the locality told me, the house was haunted, but

I never saw anything unusual there even on pitch dark night.

I thought the boy-ghost affair was a thing of the past.

One morning my father ordered that the house be vacated immediately. I asked him what the matter was. He told he had been to the bathroom at about 2 a.m. in the night. He was sitting therein when somebody caught hold of his clothes from behind and began to drag him. He turned round and found a very handsome boy with curly hair smiling at him.

My father, Mr.M.N.Nag, was the editor of the -Midinapur

Hitaishi.' He was considered an authority on black magic and knew a little about spirits as well. So, in his own way, he asked that spirit to break the shackles of worldly attachment and not trouble us any more. And forthwith the spirit vanished.

The same night my friend too had an unusual experience. The day was about to break. He awoke and was going down when a small boy went past him. He too gave us exactly the same description of the boy: curly hair, age 11 or 12, very handsome appearance. I was very sure he was the same boy of Calcutta. I felt as if I would have to wind up my business again. And within a month my forebodings came out to be true. Since 1944, I am again living at Calcutta, but that kind of phenomenon has never occurred again.

On the spot where I had seen the boy for the first time there was name-plate of the first owner of the house. I enquired about it from the people around. I was told that all those buildings once belonged to a Brahmin barrister. Almost all the inmates of that house died of cholera, one after the other. There was a very handsome boy of 11 or 12 in the house. He too died.

I cannot say for sure whether the spirit that I saw several times, was the same boy of the barrister's family or not. One thing, however, I do not understand. Twice his arrival played a havoc with my life. Still, how is it that he behaved so kindly to me?

MOTHER SAVES DAUGHTER

A couple had a daughter. Once there was a tiff between the husband and the wife. The latter got annoyed and went out of the house with her daughter. They went to a zoo where they spent quite some time. On their way back, their car was passing below a hillock. A rock fell without warning and crashed on the car, reducing it to smithereens.

The husband was sitting in the house when, all of a sudden his wife appeared before him and said,

'I was coming in the car with our daughter when the car met with an accident. A rock fell on it. I am dead but there is some life in the girl. If you rush to the hillock immediately you may be able to save her.

The husband at once rang the police and hurriedly narrated the entire incident to them. Also, he took out his car and dashed towards the hillock. There he found that the police had anticipated him long before, and was busy removing the debris. The body of the daughter and the corpse of the wife was dug out from underneath. The girl was taken to the hospital and she was saved.

Then gentleman went to his doctor. After narrating the entire incident to him, he added.

'I do not understand as to how my wife, who was already dead, came to me in human form and told me of the accident.

The doctor said, 'It is all an illusion. You did not see anything of the sort. You were perplexed over the tiff you had with your wife. So, you began to see things.

Your imagination concocted the story of the accident. You went towards the hillock under impulse. Take this medicine and you will be all right within a few days.'

The husband began taking the medicine.

A few days later, he was talking to a police inspector. The doctor too was nearby. He asked the inspector:

Inspector, I phoned to you in your office. And immediately after I started towards the hillock. There I was told that you reached the spot quite some time before me. And your men were already busy removing the debris. After all, how could you know that such an accident had occurred?'

The Inspector replied, 'I did not receive your telephone call. It must have been received by some other officer on duty.

I was informed of the accident by a white-robed lady who came running out of breath to me and told me of the accident. On hearing her I immediately shot off towards the scene of the accident with a few men.'

The description of the lady that the inspector gave him tallied with that of his wife.

The doctor too was within hearing distance. He said. to the husband, 'Now, I am convinced that the lady who appeared before you was the spirit of your wife.'

The husband took out the phial of the medicine from his pocket and handed it over to the doctor, saying, Now, I don't need this.'

WAS IT SUPERSTITION?

(Courtesy : Shri Prasad Kamal)

Mrs.Choudhury, aged 25, lives in district Moonghyr and is the wife of a doctor with a lucrative practice. Being neglected and maltreated by her husband several times, she has been living away from him for the last few years and her son of 6, lives with him.

Mrs. Chowdhury is an attractive lady with a slim figure, fair complexion and sharp features. She always smiles, but has an obstinate temperament. Being unable to adjust herself to her environments she has given up her paternal home and has begun living at Mirzapur. She is now engaged in official service.

For the last three or four years she has been experiencing several vicissitudes of life and passing through ordeals. Previous reminiscences often pain her, but she does not get anything out of them except echoes of misfortunes. Long-drawn ailment has made her temperament fidgety otherwise she was very practical and modern. Since long her husband's younger brother has been living with him. For the last several months her son is with her maternal grandparents.

Commencement of the ailment

Events began to happen since 15th December, 1969. There was a light darkness all around. Mrs. Chowdhury came back in a bus to Mirzapur and engaged an ekka (a kind of horse-carriage). There were two or three other ladies on the ekka. Hardly had the ekka gone a quarter of a kilometre, when Mrs. Chowdhury felt as if someone was calling her by name. The place was desolate and she heard her name being called thrice. She looked all around and saw no one. The other ladies on the ekka did not hear the call. Mrs. Chowdhury told me of the incident when she was back home. I assured her that it was her illusion. There was nothing to worry about.

The next day, Mrs. Chowdhury said to me, 'Today again I heard the same call. I went up to the main door, but found nobody. I asked her not to leave her place whenever she heard the voice. But she always started in the direction of the sound whenever she heard it. The usual time for the call was between 5 and 6 p.m. and this continued for about 25 days without break.

I again set a Pandit to start the worship of Goddess Durga (the goddess of Prowess). But so long as the Pandit was before her, she felt like beating him. Being unable to withstand this impulse, she left the worship midway.

Mrs. Chowdhury was scared by the incident of Dec. 15 and began to be restless. Since that day her mentality became so perverted that if she would see excreta anywhere her instinct would be to pick it up. She found it hard to control the propensity. Later on she began to see dreadful figures in her room. Sometimes she thought somebody was laughing at her. On the way, she would find a tall, bearded and dreadful man staring at her with reddened eyes. At other times she would observe fragrance of fresh roses spread over the room. According to her description, the spirit would always appear in white robes and hair scattered all over. She was mortally afraid of him and she would always turn pale at his sight. Sometimes she would find somebody lying beside her on the bed.

I was trying to cure Mrs. Chowdhry psychologically. But I failed to drive out fear from her mind. As a result of this psychosis she was rapidly losing health. Now she is not receiving those calls, but the sights of spirit continue.

Events turning serious

This happened on January 19. It was very cold with a deep fog outside. It was 6.30 in the morning and Mrs. Chowdhury was asleep. Her husband's brother had gone out to fetch milk after attending to his daily routine. As usual, he locked the door from outside. When he came back and entered the room after opening the lock he found that Mrs. Chowdhury was not in her bed. The other door of the room was, as usual, bolted from inside. He got perplexed. He came into the courtyard and called her aloud. A little later, Mrs. Chowdhury came out of her bathroom. He asked her how she entered the bathroom.

Mrs Chowdhury pointed to the staircase and said, "It was you who left me near the staircase.'

The gentleman replied that he had locked the room from outside as usual. Mrs. Chowdhury got unnerved at the reply. When they narrated the incident to me, I too got nonplussed. I pacified them and told them I would myself enquire into the matter.

The next day, on Jan.20, I had to go to those people. But it had been raining since last night. So, I felt reluctant to go. At that end, the gentleman, a usual, locked the door from outside and went out. Mrs. Chowdhury was asleep at that time. He took one of the tenants of the house, a sardar, with him and the two started for bringing milk. When they were returning home, Mrs.Chowdhury met them on the way. She was barefoot, wet and almost running out of breath. The sardar got scared as the room was locked in his presence.

When they all entered the room, her husband's brother Mrs. Chowdhury, 'How did you manage to get out today?'

Mrs. Chowdhury, I was getting wet on the roof. When I noticed it, I came down. When I found it locked, I naturally concluded that you had gone out, as usual.

So, I have come running. But I have absolutely no idea as to how I got to the roof.
The other door of the room was examined. It was bolted from inside as usual. When I got up from my morning worship, they all reached my place and narrated the entire story to me. I too could not make out anything. I decided to pass the entire day with them and keep watch over their movements. I was with them all day. Nothing unusual happened. Nor did Mrs. Chowdhury exhibit any sign of abnormality. At about 8.30 in the evening, when I wanted to take leave of them, they came upto the door to see me off. As soon as we came out of the door, Mrs. Chowdhury cried out and began losing senses.

I caught hold of her staggering body and took her to her bed in her room. I began sprinkling water on her face to bring her to senses. A few minutes later, when she came to, I helped her to sit up. She was gazing curiously at us and was unable to recognise us. I asked her name again and again, but she kept mum. Like an exorcist I caught hold of the tuft of her hair and gave her a slap. She did not feel anything. On the contrary she began laughing wildly and she gave a slap to her husband's brother.

And now Mrs. Chowdhury began to run about. Her husband's brother suggested treating her with the odour of garlic.

I asked him,'What good will it be ?

He replied, 'We have read in the book, Dracula, by an American writer, about curing people of evil spirits with the odour of garlic and asafoetida.'

I gave my assent. When garlic was brought near her nose Mrs. Chowdhury hid her face with her hands. When she inhaled the odour of garlic quite sometime, she really began to come to her own. I was flabbergasted. When we asked her why she cried out, she said, 'As soon as I came out of the door with you, the Spirit gave me a violent slap. I cried out of fear and pain. What happened after that I do not know.'

We took a little garlic and asafoetida, wrapped it in a piece of cloth and tied it around the arm of Mrs. Chowdhury as a talisman against evil spirits. I did not think it safe to leave those people at night. So, I brought them with me to my house. Since then they are sleeping in my house, but no incident of that kind has occurred again. Of course, they are never left to themselves. Somebody is always with them. Sometimes they still see that bearded fellow.

One night, the bolts of the door and window of the room in which they sleep, were inexplicably opened. Beyond that nothing untoward has happened.

Treatment

There is a certain exorcist, Noor Mohamed, in Mirzapur, who is known to cure such ills. We decided to approach him. I do not at all believe in ghosts, nor am I interested in black magic. Still, I went to the gentleman and narrated to him the entire episode. He enchanted a few mantras (hymns) written on paper and gave them to me, asking me to tie them round the arm of the lady. Besides, he wrote something else on another piece of paper as a wick in a lamp of mustard oil. Also, Mrs. Chowdhury was to sit before the lamp for three hours in a posture of adoration with folded hands.

The worship began on Jan 22. The lamp was lit, flowers and garlands were laid beside the fire, and incense was thrown into the fire. A little while after the operation started, Mrs Chowdhury lost control over herself and became violent. She talked with the masculine forms of Grammar. She wanted white garland in place of a red one. She would have essence in place of incense and so on. I provided her with both the things. She was mighty pleased. She put the garland around her neck, put the essence on her clothes and threw the entire amount of incense into the fire all at once. A few minutes later she began calling Mr. Noor Mohamad bad names and said she would settle accounts with him. She would put out the lamp again and again. We would put it on again and again. She objected to our putting the lamp. She said to us,'All of you get out of my way. I will carry this lady with me. If you do not listen to me, I will burn her to the banks of Ganga, or throw her into the river. I have no faith in God.'

She went on prattling like this. Several times she threw fire at us. Throughout the operation she went on playing with the fire. But, strange as it is, the contact with fire did not hurt her at all. When she became out of control, we would place garlic near her nose. She would regain a little consciousness. We would ask her to sit before the lamp with folded hands and utter the name of God again and again' She would do it a few times. Then she would stop and try to leave. When she would regain consciousness, she would ask us to remove the incense. But as soon as she lost her senses, she would ask for the incense. Also, she would take a bit of the fire and smell it.

Somehow three hours passed and she was brought to her senses with the help of garlic. She was feeling very week.

According to Noor Mohamed, Mrs. Chowdhury should have been normal after the worship. But nothing of the type happened. She was in no way better. Now, the Spirit would stare at her during day and night at all odd hours and almost at any place. Sometimes he put his hand on her shoulder. At other times he tried to drag her. One thing worth mentioning in this connection is that neither of us two has ever seen the spirit. However, her husband's biother sometimes gets the fragrance of flowers. This was my first experience of the kind.

Even now, whenever garlic is removed from the arm of Mrs. Chowdhury, she begins behaving violently.

THE GOLD BANGLE

I was travelling in a train. A gentleman was sitting on a corner seat of the same compartment. Putting down his newspaper, he asked me.

'Have you heard anything about ghosts?'

I was a little non plussed at the question as it was almost midnight. What a query at such an odd hour! There was no third person in the compartment. It was pitch dark outside and the train was crossing a tunnel. On top of that, my co-traveller, himself appeared to me like a ghost. He might be about 40. He was stark bald. And he had a big turn-on in the middle of his crown to boot - as if a second head was springing up!

I replied, 'No. I have not heard anything regarding ghosts. I am a student of science.'

He retorted, 'If science did not care to know anything about ghosts, it is its known fault and not that of ghosts.'

His reply was so original and weighty that I got interested in the topic and I sat upright.

I said to him, 'It seems you know a good deal about the matter.'

He turned his hand round his crown and said, 'Why not? The incident occurred exactly ten years back. I remember it so vividly as though it happened yesterday. I was living in a bungalow of Sen Thorne facing the sea.

My most intimate friend was my neighbour Krishna Kant. He was a very handsome youth. He was moneyed and well-behaved and lived in a bungalow nearby. He had a love affair with a very beautiful girl called Vimla.

Vimla too had taken to him and told her parents that she would marry him and none else. Krishna had a flourishing business which was spread over a wide area. It was difficult for him to leave Madras so he wrote to the parents of the girl to come to Madras and perform the marriage ceremony there. They gladly accepted the proposal.

The marriage was to be performed on Sunday. Just three days more were to go, when Krishna Kant received an unpleasant news from his Ceylon branch. The manager of the concern there had embezzled a goodly sum and the business was staggering. He told his would-be father-in-law that it was absolutely necessary for him to go to Ceylon and set matters right. Both parties agreed to postpone the ceremony by a week.

But Krishna Kant could not return on the following Friday according to promise. Nor was there any news about him. A terrible storm was raging during those days on the South coast of the country. No ship could sail under such circumstances.

But on Sunday the storm abated. Relations and friends assembled to take part in the marriage ceremony, but the bridegroom was not there. There was no end to the tears in the eyes of the bride. She was on the a point of losing her mind.

It struck ten in the morning. A clerk of the Madras office of the firm came running and said that a message had arrived from the Ceylon branch.

Vimla's father asked impatiently, 'What news about Krishna Kant?'

The clerk replied,'He has committed suicide.'

All were stunned. Oh, what a misfortune!

The guests were all flabbergasted. The bride's father could not control himself. And what about Vimla? She fell down and expired!

It is difficult to describe what happened next. The clerk was stupefied when he realised that the girl lost her life due to his own folly.'

I asked the contravener, 'But how did it all happen?'

He told me that the name of the manager of the Ceylon branch too was Krishna Kant.

And it was he who had committed suicide, and not the would be husband of Vimla. What an irony of fate! Such woesome tragedies occur sometimes due to a confusion of similar names.

'The funeral ceremony of Vimla was performed in the afternoon. And by six in the evening the entire party left for Madras. There was not even a soul in the bungalow when Krishna Kant alighted from a taxi.

It was I who had to communicate that tragic news to him. He received it coolly, went inside and bolted the door from inside. He was a changed man since then. During the day he would attend to his business. In the evening he would return to the bungalow and would not stir out before next morning. And no one was allowed to see him.

But he was exceptionally kind to me. One evening, when I knocked at his door, he came out and took me in. For about one hour he went on explaining things to me. I wanted him to employ a certain nephew of mine. I was talking to him while my eyes were scanning the walls and corners of the room.

The hall in which we were sitting, opened into a small room which was equipped with several kinds of articles. There was a bed in the room, which was too big for one person. There was a small round table near the bed with a chair on either side of it.

And on the table were placed two cups of milk, a fruit basket and several delicacies.

I was amazed and I was going to ask him about those articles when the clock struck ten. Krishna Kant got startled and his eyes sparkled. He said, 'It is time for my wife to come.' And all of a sudden he was reminded of my presence in the room. He cut his tongue with his teeth and said to me,'Please go out at once.' And he practically pushed me out of the room.

I did not mind this insult. But what I had seen and heard, raised my curiosity to such an extent that I did not come home. I crawled to the back of the room and hid myself behind a flower vase near the window of the room. I could see what was happening inside the room. All the lights of the bungalow had been put out, but, in the pale moonlight almost everything was visible to me.

Krishna Kant and an extremely beautiful lady were dining together. I heard Krishna Kant saying, 'Darling, Sweetest are the moments of my life when you are with me. But, how long shall we remain separated from each other? Why not let me come near you?'

The lady replied, 'Dearest, Have a little patience. We do not know what is ordained for us. But I feel sure the day is not far off.'

Krishan Kant said, 'I too hope so, Vimla.'

So, it was the spirit of Vimla, the wife of Krishna Kant. I was dumb founded. I had a good look at the girl only to ascertain if she was really Vimla and none else. No doubt, she was extremely charming and overpowering. When she smiled it seemed the whole world danced round her, and when she talked, it looked like a shower of flowers all round! Every fibre of her being appeared ethereal. Krishan Kant too was feeling overawed by her dominating personality.

All at once, she got up and said, 'Dearest, It seems somebody is observing us.'

She ran out of the room while Krishna Kant went on calling her. His voice remained echoing in the air. When he ran to catch hold of Vimla, the table over turned, cups were thrown to the ground and broken to pieces and furniture became topsy-turvy. While silence reigned supreme an hour before, there was chaos, now.

I was observing the scene attentively. All of a sudden some one hit me from behind. I at once turned round and caught hold of the person assaulting me. But, with matching agility, the person released himself (or herself) from my clutches and vanished. I could see only this much that the assaulting hand was extremely beautiful. I lost grip of the hand, but this gold bangle remained in my hand.

So saying my fellow-traveller took out a gold bangle from a pocket of his jacket. And he added, 'This bangle was left in my hand. Please see whose name is engraved in it.'

With trembling hands I took the bangle in my hand and began to look at it intently. The name; Vimla Bai' was engraved in it. I was dumbfounded. My fellow-traveller nodded in assent.

'Lo! Bombay has arrived. But now I have not much to say. I took the bangle and came back home. But, when my wife opened the door and saw me, she fainted. I laid her on the bed. But, before I could bring her back to consciousness, I had a passing glance at a mirror. I was horrified to find that the hair on my head had all vanished. I had a goodly bunch of hair on my head when I went to the house of Krishna Kant. The ghost had turned me bald.'

I asked him, 'And whence came this tumour on your head?'

He replied,'This is the after-effect of the slap of the same spirit.'

I asked him 'And then what happened to Kristan Kant?

He replied,'The same night he committed suicide by hanging himself in the same room in which Vimla expired. Sometimes I begin to doubt if this was all a fact, or simply an illusion. But, in that case, how is one to explain this tumour and this bangle?'

THE TOWER OF LONDON

(Courtesy : The Leader, March 16, 1964)

It was about 900 years back that William of Normandy conquered England. Among the first building that he constructed was the Tower of England situated in the eastern part of the city.

The Tames flows on one side of the fort. On two sides of the fort are the delapidated walls which are reminiscent of the conquerors, the Romans.

The tower is not a museum. It is a military cantonment, a royal archives as well as a palace. The jewels of the royal family are preserved therein. Moreover, it is a royal prison in name at least.

Excavations are going on for constructing new jewel house. It throws light on the way William the conqueror wanted to carry on his administration.

Certain people who have studied the tower closely are of the opinion that it is the most haunted house in the world. No doubt it contains many articles which confirm the basis of quite a few supernatural Ghost stories.

In these buildings is preserved the history of England of post 1067 times in a spectacular way. In these buildings many people were put to death who rebelled against the king, or, somehow became victims of his warmth. And many royal prisoners used to be tortured here.

The jail of spies.

In a few years after the First World War spies began being sent to the tower. There they were shot down.

The number of visitors to the tower is increasing fast. In 1964 the admission fee collected was about a lakh of pounds, Visitors can freely roam about the basements and cellars and ruminate the ghost stories connected therewith.

Annebolene was a wife of Henry VIII. She was born in 1507 and beheaded in the Tower Green of the fort in 1536. Any visitor to the tower is bound to hear the story of Annebolene.

Several generations of caretakers of the tower swear they have seen the spirit of Annebolene several times. Many of them testify that she is seen off and on. About 50 years back she was seen for the first time. The same story is narrated here.

It was in 1914. Certain German spies were imprisoned in the tower who were awaiting the sentence. A military sergeant was on guard. He distinctly saw a lady who was wearing a silk dress which used to be worn many years back. When she came near him, a cool breeze began to blow which soon converted itself into a cold wave.

The sergeant as well as the spies were all flabbergasted to see her pass through a thick, about six feet thick! They could hardly believe it and began rubbing their eyes in amazement.

Other stories

Anne was also seen by a soldier about the middle of the nineteenth century. The clock struck midnight and he saw a woman with a white dress coming out of the Tower Green. He asked her who she was. There was no reply. He was terrified. He attacked her with a bayonet by the weapon served in the air.

The soldier fainted. He was charged with drunkenness. But the other soldiers vouch sated that they too had seen the same kind of woman. The accusation was withdrawn.

The best story relating to Anne was the one narrated by a captain of guards. He was patrolling with some of the other guards when he saw light emanating from the church of the tower.

He was surprised because there used to be pitch dark at the spot. The captain managed to reach a window where he somehow tried to main his balance, and began peeping in. He was flabbergasted to see the sight. It was a wonder he did not lose his balance and fall out. The church resplendent with a terrifying blue-white light. In the middle corridor was moving a procession of men and women in clothes which were worn during the time of Henry VIII. On the forefront was a lady with a gorgeous dress and her face seemed familiar. The captain recalled that a few days back he saw an oil painting of Anne and the face resembled that of this lady.

Within moments the lights began fading and then vanished. and darkness began reigning supreme.

Some people gave credence to this story of the captain while others laughed it off. But there is one person at last who believes every word of it, and that is a sentry who used to guard the Salt Tower seven years back!

He heard a click from above the place where he was standing on guard. He raised his eyes and saw a formless white ghost about forty feet above.

He cried. The in-charge of the guardsmen as well as several other persons gathered around. They searched all around but could not trace anybody.

THE GHOST OF THE TUBE RAILWAY

(Courtesy : World Digest, November 1956)

Toni Terris

I was not at all surprised when, a few days back, the terrified passengers and the night workers of the tube railway of London told me that they had seen the spirit of my late father at the station of Covent Garden.

My father was a very prominent actor of the British stage. He was murdered at this very station during the early part of the century. His spirit used to play pranks. Those who have seen the ghost, assert that he was a handsome, smart and tall personality. And this convinced me that it was really the spirit of my father.

The ghost of Covent Garden used to wear clothes of an old fashion. He used to keep waiting for trains. And when a train arrived he would entered it and disappear. People saw him entering the train, but non of the passengers sitting in the train ever saw him entering. Likewise, many persons saw him ascending a staircase, but non could see reaching him the end of the stairs.

A member of the staff of the tube railway was a bit of a para Psychologist. Once he performed a seance in a waiting room when trains were arriving and departing. The seance was continuing when one of the members cried/Look! He is pouncing upon you.'

And at the same time, the guide of the seance felt as if somebody was calling'Terr' in a mysterious voice.

Out of sheer fear, the railway employee who was working as the guide, got himself transferred to some other station.

Many peculiar incidents took place during those days but I will confine myself with those connected with my late father alone.

About 58 years have elapsed, but to me they are as fresh as if they happened only the other day.

Willian Terris, the father had no peculiar characteristics. He was a very cheerful, active and smart person. We used to act in Shakespeare's plays and sometimes he would travel over various parts of the country with his company. He was a gay and frolicsome man even before he joined the stage.

In the beginning he used to tend sheep. Later on he became a trainer of horses. And then he began working in mines. Again he left the job and joined the navy. He earned a name in the profession.

He joined the stage with great husto, and soon his reputation grew far and wide. He played the hero in several plays of Shakespeare, and his histrionic ability is not forgotten till today.

Men were his fans, but ladies used to be simply mad after him. I was an urchin of 17 at the time. My father was 49 and was at the peak of his histrionic powers. Naturally I was extremely proud of him.

But little did I know that a mad cap was planning to murder him and some of his own friends were aiding him in the nefarious affair. During those days my father was playing a romantic part in the Adelphi Theatre. He was depicting an act of bravery which suited his genius very well. But in the same company there was a minor actor, Richard, who had an inflated notion regarding his.; Histrionic Talents, whomsoever Richard Prince met he would brag upon his acting ability and would further say that Terris was no match to him. But the latter, he would, add, was mighty jealous of him and would not let shine.

Other actors would laugh under their sleeves at this kind of talk but apparently would add fuel to the fire. They would instigate him to recite dialogues of Shakespeare's plays and would say that his histrionic ability was extra-ordinary and it was a pity he was being given ample opportunities to manifest his talents. Little did they realise that they were abetting him to evil deeds.

My father had a shadow actor, Charles. One day, when he entered the stage, he was very morose.
He told some of the colleagues that the previous night he saw in a dream that Terris was being murdered. This happened on Dec. 15, 1898.

By nature stage actors are superstitious. But somehow did not attach any importance to the dream. On the other hand, they made fun of Charles Lane. But 24 hours later, the event occurred exactly as foretold by Charles Lane.

On the night of Dec. 16, father dined at a restaurant with a friend and started for the stage. Visitors had begun pouring into the auditorium when the two friends reached the ill-lighted street behind the stage. My father had a private door for entry. Hardly had he put his key into the lock of the door when a black figure appeared from the dark and attacked him.

This was the actor Richard Prince. That very night he had to act as a murderer on the stage. So, he was clad in the attire of a killer. He was covered with black clothes and had a dagger in his hand. He showered an abuse him and thrust his dagger into the back of my father twice. When father turned round to defend himself, he attacked him for third time.

The friend of my father ran away in terror. But he repented for his cowardice for a pretty long time. And in the end he committed suicide. Prince too ran hard, but was soon caught. He passed the rest of his life in a lunatic asylum. But till the very end would go on repeating that he was the best actor in the world.

Other actors handled my father. The latter had immense strength. This is evidenced by the fact that he remained alive for full 20 minutes after though the dagger had pierced deep into his heart. And immediately before the end he said; I will surely come back.'

But this was perhaps a very natural reaction of his as he had feigned death several times before on the stage. I was informed of the event much later. But an even more astounding drama was being enacted at home, which was several miles away.

I was playing chess with my younger brother. Our mother was reading some book at seated on a chair in the same room. On her lap was our little dog. The latter was a very meek and docile animal and we had never seen him barking. A few minutes past 8, at exactly the same moment when my father was breathing his last, the dog jumped from my mother's lap, began to run round and round in the room and bark furiously.

And then he sat down under the table. He was shivering and opening and closing his eyes alternately.

We thought that the dog had suddenly gone mad. He became calm in half an hour. And suddenly knocked the door and gave us the heart-rending news.

There would be very few actors whose death would be mourned on such a vast scale. We began receiving messages of condolence from all over the world. Even Queen Victoria graciously sent her message.

The body of Cheerful Bill as he used to be called, was buried, but his name remains immortal. A newspaper of London opened a charity fund and people contributed to it liberally. The fund swelled to 10 lakh dollars. My father was a great lover of the sea. He was a sailor for many years, and had played the part of a sailor in many dramas. So, in his name was established a safety-boat house, which functioned for many years.

And now we come back to the incident of Covent Garden. I cannot say that I fully comprehended the significance thereof. I only happen to remember a line of Shakespeare which my father was very fond of.

'Horatio, there are many things which happen in the world that your Philosophy dreams of.'

THE GIRL WITH THREE DOLLS

(Courtesy : One Step Beyond)

A family consisted of a husband, wife and a daughter. The entire family went to another place for a holiday. The place was completely desolated. So, the girl could not relish staying there.

A few days later the girl appeared to be very happy and jovial. "When her parents enquired as to the cause thereof, she told them that three girls had begun coming to her for playing together. They were surprised as they had not seen any child coming to the place. So, they put off the matter.

Sometime after, the girl said to her father; 'my playmates have told me that there is a certain organ on top of an almirah in one of the rooms. Please find it out.' The father was astonished. But, at the insistence of the girl, he went to the room, put a stool near the almirah, stood on it and looked around. To his amazement he found an old organ. on the top of the almirah. The girl was too small to climb over the almirah. So, how could she know about the organ unless somebody told her. The father was really nonplussed.

After this incident the girl used to tell the father that her three playmates were teaching her how to dance and sing. And she added that she had acquired some skill in the art.

One day the parents asked the girl to accompany them for a walk out. But she refused for, she said, she would like to play with her playmates.

And soon the day arrived when they had all to return to their own home. The girl said, 'please wait a while. Let me take leave of my playmates.' She went upstairs and her father sneaked behind her. When he entered the room he found that the organ was playing on its own accord while the girl was dancing before it. On the floor were lying the three dolls with whom she used to play.

When the father enquired in the vicinity, he was told that in the house used to live three girls whom their mother tormented and often left them alone when she went out. The three played with the organ. One day, they died of suffocation due to a leakage of gas. The spirits of the three took shelter in the three dolls with whom she used to play.

A MOTHER'S LOVE

(Courtesy : Northern India Patrika)

Sachin Chowdhury

This happened in June 1942 when Calcutta was passing the days under the shadow of Japanese bombardment. My parents and other kinsmen went to our old house in Twenty-four parganas. My younger sister had been ailing for long. Her husband and I stayed at Calcutta to attend her. We were living in a rented house in College Street. The day used to be full of rumours regarding the war. There was black-out during the night. My sister was suffering from anaemia. She had been delivered of a child. Her liver was not functioning properly. She was languishing day by day.

With us used to live a boy servant who was nursing the patient with great devotion. We used to keep awake during the night by turns. But her condition went on deteriorating. We were following the instructions of the doctors scrupulously, but we were praying to God as the last solace.

A shadow-figure on the wall

It was an afternoon. The weather was very hot. My sister's husband and I were sitting near her bed. She was exceptionally weak that day. Her body was getting cold and she was breathing with difficulty. We had lost all hope of her recovery. It was evident that her end was near. We were on our tenterhooks and were waiting for the ill-omened moment. The light in the room was hazy and outside it was pitch dark. The boy was sent out to call the doctor.

The doctor came and decided to administer oxygen to the patient. The latter was in a coma. Oxygen cylinders had already been procured well in advance. She was administered oxygen. But immediately thereafter we saw a shadow on the wall. It was the figure of some human being which was appearing immediately below the photograph of my mother and disappearing again and again! For a moment we could not make out anything. But we were hearing whispering sounds from the above followed by the appearance of the shadow figure. The figure used to contract and expand alternately. And some spicy smell was spreading round in the air.

Mysterious Fear

Out of sheer panic we lighted the bulb in the room. And instantly the figure vanished. A little later we put off the bulb and at once the figure reappeared. And this time the outline of the figure was very distinct. I visualised that the spirit of my mother had come to bless my sister recoup. We were almost stunned. And the wonder was that my mother was alive till then. So, how could she appear in the form of a spirit? My brain began to reel. I was terrified of some unknown destiny. I went on cogitating and went morose.

The entire night we passed near the death-bed of my sister. Early in the morning I went out to the doctor to give him an account of the patients condition. Hardly had I come back when we received a telegram from Father giving us the sad news of my mother's death. This happened at 8.45 p.m. the previous night. That was exactly the time when we saw the shadow figure on the wall for the first time. I missed a beat. It seemed as if the universe had stopped its activities.

Miraculous Cure

The doctor came as usual. On examining the patient he found that her condition was improving. Hope again dawned upon us that she may, after all, survive. For the next three consecutive nights the shadow figures of our mother appeared on the wall. But never after that!

My sister went on improving. The doctors were agreeably surprised as they had lost all hope of her recovery. We have absolutely no doubt that it was our mother's miracle that my sister came back from the death-door. Modem Science has no solution for this riddle. But what is evident requires no testimony.

DO NOT LOOK BEHIND

At Banaras there is an old street, named Ram Ghat. In the house No. 68 there had been living a family, called the Beri Family, for the last several generations. About 50 years back a member of the family, L.Nand Kishore, lived there. He had a wife and several children. He had a younger brother, Cindu Babu, who was a celibate.

Once Shri Nand Kishore fell ill. He had already been suffering from gout when a boil appeared on his body. The boil used to ooze out pus continuously. There was ruin in the immediate vicinity of the house. The pus-besmeared clothes were usually thrown in the ruins.

One day Shri Nand Kishore went off his head. He began prattling. It seemed he was possessed of some spirit. Exorcists were called in. They besought the Evil Spirit, or, whoever he might be. After some interrogation they could emanate this much from tne mouth of Mr.Kishore.

'I am a Saiyad (a Muslim Saint). There is a niche in the ruins nearby. Every day, the clothes besmeared with the pus of the boil of this gentleman were thrown near the niche whrch is my abode. So, I have come to take him with me, and I mean what I say.'

And then the patient began muttering some sentences of Arabic. It is worth noting that MrXishore never knew a word of Arabic.

'Saint Saiyad' was implored for a long time. After a good deal of persuasion he agreed to free the patient on one condition.

"An offering should be prepared consisting of oil, cotton wick, maize and some sweets and some body should take the offering to the crossing of Kabir Chaura (a famous crossing of Banaras) exactly at midnight. He should place the offering at the crossing and leave immediately. He should, under no circumstances, look behind, but walk swiftly towards his own house. Otherwise, evil consequences may follow".

Naturally, the wife of Mr.Kishore agreed to the procedure. But

Chindu Babu said to her,'You need not take this trouble. I am a lone man. I have nobody to look after. I will carry out this task. Nobody will be the loser if something happens to me.'

Offering was prepared with due formalities. Chandu Babu took it to the crossing, put it there exactly at midnight and turned back. But when he reached home, he was almost out of senses. On being questioned, it was with difficulty that he could ejaculate so much.

When I turned back after putting the offering at the crossing I heard footsteps of horse. I ran fast towards the house. Then it appeared to me that the horses were right on my head. Then I turned my face and found

At this his tongue began to twist, his throat began to dry and he was almost speechless.

Several times we put him the same question in details. But each time, when he came to the sentence, 'when I turned my back and looked behind, I saw....' His tongue began to twist, his throat dried up and he became speechless.

Mr. Kishore began improving from the same day, and Chandu Babu began deteriorating. Within a few days. Mr. Kishore left the bed and Chandu Babu left the world.

Some descendants of the same family still live in the same house. The oldest member of the family still remembers the incident distinctly and in details. The sceptics can ask him and satisfy themselves about the authenticity of the event.

SLOW DOWN THE CAR

(Courtesy : The Daily Aaj, Banaras)

Kirti Swaroop Rawat

A cinema actor from America narrated an incident of his life thus. A few months back I was ,going to San Francisco in my car with my wife.

We had to reach there at an appointed time. Night had fully set in and I was speeding at 125 km. per hour.

Suddenly I felt as if someone was whispering to me.,'A bit slowly please.' I lifted my foot from the accelerator, and immediately my wife said to me,' Did you too hear anything?' I was in suspense, but I said to her,'Yes I have heard it, but I am again speeding up.'

As soon as the speedometer indicated 125 km. a voice again said to me, this time a little loudly,'A bit slowly, Sonny.' I was flabbergasted. I told my wife that it was the voice of my father. And she agreed.

Only about a 100 metres from the place was lying a broken trail on the road. Evidently it got itself loosened from a car only a little while I could take my car aside and avoid an accident just in time. Had we been moving with 125 km. an hour, the end could be disastrous!

The father of the cinema actor was already dead several years before the incident.

THE MESSAGE OF ONE'S OWN DEATH

(Courtesy : Daily Aaj, Bananas)

Mrs. Susheela Chauhan is a teacher of Sociology at a college in Rajasthan. She narrated to us the story of the death of her mother-in-law in these words:

My mother-in-law was at Indore during those days. All of a sudden one day we received a telegram purporting that she was seriously ill. My husband immediately started for Indore. My mother-in-law could not be saved. She breathed her last in the morning. During the day we had not received the sad news. The same evening my sister-in-law was sleeping under a quilt and I was sitting on a window with a book in my hand.

Suddenly, my sister-in-law raised her head from the quilt and said to me, 'Why are you taking off my quilt. I said to her,'I am not taking off your quilt.'

By habit, my mother-in-law used to cover the bodies of all the children carefully. This incident in itself, would not have received a notice, the same day. My brother-in-law, who was in Nepal, heard distinctly that his mother was calling him.

Another sister-in-law of mine, who was at Rewa at the time, also became conscious of the presence of my mother-in-law;

None of the two had any knowledge of the illness of my mother-in-law till then.

And thus, my mother-in-law transmitted the news of her death to all her three children within 24 hours - one was at Jaipur, a second one at Rewa and the third in Nepal - And she died at Indore.

THE SPIRIT WITH A FOUL SMELL

(Courtesy : Weekly Hindustan)

The daughter of a respectable family came to her mother and said,'I cannot sleep in that particular room. By chance a guest had arrived in the house those very days. The family put him up in that very room in which the girl was afraid to sleep, as, she said, she used to see peculiar things.

The guest stayed in the room for 20 days and did not observe any unusual phenomena. As things would have it, on the 21st day, he too experienced the same kind of phenomena as the girl used to have. That night he somehow managed to pass, but he fled away the next morning.

One day, the inmates of the house had just sat down for their meal when they heard somebody descending the staircase. It seemed some bulky fellow was coming down. Coming down to where these people were sitting. He was not visible to any body, but immediately on his arrival a very foul smell spread all around.

One day the family invited another family to dinner. Before the dinner started the same spirit arrived and spread foul smell all around. Also, it began toppling over articles of the house. The family was so much upset by these occurrences that they all decided to leave the house.

Once a very old member of the family asked the spirit,'Who are you and what is the object of your visit to this house? Can we be of any service to you? 'The spirit did not say anything in reply.

So far he used to haunt just one room of the house, but now he became visiting every part of the house. The house began to emanate foul smell. A strange tale was connected with the house. People used to say that once a very fat man used to live in the house. The door of the house was so small that it had to be broken to bring out his corpse when he died. So, they could not take out the corpse for one full day, and it began rotting.

But even though a long time has elapsed since then evil smell emanates from the house. Why? This riddle has not been solved till today.

THE ENGINE WAS TAKING WATER

(Courtesy : Daily Aaj, Banaras)

It was Nov.7, 1931. It was nightfall. A driver was driving a passenger train. The fog was so thick that no signal was visible for more than 150 metres. When he was about 2 1/2 km. from a non-stop station, heard someone saying,'Slow down.' He thought it was the fireman speaking. But the latter assured him that he had not even uttered a word.

The same voice was heard a second time:' Go Slow'. This time the voice was louder and more distinct. The driver slowed down. The outer signal was indicating that the line was clear up to the station. And the home signal was also giving the same indication. But as soon as the train was crossing the inner signal, the driver saw an engine was taking water from the water-column.

Blessed be the mysterious voice. Had not the driver stopped the train in time, a terrible accident might have occurred. The signalman permitted the engine to reach the station and forgot all about it. So, he allowed the train too, to come on the same line!

A BROTHER'S DEATH AT HONG KONG

(Courtesy : Daily Aaj, Banaras)

This experience has been narrated by Mr.Cox of Queen's Town, Ireland. She was taking care of her little nephew. She was at Devenport at her maternal house. Her nephew was being attended as her brother was a naval officer, appointed at Hong Kong.

One evening, between 8 and 9, she had left the child in bed in his room. When he came running to her and said, 'Auntie, I have just seen my father near my bed. And his voice was trembling when he was talking.

Mrs. Cox replied, 'You must be seeing some dream!

The boy replied, 'I assure you it was no dream.

And he refused to go into the room again. When, inspite of persuasion, he could not agree to go into the room, she made him sleep along with herself.

Thus writes Mrs. Cox 'Between 10 and 11, I too began to sleep. About an hour later, I saw distinctly that my brother was sitting near the fire-grate on a chair. I was astounded. I could not help noticing the paleness of his face, which was something unusual for him.

Later on, they came to know that her brother expired a few hours before the experience at Hong Kong.

THE EXPERIENCE OF LIEUTENANT ROSS

(Courtesy : Reader's Digest, November 1952)

Mr. Ross was lieutenant in the Army. He was sober and talented. His age would be about 35. He was a graduate from the Military Academy of the U.S.A. and working at a military factory. He was allotted half of a delapidated house where he used to live with his wife. Sitting near the fire-grate he could see every nook and corner of the hall and the Drawing Room. In the remaining portion of the house was living another Lieutenant, Mr. Philips, along with his wife and a 9 year old son.

It was a night of March, Ross was working at a naval problem. Two dogs were sleeping in the room. All of a sudden, one of the two dogs groaned. And immediately after, the two dogs began running inside the hall and up the stairs.

Ross raised his head. He saw somebody in the hall. The dining and studying rooms were visible and distinct.

Ross had told us that he was not surprised as workers from the factory used to come to him at all odd hours of the day, with their difficulties. But he was astonished at two things. Why he had not heard his footsteps and why should he have entered the room without tapping. This was the usual courtesy expected of him.

It did not occur to Ross at the moment as to how the man could all enter the room as the doors were all bolted from inside and the windows had glass panes. Besides, they were 7 feet above the floor.

Thus says Ross: 'It seemed to me that the man wanted to say something. So, I kept looking at him for a few seconds. But he did not utter a word. 'Then Ross got up and stepped forward towards him. But immediately the man disappeared.

Ross searched every nook and corner of the ground floor. He found nothing uncommon. He began to think like this,'As I have been working very hard, perhaps I am getting hallucinations.'

Ross's wife asked him in half sleep,'What had happened to the dogs?'

Ross replied,'Nothing the matter.'

A week elapsed. It was about 9 at night. And that is surely not the time of appearance of spirits. Ross went into the drawing room. And Lo! He saw the same man of the previous week standing. This time he was nearer Ross -at a distance of about 6m.

Ross says, 'The house was well lit. I could distinctly see each and every limb of his body. I do not think he would weigh less than 90 kg. He looked sturdy and his clothes were of a brownish shade. His skin was tanned. So, may be, he had spent the part of his life under the sun.

Ross moved forward about 2 metres. And instantly the man vanished. Ross more astonished than terrified. He consulted his next door neighbour Philips.

Philips and his wife did not take him seriously, and made fun of him. Philips said to his wife; See what he is talking about. He has seen some ghost who is not related to him.'

Nothing happened for the next 16 days, it was the dull hour of 8.30 in the evening. The two housewives were lifting up the utensils of the dinner and the two husbands were getting ready to listen to the radio. Ross observed the same man again, this time in the hall. Ross ran hard towards him. He was hardly 3 metres from him when he disappeared!

Ten more nights passed. They were having cool, spring showers. The house was quite cool. Ross suspected that perhaps the cool breeze was coming from the basement which he had forgotten to close. He went to the basement and found it closed. Then Ross turned towards the kitchen.

There was no light in the hall, but there was one in the kitchen. It was a bulb of 100 watt. Besides, there were two more bulbs of 40 watt each on the walls. But only one of the two bulbs was visible as the man was standing between Ross and the kitchen. On any of the previous occasions Ross was never afraid. But this time an invisible shudder ran across his body. And again the man vanished without giving any warning or hint.

Ross was transferred to the sea in May. He never saw the ghost again. For years lie did not narrate this story to anybody.

He thought people would think he had gone off his head. And this might even affect his promotion and career.

In his narrative, Ross would say again and again, 'That visitor would never move right or left, nor up or down. Also, he never disappeared gradually. He would almost evaporate suddenly.'

THE NEWS OF DEATH

(Courtesy : Daily Aaj, Banaras)

The grandmother of Mathew Frost, at her last meeting with the latter, when she was hale and hearty, expressed her earnest desire that he must be present at her funeral. Frost gave her the promise, and added, 'It is said that when a person dies, he can always give a warning to one whom he loves most. If you remain pleased with me till your death, will you kindly inform me before-hand of the impending event? The grandmother readily agreed.

Two years and four months later, one afternoon of April, Mr. Frost was taking tea with his wife. There was a window at his back. Suddenly he heard a tap therefrom. He asked aloud, 'Who is there' and turned around. He saw his grandmother standing. He saw her figure distinctly. She was wearing her usual clothes. One hand was raised as if she had just tapped the door with it.

The house of Mr. Frost was at a distance of about 600 Km from that of his grandmother. His first reaction was that perhaps his grandmother had undertaken the journey without giving any previous information only to give him a surprise. She had been maintaining a good health. So, there could be no surprise at her coming like this.

Mr. Frost immediately reached the door, but she was not there. He searched every nook and corner of the house but she was nowhere to be found. Nobody could have escaped from the house without being noticed. When he returned to his room, suddenly he conjectured that perhaps his grandmother had expired, and her spirit had come to give him the news at the precise moment.

And that was exactly so.

THE SHIP WAS SAVED

(Courtesy : Daily Aaj, Banaras)

This experience has been narrated by a lieutenant commander of Harwich Harbour.

The pilots of a ship suddenly realised that the gearing apparatus of their ship was not under their control, and that some invisible force was turning it the wrong way. It could easily turned in some directions. But they tried other directions, it got stuck up due to the resistance of some hidden hand. At intervals there was a sharp whistling sound which could be heard distinctly. So the pilots found that had they continued to steer the ship at her usual course, a disaster would have occurred. It was also found that the ship was carrying the corpse of a very efficient sailor who used to whistle while steering.

THE FATHER OF HAYWORTH

(Courtesy : *Reader's Digest* - November 1952)

It was a night of April. Chester Hayworth was taking a class of Astronomy at the city of Dulles in Texas. The lecture went on for a long time and he could reach home at only midnight. Other days he used to go to bed two hours before. His wife was asleep. So, he did not wake her up.

Hayworth was in bed for hardly 15 minutes, when he felt he was awakened by somebody. But, really speaking he had not slept at all. He heard someone knocking at the door and he got up. A bulb was alight in the street, though the light was faint for the street. He had hardly fixed his eyes at the door when he found his father entering. He could distinctly see his face.

Hayworth was not particularly surprised. His father was posted in California. He thought he must have arrived that very evening and had taken him by surprise. This was nothing very unusual for him.

Hayworth says `Father crossed the room, came near my cot and stood at a distance of about half a metre from me. Now I could see him even more distinctly. His face seemed to be carrying some story as I had never seen him more morose. Was it that some inmate of our house became a victim of a mishap? Father stretched out his hand. I took his hand in mine.

He clasped my hand violently and shook his head. And instantly disappeared, my hand remaining outstretched.

This incident, according to Hayworth, took hardly half a minute. During the short interval Hayworth could see this much that his father was not in his office dress, but in grey trousers, shirt and a cap. Hayworth also noticed that lie had put on braces of a brown colour and he had a pen, a pencil and a pair of compasses in the pocket of his shirt.

Hayworth says,'I was sitting stunned, when the door bell rang. I opened the door. There was a peon who handed me a telegram. It was from my brother and purported; Father expired at 8.30 can you comer.

When he reached California, he enquired as to what kind of clothes his father was wearing on the last day. He was told that day his father was repairing his car and had put on a grey trousers, a shirt and a cap. It was usual for people to put this kind of dress for doing odd jobs, like the work of mechanic. But Hayworth had never seen his father in that dress. His shirt, they told him, had a pocket containing a pen, a pencil and a pair of compasses. Thousands of people keep pen and pencil, but the third thing a pair of compasses, was something very unusual.

The Psychical Research Society of America cross-examined him very closely.

Q. Do you ever received a fore-warning of coming events?

A. Ordinarily not. If I get it, It is always wrong.

Q. Do you see dreams very often?

A. Very rarely.

Q. Do your father ever have Psychological experiences?

A. He used to make fun of such things.

Q. Is it possible that you were asleep at the time and you saw your father in a dream?

A. I was never more fully awake.

Q. Do you think you possess any parapsychological powers?

A. Absolutely not.

Transmission of the news of a death is by no means uncommon. When someone near and dear one dies, he comes to him in his astral body and breaks the sad news. Later on it transpires that the death occurred exactly at the moment he expired. But, in the instance of Hayworth there was a time gap of two hours.

But researches provide an answer to this question too. They indicate that hallucinations take shape only when the dying person has an intense desire to communicate the news. But if his mind is involved in something else, it will wait for an opportuned moment for communication.

In the above instance, the Hayworth was taking a class at the moment his father died. So, the message waited. And it was communicated when Hayworth reached the bed, for that was the most opportune moment.

SAVED FROM THE GERMAN BOMB

(Courtesy : Daily Aaj, Banaras)

Western Hopkins was a famous scholar and writer. One night, as he was coming out to walk as far as the hotel, he went inside the hall to take his hat. He heard someone coughing and murmuring.He opened the door of that side. He cast a glance at the road opposite, but could not see anybody.

Hopkins returned to the hall but became excited as, during those days, pilots of aeroplanes that crashed would take shelter behind trees and bushes, near his house. Only a few days back he helped a local policeman in taking a wounded German pilot to my house for the time being till the ambulance arrived.

Hopkins gave up the idea of walking. A little Iater heard the same kind of sound of coughing and murmuring from outside the window. He felt as if somebody (Whosoever he might be) was anxious to communicate something to him. He had something important to tell him, but somehow found himself unable to convey it.

Only a few minutes later there was a loud bang of a German bomb exploding outside. Hopkins says, 'Only then I realised that the mysterious person wanted to forewarn me of the impending explosion.This reminded me of the German soldier whom I gave shelter in my house a few days back. While going back he greeted me and expressed his high sense of gratitude for my hospitality. I heard later on that he died in the hospital a few days later.

FULFILMENT OF A PROMISE

(Courtesy : Daily Aaj, 1971)

Dr.Celtagiron was talking to his friend Benjamin Sirchia on matters parapsychological. His friend said, Hark, doctor, if I die before you, which is very probable as I am old and you are young, I promise to come to you to give you testimony of the existence of after-life, if such there be.'

Dr.Celtagiron half humourosly replied,

'In case, please furnish me proof of your arrival by breaking something in this very room. For example, the lamp; that is hanging above the table.(This dialogue was going on in the dining room). And I too give you my word that I will give you proof positive of the existence of life in the form of a spirit;, if I die before you.'

Some time after this talk, Benjamin settled down at another place and lost all contact with Dr.Celtagiron. This conversation was held during the month of May.

The same year, on December one or two, Dr.Celtagiron was sitting in the same room with his sister at about 5 p.m. All of a sudden his attention was drawn towards the lamp hanging above the table. It seemed as if someone was tapping at the shade as well as the pulley of the gas-lamp gently. Gradually the sound increased in volume.

The doctor could not find any visible explanation for the phenomenon. The sounds stopped when he finished his dinner. The same thing occurred for four or five consecutive evenings. This increased the curiosity of Dr.Celtagiron and his sister, to find out what the matter was.

The doctor writes,'I write in all sincerity that during those four or five days I never thought of either my friend Benjamin or the conversation that I had with him during May last.'

On the evening of the fifth or sixth day, the doctor was in his study room and his sister was standing in the Balcony. Suddenly they heard a loud Bang from there dining room. They both went into room. They found half portion of the pulley of the gas lamp in a broken condition, on the table. This was all the more surprising as the part of the pulley could not have fallen without breaking the chimney. It seemed some blow had been given to the pulley as it fell exactly below the lamp.

Two days later a friend of Dr.Celtagiron told him that his friend Benjamin expired on Nov. 27 or 28. And at once the doctor began to suspect whether the mysterious events of the previous week were in any way connected with the death of Benjamin. Those phenomena occurred from Dec.1 or 2 and continued till Dec. 5 or 6. And it was evident that lamp was broken as promised during the conversation of May.

LORD CASTLEROW

(Courtesy : Daily Aaj, June 5, 1960)

Lord Castlerow was the foreign minister of England in 1812. During his youth he used to live in North Ireland. Once he lost his way, while hunting. He strayed into a big house. There were many guests in the house already. Castlerow was asked to sleep in a very big room. Due to a lack of proper beddings a firegrate was burnt near his bed and lie managed to sleep under a quilt.

About midnight Castlerow was awakened by the advent of a dazzling light in the room. First impression was that perhaps his quilt had caught fire. But he was astounded to find that the fire in the grate had already extinguished and a peculiar kind of bright light was emanating from the chimney!

But lo! A child appeared from the light. Castlerow was stunned. The child looked at him for a few moments and then vanished. There was a superstition abroad that prosperity reigned over the person who had a glimpse of such a child. But soon after he reached the peak of his fortune he would die in mysterious circumstances. Lord Castlerow met the same fate. He died a pitiable death.

DEATH WITH A CAP ON

(Courtesy : Daily Aaj, September 12, 1971)

As certain gentleman saw his grandmother in his room at about 2 a.m. He was very much taken aback by the fact that she was wearing a cap of a very old fashion.

Next day, after the morning breakfast, when he was narrating the last nights incidents, his father at once got agitated and left the dining chair. He left the room and the breakfast remained half-finished.

The gentlemen's mother said, 'Sonny, I am telling you the reason of his becoming so agitated. This very morning he told me that last night he got up suddenly and saw his mother standing near his bed. But, as soon as he began to talk to her, she disappeared'.

Not only that his father's sister too saw her the same night.

All the three experiences were felt at 2 o'clock in the night, whereas the mother had expired at 12.15 midnight!

His uncle was at the death-bed. He told them that at the time of death she was actually wearing that very kind of cap. She used to wear the same cap throughout her illness.

THE HAUNTED GALLERY OF HAMPTON COURT

(Courtesy : Daily Aaj, June 5, 1960)

A spirit is frequently seen in the gallery of Hampton Court. A tale goes that when Catherine Howard, the fifth queen of Henry VIII (1509-1547) was arrested for corruption, she escaped from the prison. She wanted to fall at the feet of her husband and apologize. But she had not been able to get out of the church when she was waylaid by her guards. She cried and cried but in vain. They virtually dragged her from the gallery.

Many people have testified to the fact that they have seen a white figure emerging out of the dark room and walk towards the church. She goes upto the door of the church, cries fiercely and returns by the same route.

Many stories of a similar nature are connected with the Hamton Court. The tomb of Pan, the God-Mother of Edward VIII was broken open. This became necessary for the rejuvenation of the Hampton Court. A little later mysterious whispers, murmurs and whirling sound skin to that of a spinning wheel were heard. Instantly labour was employed to trace the origin of the voices. It led them to a room about the existence of which nobody knew anything. The greatest surprise of them all was that there was a spinning wheel of a very old type in the room. And it seemed as if someone had been spinning over it continually.

Some people have vouchsafed that they have seen Pan moving in the verandah and she had exactly the same dress that is put on marble statue on her tomb.

MISCHIEVOUS ACTIVITIES OF AN EVIL SPIRIT

(Courtesy : Weekly Hindustan)

Experiences of Hariword Carrington

I was invited to the town of Stockton for delivering a lecture. In course of the lecture, a lady approached me and said, 'I am very much disturbed by a voice. It emanates all of a sudden and goes on for some time. I feel as if the voice is that of my late husband. Many years have passed since he died. Sometimes the voice is full of emotion. At other times it is insipid. It seems to interfere with every activity of mine and has began hold of me. It is getting of my nerves and sometimes I cannot even sleep properly.

Her statement appeared to contain a good deal of truth. She did not know anything about supernatural subjects. I understood that some spirit was wondering around her. She is short statured. Her hair are black. Her head is also small. Sometimes she would spell her to be liberal; at other times miserly. Her voice and activities would become more prominent at night.

Since that day the lady began to feel as if some person is embracing her at odd places. He found many signs on her body which indicated that she was embraced by somebody. The spirit could not be that of her late husband. The latter was a thorough gentleman and loved his wife dearly. This was some evil spirit in the garb of her husband.

First of all, I tried to persuade the spirit and asked it to leave the lady alone. This did not have any effect upon it. At last I invoked some sublime spirits and asked them to get rid and lady of his visitations.

I could see it clearly that several spirits came and virtually dragged the evil one. Since that day the lady was not troubled any more by the mysterious voice.

THREE SKELETONS

(Courtesy : Daily Aaj, June 5, 1960)

In the north of Engalnd there is a landlords' mansion of an old type which was built in 1860. It is said that during the reign of Queen Elizabeth the owner of the house, Sir John Southworth, who was a staunch Roman Catholic, one day got a hunch that one of his daughters was in love with a protestant. This enraged him.

He upbraided her and said, 'If ever in future you try to meet him, I will deal with you very severely.'

The girl was egoistic and stubborn like the father. She met her lover and the two conspired to get married clandestinely. But ill luck would have it, her brother came to know of the ploy. The day her lover reached along with two of his friends, several persons pounced upon them and killed them.

After this nefarious deed the inmates of the family sent her to a convent where she languished and died. People say that even now her spirit comes out to meet her lover in the astral form. As soon as she comes out of the convent her lover welcomes her by bowing down before her. Then the two walk together for some distance, embrace each other and disappear.

A testimony to this episode was provided by three skeletons which were found when the ground near the house was excavated.

A NAKED BOY

(Courtesy : Daily Aaj, June 5, 1960)

Some spirits are liberal-minded and helpful.'Naked boy' has been given the name to such a spirit.

The haunt of this spirit was the Dilton Fort near Sunderland. When all the servants of the fort would go to bed, this spirit would come, churn the butter, wash the dishes and finish the daily works which were left unfinished by the servants. And then the spirit would leave. He was so fond of doing such odd jobs that if some day, the servants would not leave any such work unfinished, he would lose his temper and began breaking utensils and turn everything topsy-turvy in the room. The next day the servants would deliberately leave a few things unfinished and thus pacify the naked boy.

One day, out of sheer compassion a servant left a suit of clothes for him. When the boy came at night his joy knew no bounds. But alas! Since that day, the spirit never returned. And now the servants had to finish all the household corps themelves.

TELL HELEN

(Courtesy : Reader's Digest, November 1952)

Mrs. Harris was an inhabitant of Philadelphia (America). Her close friend Helen Hoyet was divorced from her husband. She had never seen Mr.Hoyet. One day she was told that he had expired. She was retiring at night when she was reminded of him.

She felt as if some gentleman was near her. He was medium sized, had a round face and his eyes were showing signs of impatience.

The spirit said to her in a commanding voice,'Tell Helen; tell Helen.

Later on Mrs.Harris came to know that Mr. Hoyet was a rough and ready man who sometimes became even discourteous. She asked him,'What should I tell Helen.

The spirit answered, "At my house. Wooden box with a brass handle. The upper drawer containing my handkerchief. Black purse. File...Tell Helen."

Mrs. Harris conveyed the message exactly in the same form to Helen.

With reluctance, Helen went to his house where she had not gone for 15 years. His co-wife was living there. She opened the drawer concerned. The black purse and the file were there in tact. The file contained the appendix of the will of Mr. Hoyet.

WILBER FORCE

(Courtesy : Daily Aaj, June 5, 1960)

Clergyman Wilber Force once narrated his very strange experience. One day he went to a friend of his. While going for dinner he saw another clergyman in the verandah. At dinner he spoke about the other clergyman to the lady sitting next to him. The lady almost jumped up and said,'You have seen the spirit of an inmate of this house.'

Wilber Force was astounded but still he did not pay much attention to the matter. The same night he was studying in his library when the door opened and he saw the same person entering. Without even looking at Wilber Force he went straight to the almirah of books and began searching something. Being disappointed he went back the same ways. Wilber Force was stupefied and lie remained seated as if pasted to the seat.

The next day he decided to accost the spirit when he came. At night when he was seen again, Wilber Force asked him,'Gentleman, what is it that you want?' The visitor was almost enraptured, and said to him gratefully/Before death I placed a bundle of papers in this almirah. In case it is read by the inmates of this house, it would create a furore. I want to destroy it, but I am unable to find it out.'

Wilber climbed over the almirah and brought out the bundle from behind. Then the two burnt it together. The visitor said,'Now I will be at peace. 'The same instant, he left the room and was never seen again.

THE MYSTERIOUS BOX

(Courtesy : Daily Aaj, June 5,1960)

A spirit used to appear in an old fort. A daring lady relieved him of the predicament.

The Earl of the fort was in London along with his family. The lady mentioned above applied to serve in the family and she was appointed during the absence of the Earl. She was given a very big room to sleep. The old lady was flabbergasted when she examined each and every article of the room. But little could she realise that the servants had put her in a haunted room only to harass her. But she quietly began reading the Bible.

A little later a rather rich man entered the room, and after staying for a few minutes left without a word. A few moments elapsed. Again the same person entered, remained standing for a few minutes and went away silently. The old lady was convinced that the visitor was some spirit. She recalled the name of God and decided that she would talk to him when he came again.

A little while after, the visitor came again. The lady asked him,'What do you want, for which you have come here three times.

The spirit said, Follow me.'

The old lady walked after him. Stopping at the door of a small room, the spirit asked the lady to enter it. He assured her that no harm would result to her therefrom. They went a side. After lifting a plank from the floor of the room, the spirit said to her,'Do you see a wooden box in pit below? Send it to the Earl in London. Thereafter I will never come to this house again.'

The lady promised to do the needful. What the box contained, only the Earl and the spirit knew. But the Earl was very much pleased to receive it and he gave a life-long pension to the old lady.

THE GHOST OF RAJA TALAB

(Courtesy : Mrs. Shakuntala Mohan)

My father was a very prominent citizen of Banaras. Till 50 years he used to practise at the bar. He was one of the toppers in the profession. After returning from the court he would go out for a change in his horse-carriage. A servant and his two elder brothers would accompany him. He gave the utmost importance to outings as well as delicious dishes.

He was equally fond of horse-riding. In the afternoon when his brothers were not inclined to go out with him, he would ride his white mare. And he always preferred to visit solitary places.

'Raja Talab' is a small, but well-known locality, about 16 km. from Banaras. 50 years have elapsed since this event. During those days the place desolate, people would not dare go there after sunset. The tank, as the name indicates, was very big and there were several banyan and peepal trees near it.

My elder uncle was an expert in cooking. When he accompanied us, we never bothered about our meals. He would keep all victuals and paraphernelia required in the carriage before hand. As soon as he saw a suitable spot for the purpose he would stop the carriage and begin preparing for the picnic. The servant would clean the place and my uncle would set himself to prepare the various kinds of dishes.

The servant would only clean the place. My uncle would take care of the rest. Before we would sit down for the meal, my uncle would set apart plentiful of dishes as the latter was of an orthodox type.

The servant was a few years older than my father. In our seven storey house, the ground floor was occupied by the servants. The name of this particular servant was Chhedi. He was a very sturdy fellow. He had a wife, a mother and a small child. The servant was almost a shadow of my father. He too was very fond of Chhedi.

The spices and condiment were all brought from a particular shop which used to specialise in them. One day, when father returned from the court, his elder brother said to him,'Tomorrow is Sunday.

Where do you propose to go for picnic? Father replied,'Let us start early in the morning and prepare a winter picnic. Have you thought of any suitable place. His brother replied, will not Raja Talab be a fit place for the purpose. Father agreed.

Uncle called Chhedi and got all things ready in the carriage in the evening. He did not forget to bring the condiments.

Next morning we started in our carriage at about 5. The weather was exceptionally good. By dawn we reached Raja Talab. After finishing with the morning ablutions Uncle began searching for a suitable place for setting the oven. He came across a delapidated room nearby and he chose it. Chhedi washed the place carefully.

Uncle took a bath and prepared for the meal. It was got ready by noon. Uncle called Father, who said,'this place is emitting pleasant smell. Uncle remarked that it was the fragrance of the spices. Chhedi's meal was set apart and then we all sat for the meal. The food was really very tasty. Every one of us took meals to our fill. Then we asked Chhedi to take his food which had already been set apart. Chhedi said that he would partake of his food after his daily routine of a bath and physical exercise. He took his exercise underneath the peepal tree and then took food.

Chhedi put the articles in the carriage and beckoned to us to start back. But father said that lie would like to take rest for a couple of hours before going back. This belated things and we all started about two hours later.

It was about 6 in the afternoon. Father was chatting with his brother. All of a sudden we heard a bewailing sound from the room of Chhedi. Father thought, perhaps, he was beating his wife as he sometimes used to do. But when the cries became even more shrill, Father started coming down to take Chhedi to task. On reaching the ground floor he found that Chhedi was lying, face downward, and his mother and wife weeping. Father was flabbergasted as, only about 15 minutes back, Chhedi was hale and hearty, and had come down after having a chat with father.

Cold water was requisitioned. It was sprinkled on the face of Chhedi. Only then could lie mutter a few articulate words. Father asked him in an aggressive tone, 'Chhedi, what is all this hulla baloo about? Chhedi replied, 'This rascal ate up all my victuals? I am not going to leave him. Father was truly nonplussed. He never believed in ghost stories.

Even then, he asked Chhedi; 'Who are your the reply was 'I belong to the chamar (low) caste. I was drowned in the tank near. Since then I have been living on the peepal tree abode it. Today, where you set apart my food in the room, this fellow ate it up. On top of it, he challenged me to a bout of wrestling. Now, just tell me whose fault it is. Let him suffer for his misdeed.

Father drew up a sketch of the scene of Raja Talab in his eyes. How Chhedi took physical exercise which appeared to an ignorant man like a challenge for a wrestling match. Chhedi had taken his own meal. How could he realise that the ghost would take it to be his own meal and thus get infuriated by taking it. Father said to Chhedi, 'Please leave Chhedi alone. We shall do according to your bidding.' They got elicited this reply, 'At exactly the same place a similar meal should be prepared. The same kind of condiments should be introduced in it. The meal should be placed at the same place as before at midnight. Then alone I will leave Chhedi. Otherwise I will take his life.' Father replied, 'We shall follow your instructions scrupulously. But then, for sure, you will leave Chhedi alone.' The reply was, 'Most certainly. But there should be no lapse in the details.'

Five minutes later, Chhedi opened his eyes. He was astounded to see Father in his room, for it was something unusual. He asked his wife what the matter was, and why his master had come to his room. What reply could the poor woman give? Father told him that he had gone into a swoon. So, he had to come to see him. Pressing his head, Chhedi said; Yes, Babuji, I have got headache. But about the swoon I did not know anything. Father took his mother and said to her, 'Just do exactly as has been told. Otherwise, Chhedi, may fall ill again. The mother replied, while weeping. At my house there would be nobody willing to do this kind of job.' Father had to keep quiet.

The same kind of balechoo began to recur in the room of Chhedi. This went on for about 6 months. Nobody offered to do the job. Chhedi began losing his health. When the mischievous activities reached a climax, some neighbours sent him to the lunatic asylum.

The inmates of the house heaved a sigh of relief.

One day, while coming back from the court, Father sent his tiffin on the ground floor, the servant placed a sumptuous dinner on the table in the room. Father had not picked up even a morsel when he saw Chhedi standing at the door.

Father was nonplussed as to how he got out of the asylum. He stared at Chhedi to make sure whether his eyes had not been deceiving him. Sure, he was Chhedi himself. The latter said, 'Will you take the meal alone' Father replied,'No, you better take it.'

Chhedi consumed the entire meal, and said,'It was very tasty. Now, I am going.' Father was dumb found as it were.

A little later, Father enquired of the asylum on the phone as to why they had let off Chhedi. They told him that they had not let him off. He was still in the asylum. Father was flabbergasted. He was sure his eyes were not at fault. He had himself offered the food of his dishes to Chhedi. There could be no mistake regarding the matter. Then, how did it all happen?

About a year later Chhedi was discharged from the asylum. The members of his family had placed the requisite meal at the appointed place according to the bidding of the spirit. That was why Chhedi had got quite well. This even impressed Father so much that his interest in the subject began to grow. He studied many books on the topic. In the end he had to admit that there was some kind of invisible force in existence, call it a spirit or a ghost. If the wishes of some person remain unfulfilled in his life-time he carries the desire to his after life. Only then his spirit wanders recklessly. Chhedi is alive till today. When we ask him about those occurrences, lie laughs and says,'How can I say whether I was possessed of a ghost or not. You may ask Babuji.'

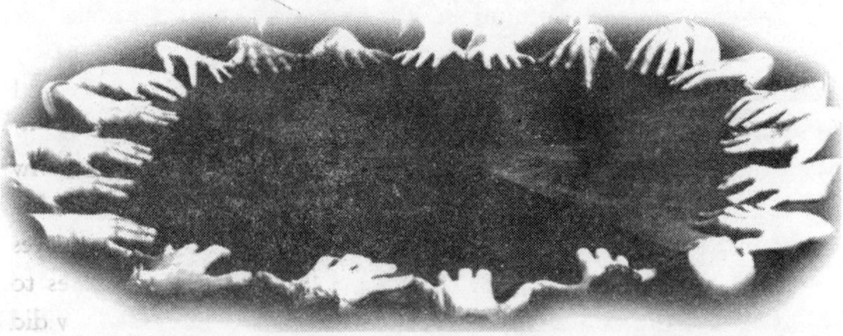

PART–II

Seance

INTRODUCTION

In the modern form this activity is not very old. Even then about a century has elapsed when it began. But it has not yet been given the status of a science. For, quite a few educated people regard it with suspicion and do not recognise it as a full-fledged branch of knowledge.

It is nightfall. There is silence all around. A light three-legged table is standing in a room which is lighted with a rather low light. Camphor, incense etc. have been burnt in the room during the day. So the room is full of pleasant smell. Religious books have been put in an almirah of the room. Pictures of great men and incarnations are hanging from the walls. There is a photograph of a certain person who has died recently. Five persons are sitting around the table for evoking the spirit of the same person.

One of the five persons is the guide who seems to be conversant with the procedure. He says to the remaining persons:

'All of you kindly open out your hands and place them on the table consecutively so that the fingers of each of you may touch those of the next persons on either side, so that the circle may be complete.

The others follow. And then the guide addresses them again:

'All of you, please think of the soul that is gone and call him. If the table seems to tilt on a side, please do not stop it. But do not put your hand's pressure to tilt it voluntarily.'

All of them keep silent for a few minutes. And then the guide says :

'If some spirit has entered the table, please give it a click.'

And lo! The table tilts to one side, and gives a click and again stands still. The guide goes on:

'If you are the same spirit whom we are evoking, please give two clicks, otherwise, three.'

The table will give two clicks or three as the case may be. And then will start a series of questions and answers.

This is Seance.

It is evident that every question cannot be answered in the form of Yes or No. So, a different procedure is adopted. The five persons are given the numbers 1,2,3,4,5. Then the guide asks the spirit:

'Would you like to give your answers with paper and pencil if so, through which medium? Give us many clicks as the number of the persons of your choice.'

The medium thus selected is provided with a paper and pencil. The guide says to him:

'Leave your hand loose. If the pencil moves of its own accord, do not stop it. But, do not try to write of your own accord.' And then the real session begins.

A small plank is sometime requisitioned which is constructed specially for the purpose. It has a hole in it, in which a pencil is inserted there are three wheels under the plank. The medium places hand gently which is called planchette. It facilitates the process. There are several variants of this procedure. Some people call the spirit on the jar instead of the table. Others put a tumbler on a broad dish. The other details are almost the same.

There are no set rules as to who can serve as a good medium. It is surmised that one with a clean heart and a simple nature ordinarily provides a good medium. Some media do not require even a table. They go into a trance and began answering the questions with their own tongue. A trance is a kind of suspended animation, in which one forgets his original self and adopts a secondary personality.

Usually 3, 5 or 7 persons sit at the table. As to why the table should be light, the cause is obvious. We should make things easy for the spirit or whatever entity enters the table. If the table is heavy, it would be difficult to tilt it, but why should it be three-legged, and why round, as also why should only an odd number of persons should partake in the seance, we cannot answer such questions. We can only say this much that all the persons who carry on this activity say that success comes only this way. And our experience corroborates this statement. This art if it can be given that name, is, as yet, undeveloped. It requires good deal of research work. We shall reach at the bottom of the secrete only after years of search

But this happened sixty years back. A friend of mine, Dr. B.L. Atreya, who is no more, was performing a seance one day. He had been the Head of the Department of Philosophy at the Banaras Hindu University. He was very fond of the seance during his youth. And he was quite successful at that. One day, a spirit entered the table. A near and dear owner of the house, where the seance was being performed, had expired.

They wanted to invoke his spirit. But it was some other spirit which entered the spirit. And the following conversation took place through the medium:

Q. Who are you and when did you die?

A. I am the spirit of an English soldier who was killed during the mutiny of 1857.

Q. Why has not the spirit, whom we are evoking, come?

A. Today, a very high personage of Kashi has expired. Many spirits are engaged in welcoming him. That spirit too has gone out for the same purpose.

Q. So far as we know no reputed personality of Kashi has kicked the bucket today. If such a thing happened, we must have known it.

A. The person is not high according to your standards. He is according to ours.

Q. In which street of Kashi has it taken place?

A. I do not remember the Indian names of the streets. But I can draw a map on a piece of paper to indicate the place.

Through the medium, the spirit drew a sketch on paper which indicated the turnings and crossings through which one would have to pass, for reaching the place. The spirit also told them that the departed person was a hermit belonging to an order of mendicants. People were turning from the cremation ground and a funeral dinner was in full swing in the street. This much information was further supplied by the spirit.

A man was run for the street with the sketch. He went on following the route indicated on the map. When he was nearing the place he found the street aglow with light. He asked the people around and found that a hermit of mendicants' has left for his heavenly abode the same evening.

The funeral dinner was over and people were busy removing the dishes.

When I was told the story I began to take interest in the subject. I practised concentration for some days. On a few occasions, I partook of the seance along with Dr. Atreya. After a little practice I could do it myself. On most of the occasions I was successful. On two and three occasions I failed. I am narrating my experience of several occasions:

(I) This happened at Moradabad, my native place. The patriarch of a family, Brij Bhan, had expired.

His descendants had come to know that I was interested in this activity. So, they called me and invoked the spirit of the deceased.

Several people were sitting at the seance including a son and a grandson of the deceased. The spirit was asked as to through whom he would answer our questions. He pointed at his grandson. I put a paper and a pencil in the hands of the grandson and asked the spirit to sign his name. Strangely enough he signed his name in the form of: Breej Bhan.

I was not a little surprised for this was a definitely wrong way of signing his name. Then his sons told me that the deceased knew very little English. And throughout his life he used to sign his name in this very form. His accounts books were sent for. And it was found that his signatures tallied with the one put down here.

(2) A seance was going on at Banaras. A spirit said to us through the table.

'Among you there is a man who has been beating his mother a little time back.'

The person concerned immediately began to shed tears. He admitted that accusation was true.

Another incident from Banaras: five persons were performing seance. B.B's father-in-law S, the latter's son, P and two sisters of P : I and U.

(3) B called the spirit of his mother-in-law who had expired recently. Afterseveral questions, she was asked,'You know B's wife is expecting. Will that be a son or daughterT

A. That will be a son, but

Q. What is the meaning of this but?

A. I mean she will have a son and

Q. Yes, if everything goes smooth, then for the son, a p

On repeating the question a number of times, we could elicit the answer that she wanted a perambulator for the son. The departed lady was only semi-educated. She could not pronounce the word, 'children's carriage instead.

The spirit was asked several times to spell out her statement, 'If everything goes well' elaborately. But we got no clear answer. We were convinced that something untoward was being indicated.

About a month later the wife B delivered a male child who was still born.

S was a non-believer. We asked him to put a question, the answer to which would convince him that it was really the spirit of his wife who was responding and none-else. S replied.

'I am taking a question in my mind which none but he and his wife knew about it. If the spirit refers to it in her reply, I will be convinced.'

We put the question to the spirit. The reply was characteristic.

'I know what he was hinting at. But does he not realise that it is such a delicate matter that it cannot be talked of in the presence of the children ?

S had to acknowledge the truth of her statement.

(4) We were sitting on the roof of a house in the Banaras Hindu University campus. Besides Dr. Atreya, we had one more companion who was still in our midst.

After a few questions we put him another poser. We asked him to give two clicks if the answer was affirmative, otherwise three clicks. The table gave us 12 clicks. We repeated the question. This time we got 20 clicks. We put the question again and again. Every time we got meaningless reply. Then Dr. Atreya realised that some evil spirit had captured the table. He addressed the spirit thus :

'We have understood that you are an unwanted spirit and have come to harass us. Please give us two clicks and be off.'

In response to that the table began to rotate. We repeated the same thing. Believe it or not, the table began hoping round the roof!

Readers, please bear with me. Neither am I out of head, nor am I wilfully distorting the facts. There was no fourth person in the house. Nor was there any string or rope or hidden apparatus. So, there could be no question of any wilful deception. This is no hearsay. We were eyewitnesses to the incident.

There is a rule of seance performers that the sitting must be held inside a room. There may be some mystery about it. We had broken the rule and were holding the session on the open roof.

Now, we shall narrate a few incidents taken from clippings of newspapers. We are sure the writers have not wilfully exaggerated matters. We are not inclined to believe that any educated man would try to deceive the public deliberately.

THE NEWS OF ONE'S OWN DEATH

(Courtesy : *Northern India Patrika*)

A Bengali doctor had to migrate to U.P. for reasons of health. He had absolutely no faith in spirits and seance. Still, at Allahabad, some of his friends succeeded in persuading him to sit at a session of seance.

Five persons were performing the seance in dim light. A little later the guide informed them that some spirit had entered the table. A black curtain was hanging on one side of the room, on which a dim figure was taking shape. Gradually the figure took the form of a man. The medium was in a trace.

The guide asked him, 'Who are you?

The medium answered, 'I am Panchoo of village. I have a paternal house in that village.'

The doctor interrupted. But I know it for certain that Panchoo of that village is still alive.'

The medium replied, 'I am definitely Panchoo of that village. Last night I have committed suicide by hanging myself from a tree outside the village.'

And the figure disappeared.

The doctor enquired of his relatives of that village. The event described was cent per cent correct. Panchoo had actually hanged himself from a tree outside the village the previous night.

THE MYSTERY OF MURDER

(Courtesy : Northern India Patrika)

This happened in Burma. The husband of a lady Ma Omkin suddenly disappeared. Two weeks later the lady arranged for a seance. The medium was a lady. She said in the voice of her husband.

'That day I won 600 kyat (a coin) at a gambling spree. I was returning home when I was attacked by robbers. They were five and all masked. They met me near the bridge between the villages Changan and Myagan. They dragged me to the forest. There they attacked me with a dagger and beheaded me. And then they burnet me in the jungle. Please dig my body out of the pit and perform my funeral ceremonies duly.

Hearing the heart-rending story a search was made around the village Mbehock. A head constable was helping us in the search.

At a spot he caught a sight of a piece of coloured cloth protruding out of the ground. He drew it out. It was a loincloth besmeared with blood. And the ground around was ejecting foul smell.

We succeeded in digging out the fragments of the body of Mr. Ko Kee Chan, the husband of Ma Omkin. As to why he was murdered we could not say. Nor we could ascertain as to whether the deceased had actually won anything in the gambling. There was no money on his body. But this much could be gathered that he was the leader of a gang of freebooters who held away over the neighbouring villages. And so he had created many enemies. Possibly some of them had taken revenge upon him in the form.

A MESSAGE

(Courtesy : Northern India Patrika)

Tushar Kanti Ghosh

This incident pertains to the family of Shri Vidhu Bhooshan Mallick who has been the Chief Justice of the Allahabad High Court. Justice Mallick was married to Smt. Leela Devi, a daughter of Shree Sharda Charan Mitra, a judge of the Calcutta High Court. A maid of the name Hari Dasi accompanied the bride to the bridegroom's house. She had nurtured Leela Devi in childhood. So, she was sent to attend on the lady.

Leela Devi died at a comparatively young age after a protracted illness. The youngest son of Mr. Mallick was not so considerate to Hari Dasi as was expected of him. So, he decided to go back to the village. Mr. Mallick tried hard to dissuade her but she was adamant. Mr. Mallick decided to give her life-long pension of Rs.15 per month. He began sending the amount to her village every month.

Some time later Mr. Mallick received a letter from Hari Das. The addressee's name was written not as Vibhu Bhooshan but as Vibhuti Bhooshan. Mr. Mallick was surprised. He thought Hari Das has lived with him so long that she could not commit a mistake of this kind. Perhaps, he thought to himself Hari Das is no more and her pension is being grabbed by some one else. He tried to find out the truth but could not come to any definite conclusion. So, he gave up sending the pension. Some days later, he received another letter from Hari Das. In this letter also, he was addressed as Vibhuti Bhooshan.

Now, he was convinced that Hari Das had expired and the letters were written by someone else. So, he did not recommence sending the pension.

Shri Praphull Kumar Sarkar was a relative of Mr. Mallick. He was a very high officer in the Finance Section of the Railway. This should be enough proof of his credibility. Even otherwise many people could vouchsafe to his honesty and truthfulness. So, his evidence cannot be brushed aside.

Mr. Sarkar had been to England for treatment of his eyes. He was once partaking of a seance of Sir Oliver Lodge Physical Research Society. After several questions and answers, the medium asked the participants, 'Is anybody connected with the Chief Justice of Allahabad High Court sitting amongst you. The wife of the judge wants to convey a message.

Sarkar said that he was related to Justice Mallick. 'The wife of Justice Mallick wants to send him three messages:

1. These days you are working very hard. Please discontinue it.
2. Be in taking interest in Psychic matters.
3. Do not dismiss your erstwhile maid.

Mr. Sarkar sent all the three messages in a letter to Justice Mallick. A photostat copy of the letter was published in the Northern India Patrika. We have no record of the date concerned. But from the stamps on the letter it appears that the letter was posted in London on Oct. 31, 1951 and received at Allahabad on 6th Nov., 1951.

On receipt of the letter, Justice Mallick enquired again. It was found that Hari Dasi was still alive. He began to send her the pension again. Also, he paid her all arrears.

THE PEARL TIE-PIN

(Courtesy : Geraldine Cumins: Mind in Life and Death-The Aquasian Publishing Co. Ltd., London 1956)

An army officer of France was killed in World War I. About a month later his sister was performing a seance when she got a message from her late brother:

'Kindly ask mother to give my tie-pin to the girl I was going to marry'

The sister asked him the name and address of the girl. The spirit gave her the name and address required. A letter was sent to that address which came back, undelivered.

The post office wrote that there was nobody bearing that name at the place. So, people thought the message was false.

About six months later the Army officers sent all the belongings of the deceased officer to his next of the kin in Ireland. It transpired that he was really betrothed to a girl of the name given. The girl's address was given therein also a pearl tie-pin. He had not disclosed the fact of his betrothal to anybody and he had gone to the battlefield soon after.

When a person goes to a battlefield he is asked to name his next of kin. The departed officer had given the name of that girl. The name of the girl was given correctly, but not her address. It is possible that his sister took the address wrongly.

At the time of seance the sister knew of the death of her brother but she had never heard the name of the girl.

A HIGH SOUL

Shri Ram Chandra Verma, a famous writer of Hindi, received a letter from Bharat Ratna B. Rajendra Prasad, President of India. We are here appending a copy of the letter. The original letter can be seen at his address :

47, Lajpat Nagar, Maldahia, Varanasi 22.

Rashtrapati Bhavan New Delhi

Jan. 6, 1955

Dear Shri Ram Chandra Verma

Kindly accept my thanks for a copy of a book 'Dev Lok' translated by you. These days I am hardly getting any time for reading and writing. Still I was anxious to read this book. I would not do so for it was printed in small type. So I have got it read for me. I am writing this letter after having gone through about three-fourth of the book. The matter given in the book may not be acceptable to Physicists, but I feel the basis of the statements therein is not false.

I have got myself interested in the book due to certain personal experiences. A good deal of interest is being taken by the western in spiritual subjects and quite a voluminous literature has sprung up on such topics.

It would not be out of place to mention a few of my own experiences.

There is a gentleman here through whom high soul sends us messages which come to us in such mysterious ways that this can by no means be called a case of fraud or deception. Write out your questions on a piece of a paper and put it at a place indicated. You may put your seal on that you may feel sure it has not been tampered with. When the soul will feel inclined to do so. The envelop or the covering will remain in tact. But when you will open it you find the answer to your question written therein. You may place several such envelopes together. And each envelop will carry a mark whether it has been attended to or not. Sometimes there will be a hint that it should be placed again. Such directions will be written very clearly and legibly. When the envelope is opened the questioner will find an answer to his question.

That is not all. When the medium prays and offers some incense, fragrant flowers etc. he puts a paper and a pencil along with them. The medium and the questioner sit or stand at a distance from the place. The flowers began to tremble, the pencil stands erect and begins to hover round the paper. After a few moments, the paper gets turned upside down, the pencil gets up and writes up a message. If there is no paper the pencil does not move. Then another paper is put there and then pencil begins writing. When the message is completed, the pencil no longer lifts up. This I have seen several times myself. Besides, see articles appeared at the place from nowhere as it were, like a talipearls, sapphires, small amulets etc. Sometimes, from the midst of flowers the figure of a hermit takes shape. He has long beard and a very pleasant light of compassion emanates from his eyes. Sometimes the figure disappears immediately after appearing. At other times it stays longer. In exactly the same way sometimes we get glimpse of Ram, Krishnas other gods. Sometimes even more mysterious things take place. Some of the articles and pictures that I have got this way,I have treasured like an heirloom.

As I knew all these things naturally I was interested in the book and I began reading it.

Hoping you are quite well,

Sincerely yours,
Rajendra Prasad

THE CHILD OF LINDBERG

It was March 1, 1932, when this nefarious crime was committed by the most demonical wretch of the twentieth century.

The house of Col. Charles Lindberg was at some distance from Hopewell in New Jersy. The rascal in question left his car a little away from the road which led to the house of Lindberg. He lifted up his folding ladder from the back seat of the car and took it to the lawn of Lindberg. He adjusted the pieces of the ladder and set it against the window of the room where the baby of Lindberg, 20 months old, was sleeping. A few moments later he descended on the ladder with the baby in his hands. But the ladder gave way and the two fell down on the ground. And so, the police which reached the spot next day, got a clue to the crime.

The whole world was aghast at the news which ran like wild fire. Everybody who heard it cursed the culprit from the bottom of the heart. Quite a few persons were interested in the matter out of curiosity. They hindered rather than helped the police in the investigation.

A merchant of Norfold in Virgina had said that the culprit had contacted him. Several days passed when it became evident that the matter was a hoax.

A letter was received from the criminal which supported that the baby was in his custody in a boat. The authorities searched hard but could not get any clue to the boat. The letter was genuine but there was no trace of the boat.

There was a crazy schoolmaster of Bronx who gave an advertisement in a newspaper. As luck would have it, the culprit used to read that very paper. It was advertised that the child could be restored on payment of a specific ransom.

The ransom money was given in the form of bonds of gold which were no longer in vogue. Through the bonds the police caught hold of a certain old German soldier, Bruno Hoptman. He used to live in a small house of Bronx with his wife. He was not employed but he had ample money which he procured through illicit means of a like nature. The Government cast such net around his neck that he could not escape it, and ultimately was sent to the gallows.

Certain things happened in connection with this episode which could not be made any head and tail.

It is definite that Hoptman had at least two accomplices in his nefarious activities: a man and a woman. But, when Hoptman was caught, nobody bothered to trace his accomplices. An amount of the ransom money was found with Hoptman, but the remainder could not be traced. And to be sure, the criminal knew as to which persons were present at the house of Lindberg the night he committed the act, and what they were doing. This is evidenced by the fact that the nurse baby's, Betty Gow committed suicide.

The police left no stone unturned in finding out the baby. They were hovering round the house of Lindberg day and night to find a clue. But now they were becoming desperate. But instantly rang the telephone bell. The speaker was the clergyman of Brooklin. He told them that he had the knowledge of something regarding the missing baby. But he could leak out the information only when he came to the house of Lindberg personally.

Members of the C.I.D. met the clergyman the next day at Hopewell. The latter told them that a client of his was a very successful medium at seance. She had solved many a mystery till then. She could give some positive information about the missing baby if she was left in the baby's room for an hour.

The C.I.D. men were very much annoyed at this. Mrs. Lindberg was very much upset those days. Even otherwise she was in the family way and the time of the delivery was very near. They did not take the medium to her room. But they took her to another room just opposite that one. The medium went into a trance. She remained in that condition for two-and-a-half hours. She told them that the baby was in an uncoloured house about 7 km from the place in the north-east direction. The kidnappers of the baby were sitting in the house with a telescope pointed in the direction of Lindberg's house. If anybody dared to near that house they would kill the baby.

About three weeks later, the body of the baby was found in a house at a distance of about 7 km from that of Lindberg in the north-east direction. About a few hundred metres from that house was a cottage which was uncoloured. A glimpse at the house could convince anybody that a child used to live in the cottage till very recently. And, as told be the medium, a woman with red hair used to live with the child. Also, that they had to leave the place in a hurry.

The C.I.D. people ignored the reading of the medium, but the subsequent events testified to their truth. And our conventional science has no explanation for the phenomenon.

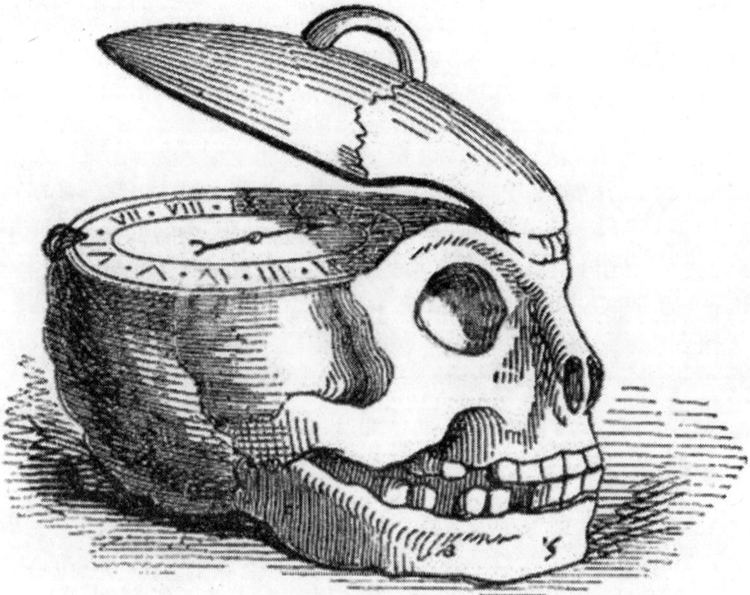

PART–III
Reincarnation

INTRODUCTION

It was a night of Kartik, the 8th month of the Hindu lunar calendar, when winter begins. An old woman is sleeping in a hut. There is small courtyard outside the hut, which is full of creepers and plants. In the middle of the courtyard, there is a bed of Tulsi plant, sacred to Hindus. In a corner an oil lamp is burning which contains oil enough to last for the whole night.

Midnight has passed. The Tulsi said to the lamp.

'Can't you give me some lay story for passing the night. The lamp readily agreed and narrated the following story :

'In olden times there was a blind king, by the name of Dhritrashtra. He had a hundred sons who were called Kauravas. And he had five nephews called Pandavas.

'Once Kauravas and Pandavas went to war. Lord Krishna was supporting the Pandavas. During the war of 18 days, all the Kauravas were killed, but the five Pandavas remained safe. Also, lots of soldiers were killed on either side. The Pandavas were the winners.

'Dhritrashtra was bemoaning the death of his sons. One day, he asked Lord Krishna: Worthy Sire, what sin had I committed to deserve the sight of the death of all my sons? During my present life at least I have not committed any sin of such dimensions.

Lord Krishna replied, 'You are a yogi (foreseer) yourself. Contemplate and find out yourself. You might have committed a sin of the type in some previous life.'

Dhritrashtra went into a trance. When he came to, he said,'My lord. I have gone through my previous hundred lives. I could not find any such sin.

The lord said, 'Have you had only a hundred previous lives? Why do you not deliver deeper?

Dhritrashtra said, 'I do not have that much capacity.'

Lord Krishna provided him with the requisite amount of power. Dhritrashtra again went into a trance, this time for a longer period. When he opened his eyes, he said, '0 lord, now I have understood the matter.

Krishna: What do you make of it?

D : Lord, you are a seer of all times. Why are you asking me then?

K : I want to hear from your own words.

The Dhritrashtra narrated the following story:

'This happened during my life, 140 lives back. I was a king of a territory. I was very fond of gardening. Every day I would have a stroll in the garden. There was cistern in the middle of the garden. There were dozens of gardeners. The garden contained hundreds of types of plants and flowers. The garden spread fragrance all round . I used to enjoy the strolling for hours.

One day I was walking in the garden when a couple of swans met me and said,'We are both going on a pilgrimage. We are depositing these hundred eggs of ours with you. Kindly take care of them. We shall take them back on return. They will develop into swans. Kindly nurture them.

I said, 'No problem. We are bringing up hundreds of animals and birds. A hundred swans will make hardly any difference. Please keep them with the head gardener.

The couple deposited the hundred eggs with the head gardener and went away.

Time passed and my hobby of gardening waned. My daily walks in the garden began decreasing in frequency and finally stopped altogether.

One day, my cook told me that there was no fresh meat in the kitchen. I told him that the meal would be insipid without meat. I asked him to go out and try again. The cook went out and brought a young one of a swan. The cook killed it and prepared the same for meal. It was very tasty. I asked the cook to bring the same type of meat every day. This he did every day.

A few months later the couple of swans returned and asked for their ducklings. I asked them to go to the head gardener and take them. The couple entreated me to accompany them and deliver the same to them.

I went to the garden with them. The garden was changed out of recognition. The gardeners had ceased to take any interest in its upkeep due to my continued absence. It was full of shrubs and bushes. I called for the head gardener and asked him to deliver the ducklings of the swans to them.

The gardener said to me,'where am I to bring the swans now: They were all taken, one by one, by your cook every day. Thus, the ducklings have all been killed.'

I was flabbergasted. I said to the couple, 'Look here. I have eaten up all your children. But I have committed this sin unknowingly. I beg to be excused.'

The he swan said; Every body commits mistakes. You have killed our ducklings unknowingly. So, I excuse you.'

But the she-swan was not to be pacified so easily. She said,'My husband can excuse you. But I know what it means to carry child in the belly and nurture it. It is only a mother who can realise it. I cannot excuse you. I curse you. You will bemoan the death of your hundred children bitterly as I am doing today.'

Lord Krishna said,'King Dhritrashtar. Now you must have realised that no injustice has been done to you.'

The latter replied,'Yes, my Lord. Now, I am satisfied.

Whether this story a fact, or the figment of the imaginatic of some fertile brain, we cannot say. But, the underlying principle, the Theory of Action and Reaction, transmigration and reincarnation is certainly not wrong. There was a time when the scholars of west used to make fun of this principle. And quite a few of them do so even now. But those of them who have studied the literature concerning the matter and have examined the stories of this type as to the veracity, are slowly coming round to have implicit faith in its authenticity. The number of such tested and examined incidents has run into thousands. And reputed Philosophers and Scientists as well as Psychologists have testified to the genuineness. Then, turning our face from them would be tantamount to denying the truth. ,

In our childhood we listened to many stories beginning with the lamp of Kartik. What is the significance of the lamp of Kartik. Our ancestors would give a religious tinge to almost everything that they wanted up to follow, so that people may have an unquestioning faith in them. Many people take a morning bath in some river during the month of Kartik. Winter begins in that month. If one begins taking a river bath during this month he will get used to it and will be able to sustain it throughout the year. Otherwise, if one does not begin it in early winter he will be hard put to it to begin it when severe winter sets in.

Another function which the ladies have to perform during Kartik is that every evening they would take an earthen oil lamp to the peepal tree outside the village and put it underneath it. During those days trees used to be at some distance from the village. This way the ladies would get a walk of two to three km. every evening. A sufficient quantity of ghee or oil was poured into the lamp to last the whole night. This had the additional benefit of serving as a beacon to the pedestrians at night.

Another variant of this custom is that an earthen lamp is placed on top of a bamboo and the bamboo is erected at some prominent place in the village. It was given a special name: The Sky; Lamp. A remnant of the custom is that now they place an earthen lamp on the threshold of the house and keep it burning throughout the night.

Winter nights are longer. This fact is hinted at by the statement of Tulsi,'Give me some lay story to pass the night, 'We do not think the kartik lamp has any spiritual significance.

So, we come back to our narrative. Amba had to take revenge upon Bheeshm. So, she came back to the earth in the form of Shikhndi in the next life.

Our religious books are full of episodes of reincarnation. Even we do not give any credence to them, can we ignore all such stories that appear in newspapers, quite a few of which have been tested and authenticated? We are presenting some of them in this book.

A certain man was extremely miserly. One day a friend of his was narrating to him some ghost stories. Hearing them he said,'Is that everybody has to pass through the ghostlife necessarily? Then, will I too have to pass through that life.'

The friend retorted, 'I have already told you that nobody gets the same kind of life in two successive lives.'

PARAMANAND

This incident was described in the issue of Aug.25,1949 of the Northern India Patrika and several other newspapers. For quite some time it was the talk of the day. There can be absolutely no doubt about the truth of the story. In the test thereof, given in the following pages dozens of educated people-Advocates, Doctors, Teachers and others participated. My late brother,, a school teacher, was also an eye witness of the incidents connected therewith. And he used to assert that the narration given in newspapers of the day, was cent per cent true. In particulars, he was reputed for his honesty and truthfulness. So, there is hardly any room for doubt regarding the following account.

Near the office of the municipal committee of Moradabad, there is a famous shop of tea, biscuits etc. The name is 'Mohan Brothers.' Of three brothers, Mohan Lal was the eldest.

The next was Parmanand. The shop had a branch at Saharanpur. Some time before, they had a third shop in the Civil Lines of Moradabad, but it was closed before the following events occurred.

On May 9, 1943, Parmanand died at Saharanpur. Exactly 9 months and 6 days later, a son was born to Pt. Bankey Lal Sharma M.A. Shastri of District Budaun in the township of Bisauli. Mr. Sharma was a professor at an intermediate college of Bisauli. It was a sheer coincidence that, according to the readings of the horoscope, this child too was named Parmanand. But the elder brother of the child was named Vermod. So, he was named Pramod.Pramod had hardly begun speaking when he began uttering the names of the cities Moradabad and Saharanpur. When he grew a little, he could distinctly pronounce the name 'Mohan Brothers'. Whenever the inmates of his house brought bread, butter etc. from the market, he would say that he owned a shop of the kind at Moradabad, which dealt in such articles of food. Time and again he asked his father to take him to Moradabad. When they called him 'Pramod', he would resent it and say that his name was Parmanand. Also that he had a wife, brother, son and daughter at Moradabad.

It was early in 1949. One, Shri Raghunandan Lal, of Bisauli, went to Moradabad and stayed with a relative of his. He narrated the story of Mohan brothers and Parmanand to him. And the latter talked about it to Mohan Lal. The latter went to Bisauli along with several brothers and nephews, in July 1949 and met Prof. Bankey Lal. Pramod had gone to some other village that day. So, they asked Bankey Lal to bring Pramod to Moradabad at his convenience. It was decided to undertake the trip on Aug. 15, 1949, the Independence Day.

The news started a commotion at Moradabad. The public was eagerly waiting for the appointed day. Dozens of educated persons as well as uneducated people, accompanied Mohan Lal to the railway station at the time of the arrival of the train. Pramod had never been to Moradabad before. As soon as they got down from the train, he ran hard to Mohan Lal and clung to him calling him, 'Bhai Saheb' (Elder Brother).

Pramod was seated on a tonga. When the same reached the Municipal hall, he at once cried, 'My shop is very near.' The tongawala was instructed before hand. He bypassed the shop concerned.

And at once Parmanand ejaculated,'Stop. This is my shop.'

Going to the shop Parmanand sat at the seat occupied by him in previous life. Then he went to the machine which prepared soda water and tried to operate it. His father told everybody present that the boy had never seen such a machine in his present life. The machine could not be started as its connection with the water-supply was deliberately broken to put him to test. When he could not prepare soda water he said, the water-connection has broken.

Then Pramod was asked to go to his house which was exactly opposite the shop on the upper storey. Pramod ran to the house and went up stairs very rapidly. His wife of the previous life was sitting there. At once he said to her,'Why have you broken your bangles.'I am alive (Breaking the bangles is a sign of widowhood.) The wife began crying bitterly. He recognised all the other ladies of the house and narrated several incidents of his previous life which were literally true. When he said,'At this spot all the three of us used to take lemon syrup, the brothers too could not help shedding tears.

Paramanand had a cousin Karamchand who owned a'Victory Hotel at Moradabad. Pramod expressed a desire to go to the hotel. All of them started for the hotel along with him. Here too he was leading the way. He went straight to the hotel. When they took him to the upper floor, he said"'These rooms seem to be newly constructed'. And it was a fact.

A reputed nobleman of Moradabad took him to the Meston Park in his car. And he was asked to locate the place where there used to be a branch of Mohan Brothers, in the Civil Lines. He took them to exact spot. On the way, he recognised several buildings: Allahabad Bank, Water Tank, District Jail etc. Also, he recognised many persons on the way who frequented his shop.

The next day a public reception was arranged in honour of Pramod. His father described how the memory of the boy developed since early childhood.

Pramod was very reluctant to leave Moradabad. On the night of 17th Aug., he was carried to the railway station while asleep. Everything that he said proved to be absolutely correct. He never shied or hesitated while describing the events of previous life.

THE STORY OF A GIRL

(Courtesy : Daily Aaj of April 2, 1962)

Mr. Harendra Lal is an employee at the law-court, who lives in the village Gonhia Chhapra of district Balia. In 1957 his daughter 'Asha' died a few days before Holi. The girl was 6 years old.

The manager of the Usha Company of Balia was Shri Bhagvati Prasad Agarwal. In 1958 he begot a daughter in village Bayan of Bharatpur his native place. When she reached the age of 4, she began asking her father to take her to her'Father.

The father took the girl, who was named Gaytri, to her Father of the previous birth, Harendra Lal. There she at once recognised her Father and Mother of the previous life.

In 1962, on the Holi day, when her father, Mr. Agarwal gave her a new frock, she began crying. She said,'This is not my frock. My own frock is kept in a box at my Fathers house. Her father took her to Shri Harendra Lai. She was told that, due to illness, she could not wear the new frock on the Holi day. And thereafter she died. The new frock was still there in a box of Harendra Lai.

Hearing this story certain journalists approached Gayatri for interrogation. She told them that during her previous life she had a playmate Susheela. They found out that Susheela was still there. At the adolescent age of 4 she amazed the reporters by reciting the Gayatri verse of the Geeta.

Hundreds of visitors came every day to have a glimpse of Gayatri and this continued for months.

THE STORY OF A BOY

(Courtesy : The Leader, July 20, 1961, and Aaj, July 21, 1961)

Shree Braj Lai Varshney is a middle class shopkeeper of the township Chhata in Muttra district. When his son Prakash reached the age of 5, he began saying that he is a son of Mr Bhola Nath Jain of Kosi Kalan, a small town on the Muthra-Delhi road. Also, that his father owned a shop of general merchandise. He added that he 'died' of small pox at the age of 10.

The boy insisted several times that his father should take him to Kosi Kalan. On several occasions he ran away towards Kosi Kalan, but each time his father traced him out and brought him back. Once, just to pacify him his father sat down on Muttra bus and took the boy with him, But, as soon as the bus started, the boy cried out.

'The bus is going to Muttra. Kosi Kalan is on the other side.'

Once the father actually took him on the bus to Kosi Kalan. As soon as they reached the place, he recognised his previous house, his father's shop and even his neighbours. His father had gone out somewhere along with his family. On returning the entire story was narrated to him. He at once started for the town of Chhata along with his daughter Ratna Devi. The boy immediately recognised both of them and began to weep bitterly. His father and sister also were much moved.

Shri Bhola Nath was eager to take the boy to his house for a few days, but Mr. Varshnay did not agree. Later on, at the insistence of the boy, he was again taken to Kosi Kalan on July 14. The news of his impending visit ran far and wide and about ten thousand persons assembled to witness the sight. In the presence of all of them the boy recognised his

Father, Mother and other kinsmen of the previous life. And the wonder was that there was a good deal of resemblance between the faces of Ratna Devi and Prakash.

Bhola Nath offered to get the son educated at his own expense but Shri Varshnay did not agree. He said that he would have him educated on his own.

THE ADVENT OF A SPIRIT IN A BODY

(Courtesy : *Nav Bharat Times, New Delhi, May 30, 1965*)

It was March 1960. A three-year old boy, Jasbeer, a son of Girdhar Singh Jat, of Rasulpur in District Muzaffarpur, died of small-pox at 6 p.m. Next day, at 4 in the morning, when they tried to lift the corpse, the corpse trembled and the child got up. He said, I am a son of Shanker Tyagi of Village Behari. That boy has just now died of a fall from a chariot.

Behari Village is about 25 km. from Rasulpur. All the people were astounded to hear this story. They sent a man immediately to Behari to find out the truth. The statement of the child was true.

Shanker Tyagi and his kinsmen came from Behari to Rasulpur to see the child. The child recognised all of them and called them by their names.

Then they all took the child to Behari. He recognised his house and entered in it.

REMEMBRANCE OF TWO LIVES

(Courtesy : Daily Aaj, July 23,1960)

Dr. Kailash Nath Katju was the Chief Minister of Madhya Pradesh. During my last sojourn at Jabalpur, I met the 11 years old girl Swarn on july 6 at Chhatarpur. We were told that the girl could narrate the events of her previous two lives. It is said that her story was published in several newspapers of repute of the country. And so, Dr. Katju was anxious to meet the girl. Parliamentarian Shri Govind Das Gupta had also talked to the Chief Minister about the girl. So he called the girl to his residence at Jabalpur.

When Dr. Katju returned after a dinner from the residence of Seth Govind Das he called Mr. M.L. Mishra, the father of the girl, and her maternal uncle Shri Rang Nath Pathak. Mr. Mishra was attached to the education department at Chatarpur. Dr. Katju talked to the girl Swarn Lata, for about 40 minutes, in the presence of the following personages:

1. Shri Kunji Lal Dube, Speaker, Legislative Assembly and Vice Chancellor, Jabalpur University.
2. Mr. Kashi Prasad Pandey, M.L.A.
3. Divisional Commissioner, Mr. Chhadammi Lal Gupta
4. Dt. Magistrate Shri Ramesh Chandra Mishra

Dr. Katju put several searching questions to the girl regarding her previous two lives. He was very much impressed by her intelligence and memory at the raw age of 11. Swarn Lata performed several dances of the Assamese style and sang a few songs. It is worth noting that during her present life the girl has never been to Assam or West Bengal, nor has she received any training of music at any school.

A CHILD OF NINE

(Courtesy : Amrit Bazaar Patrika, March 25, 1965)

Gopal was the name of the owner of a petrol pump at Asaf Ali Marg of Delhi. When he was only two he began talking about his previous life. He said to his father, 'My Father Shakti Prasad, is a resident of Muttra. In 1948, when I was 35, my younger brother shot me dead in our factory. Property was the point of dispute.'

In the beginning Gopal's father did not pay any heed to his words. But when he repeated the story over and over again, he took it seriously. He took the boy to Muttra. The boy recognised his house as well as shop. He had never been to Muttra ever before. Nevertheless, he was leading the party along the way. A friend of his previous life brought an album of photographs. He recognised each and every member of his family in the album. Besides, he recognised several persons whose photographs were hanging on the wall, and told their names.

Gopal recognised mother of the previous life too, but did not greet her. He said, 'I had a quarrel with her. He asked her for Rs.5,000. She asked me to take the amount from the factory. I went to the factory and it was there that my younger brother put me to death.'

On scrutiny it was found that the narrative was true in each and every detail. He was murdered in 1948 and Gopal was born 8 years later. Somebody asked him as to where he passed the interval of 8 years. To that he replied, 'I cannot say.'

A CHILD OF TEN

(Courtesy : Amrit Bazaar Patrika, Aug. 7, 1970)

This is the story of Subhash, a son of an Income-Tax Officer of Gaziabad. The officer has told us that a few years back he was employed at Bareily. Subhash sometimes used to spread a piece of cloth on the ground and perform namaz of the Muslim style. One day he picked up a quarrel with his elder brother about some point relating to carrom. And at once he began recollecting event of his previous life. He said, "I am by no means poor. I possess Rs. 90,000 at Lucknow. I can purchase; not one but a thousand carrom boards. So saying, he threw away the carrom board.

The same day he began narrating incidents connected with his previous life, thus:

'In my previous existence I was a rich musalman. My name was Jan Mahomed Khan and that of my wife Soofia Khanam. I hoarded Rs. 90,000 for saving on income-tax. Besides, I opened a separate account in the name of my wife at the State Bank. I had a house at Lucknow. The number of my car was U.S.J.3289. I had two daughters, and two of my sons were being educated at the Usmania University, Hyderabad.

I was on the roof of a three-storeyed house. I ran to save myself from a monkey. I fell down from the roof and died.'

The parents of Subhash took him to Lucknow. Each and every part of his narration was found true to the hilt.

When he was 7 or 8 he would write letters to his previous wife. But he would tear the letter to pieces after writing. He was very anxious to meet her. But now he had lost all interest in the matter.

A PECULIAR STORY OF REINCARNATION

(Courtesy : Daily Aaj, Jan. 19, 1961)

There is a village about 8 km. from Gaya, inhabited mainly by members of the Kshtriya class. A child was born there in 1957. When he began speaking, it was in a dialect, not his mother tongue. The inmates of his house were astounded at the phenomenon.

He would say to his mother, 'My mother is in Ceylon. My elder brother who uses spectacles, as well as my preceptor, live there. I will surely go there when I come of age.'

His kinsmen did not take him seriously. When the boy was four, a Buddha mendicant came to the village. He was eager to meet the members of the family of the boy. On being questioned he told them,'In 1955, a son of my preceptor died. From theBook of Astrology, named NaaRee I have found that the boy is reborn in this village. I have come so far only to find him out.'

The boy was taken to the mendicant. And at once he leapt and sat down in his lap. When the mendicant started back the boy was visibly moved. Many people pay a visit to the village only to see the boy.

THE RIDDLE OF LIFE AND DEATH BY SANT RAM

(Courtesy : Navneet, January 1966)

I am an inhabitant of village Purani Basee of District Hoshiarpur. There is a big village Jaijon, at a distance of about 50 km. from my village. An inhabitant of the village was a widower. His daughter Chandra used to attend to all family cores. She was about 10-12 at the time. Suddenly she fell ill and took to the bed. When she was on death bed, her father began to weep bitterly. The girl asked him as to whey he was weeping.

The father said, 'You are leaving me in lurch. Where shall I find you?'

The girl replied,'At a short distance from here there is a village named Nandan. I will be reborn of the wife of a Chamar Kesri of the village.' And at once her eyes languished. A relative of her who lived at Purani Basee, came to the house of condolence. Chandranan's father asked her about Kesri Chamar. She replied that there was not a single house of Chamars in her village. But, there were several houses of that community in a nearby village Nandan. Chandranan's father had never been to Purani Basee or Nandan. He narrated the entire story to the woman, Shiva Devi, of Purani Basee. The latter came to jaijon and told me the entire story. 'I found out that at Nandan village there was a Chamar, named Ratan Singh, whose wife's name was Kesri. She was married only about 1 1/2 years back, and was expecting.

A few months later Kesri was delivered of a female child. Chandranan's father went to offer cloths to the baby. She was, named Swarn Kaur.

An amazing thing about the girl was that she never talked about her previous life to anybody.

SHANTI DEVI

This girl used to say that she had a previous life. Sceptic scientists tried hard to find out the truth behind her utterances but failed. They could neither prove her to be right, nor disprove her utterances.

Shanti Devi was born of a middle class family of Delhi in 1926. Her parents were leading a peaceful life when she was born. Nor was there any peculiarity in the circumstances of her birth which could indicate that the girl was out of the ordinary.

When Shanti began to pass through adolescent age, her mother found that she was usually agitated about something. She was fond of solitude and she used to talk to some imaginary personality when she was alone.

When she was seven her parents began to feel that she was perhaps of a retarded mind. The same year she told her mother that her real house was at Muttra. She gave a vivid description of the house of her previous life.

The mother talked to the father. The latter took her to a Doctor who examined her closely.

When she narrated her peculiar story, the Doctor said, 'If this is a vagrancy of mind, it is of a very peculiar type. But if it is something else, I shudder to think of it.' The Doctor asked her father to go Yon cross-questioning her after intervals, and if she stuck to her story, he would like to examine her once again.

Shanti never changed a word of her story even in minor details. When she reached nine her parents were convinced that there was something wrong with her mind. So, they gave up taking her seriously. In 1935 she told her parents that in her previous life she was living at Muttra; she was married and had three children. She gave a detailed description of the children and told their names. She added that her own name in the previous life was Ludgi. The parents were filled with sadness at the narration, but apparently gave a insincere smile.

One day, Shanti and her mother were taking their evening meal when somebody knocked at the door. Shanti ran out and opened the door. When she did not return for a pretty long time, her mother began to feel anxious. She ran to the door and found that a stranger was standing and Shanti was constantly gazing at him. Shanti said, 'Mother, he is a cousin of my husband. He too lives at Muttra at a short distance from our own house.'

That man actually belonged to Muttra and had come to talk to Shanti's father about some business matters. He did not recognise her but'admitted that a cousin of his was a widower, whose wife was named Ludgi. She expired after a delivery ten years back. The parents of Shanti told him the entire story of Shanti. He said that he would bring his cousin to Delhi and see if Shanti recognised him.

The girl was not given any previous information about the plan. But when the person concerned came, she embraced him, began to weep bitterly and said that he was her previous husband and she was lucky enough to meet him again. The husband was astounded. Then they all went to the District Magistrate and narrated the entire episode to him. The Government of India formed a committee of scientists to find out the truth behind the story as, by this time, the attention of the entire nation was focussed round the girl.

Was Shanti the new incarnation of Ludgi?

The Scientists took Shanti to Muttra. As soon as she got off the train, she at once recognised her mother-in-law as well as her elder son, and spelt their names.

And the wonder was that she began talking to them in their local dialect, though her parents had taught her only Hindustani.

The scientists were stunned. But they continued their investigations. They blind folded the girl and sat her in a carriage. They too sat near her. She went on leading the way without the least hesitation. She named each and every place on the way and asked them to stop the carriage at a narrow lane. She said, 'We used to live in this very house.' When the bandage was taken off her eyes, she saw an old man enjoying his hubble-bubble. She told all the people that he was her father-in-law. And he was really so.

Shanti recognised her two elder children, but not the youngest one in whose delivery she expired.

The scientists were very careful about their report. They said that there was no doubt that the girl who was born at Delhi knew the entire life of a girl at Muttra, even in the minutest details. There was absolutely no deception in the matter. But they could not explain what they had seen with their own eyes.

Shanti Devi is spending her life happily and peacefully with a Government servant at Delhi. Her entire story along with documentary proofs is registered in the files of the secretariat as well as medical reports. In 1958 she told the specialists that now she had compromised herself with her present life. She no longer worries about the matters concerning her previous life.

The life of Shanti is a challenge to the scientists of today.

SPIRIT GIVES ITS OWN DEATH NEWS!

Sir, The story I am revealing here was told me by my late lamented father, who was a qualified medical graduate with the doctor's typical half amused and half-cynic attitude towards spiritualism and ghost stories. He had to leave his native province of Bengal in his youth and settle down in the U.P. for reasons of health. Apart from his profound knowledge and professional experience in medical science, he had a wide and varied interest in all cultural and literary matters.

Some of this spiritualist friends induced him one evening at Allahabad to take part in a "séance" just to convince him about the existence of spirits. All arranged and the stage was set for the appearance of the spirit. The four friends sat at the table in deep meditation with the light so arranged that the room was in semi-darkness. After some time the leader of the "séance" whispered that the spirit was approaching. A luminous haze was discernible against the dark curtain and it took the blurred appearance of a human form. The medium seemed to be in a trance.

"Who are you?" asked the leader of the "séance".

"I am Panchu of the '___' village" replied the medium in a scarcely audible whisper '___', village was my father's country home.

My father caught the words and exclaimed in an incredulous tone. "But I know that Panchu '___' of village is still alive and is in perfect health."

A distinct reply came from the medium. "I am Panchu. I have committed suicide last night by hanging myself from a banyan tree in the outskirts of the village.

The spirit hereafter disappeared.

My father wrote to his relative in '___' village who confirmed that Panchu had actually committed suicide by hanging himself from, that tree.

Sir- In his "Malice' column (HT June 4) Khushwant Singh's doubts about life after death arise out of his intellectualism.

My mother died in 1947 when I was 38. For the last 36 years the departed soul of my mother has been physically appearing before me. She helped me to write my best novel "Walking Walls" in Hindi and it was prescribed as a text book by Panjab University, Chandigarh. The art was not ingrained in me and I never studied novels before writing my own novels.

In 1957 I was devoid of cash, I had seven grown-up children for whom I had to manage university education in my poverty. My mother appeared before me and ordered me to join Delhi University's Law Faculty as a day student. She promised to do every thing for me and for my sons.

In 1979 my mother's smoky form appeared. She gave me the address of a person who was unknown to me and she ordered me to contact him without delay. I did so and this man published a huge manuscript of mine which was not accepted by any publisher for the last forty years.

When left in the open air mercury, thought a metal, evaporates and becomes a part of the cosmic dust which is raised by the cosmic rays.

All spokes in the cosmic wheel are not grasped by man. Mysticism and not cynicism is needed to understand life after death. A cosmic mind can catch the mercurial activities of the so-called dead. The persons whom we call as the departed souls are actually living in a form which is known to the ancients of India as the "sooksham sharir" (mercurial body).

Psychic phenomena arise with the help of cosmic rays which are well known to the students of science–

Yours etc.

(Prof) Piare Lal Sharma,
House No. 2805,
Sector 22-C, Chandigarh.

II

Sir, On "Life after Death " narrated in the "Malice" column (HT June 4) I had a different personal experience.

Through the system called "Planchet," which operates through two or more suitable mediums, one can communicate with the souls of known people (if they are not already reborn.) I had myself communicated (through this system) with my grandfather and a few others. To make sure we were talking to the right soul, and not to any imposter, we asked about some past happenings which were known only to a few of us and only after being convinced we proceeded further. We even talked to actress Meena Kumari about her previous life.

But, a main drawback of this system is that it creates a bad effect on the minds and the health of the mediums. We had to give it up forever mainly because a few of our friendly souls advised us not to call them as they did not want to remain attached with the relations of their previous life. All this may sound surprising or even untrue to many but "Sitaron Se Agey Jahan Aur bhi Hai". (there are other planets also beyond the visible stars.

Vinod Pal
D- 23, IARI Pusa Campus,
New Delhi-110012

III

Sir- In a "Malice" column on "Life After Death" (HT June 4) Khushwant Singh desired to know from his readers if anyone has an experience of talk with deceased persons.

A great saint, Malik Sahib of Adhyatm Niketan, Koteshwar Road Gwalior - 12, passed away on Feb 12, 1983. But to our surprise we were having communion with him every night from 8.30 p.m. to 1.30 a.m. from Feb 17 to 23 through a medium. We listened to his posthumous sermons with rapt attention and freely put questions to him and got answers to our full satisfaction.

I recorded the sermons of Feb. 20, in two cassettes which I have brought here from Gwalior. If Mr. Khushwant Singh is interested, he may, immediately contact (Tel No. 521633) me with a tape-recorder at my address. I shall play the posthumous sermons to him.

Yours etc.

P. N. Vijayvergiya

C/o Rishi Kumar Gupta

18, U.F. Delhi Cloth Mill Road,

Delhi-110006

AFFECTIONATE GHOST

(Courtesy : Kailash Pati Srivastava)

During the summer weather in 1951, we were at Jhansi. My newly married aunt had died of heart attack in the house we were living in. She was very affectionate to me and being of the same age, we were very fast friends. It was quite natural, therefore, that I , very often, used to think of her.

We used to sleep on the roof. I used to sleep just in front of the room in which she had breathed her last. My mother's cot was next to that of me and others slept on the other end of the roof. Only my grand-mother used to sleep on the ground-floor with my youngest sister who was four months old.

We used wrappers as the nights at Jhansi are fairly cool. One night, I forgot to have my wrapper and felt light shivering at about 2 a.m. I awoke and was going to ask my mother to give me a wrapper when my eyes fell on a human figure standing near my cot. I recognized it. It was she, my aunt standing in front of me with her old graceful smiles and charm. Seeing me shivering she said, Didi (she used to call my mother Didi) has gone downstairs. I shall give you the wrapper" -- and before I could think anything, she threw my wrapper on my cot and while I gazed at her, she disappeared. I looked at my mother's cot. She was not there and later on I knew that she had actually gone downstairs as my sister was crying.

I sat there thinking. I was least afraid -- so much did I love her. I thought what that could be. It was surely not a hallucination because it was not known to me that my mother was downstairs and moreover, the wrapper was still lying on my cot. I thought for half an hour, then covering myself under the wrapper, I slept, from that day I firmly believe that there are good spirits also who sympathies with and help their near and dear ones of their previous life.

GHOST ON TELEVISION

Grandfather's ghost won't get off the television set of Mr. and Mrs. John Mackey of Indianapolls, U.S.A. They contend that the mustached image in their TV screen (above) is the face of Mrs. Mackey's grandfather, George R. Shots, who died last April at the age of 74. The Mackeys and Mrs. Marie Johnson, Mrs. Mac Mackey's mother, declare the TV image wears the clothes in which shots was buried. It appeared during a network drama and became more intense the following day and persisted regardless of what channel was turned on. The police, called in by the Mackey's had the set torn down and when it was reassembled, there, clear as ever, was the image. Engineers suggested that an image, possibly of a performer in a show, has been "burned" into the phosphorescent back on the set's picture tube, an explanation given for a similar phenomenon in Long Island, N.Y.recently.

NINE YEAR OLD BOY REMEMBERS PAST LIFE

For nine-year old Gopal Agarwal his first visit to Mathura on Sunday was in the nature of a pilgrimage, but a pilgrimage with a difference.

He went there to see the house in which he says he was born in his previous life and the factory where he was shot dead by his younger brother.

Gopal, son of the manager of a petrol filling station on Asaf Ali Road, Delhi, mentioned incidents from his previous birth for the first time when he was two and a half years old.

His father recalled in an interview on Wednesday: "On a summer evening Gopal came to me and said that he had a father in Mathura. I thought he was joking. But he was not. He said he was born in a prosperous family of Mathura. His name was Shakti Prasad, In 1948 when he was 35 his younger brother shot him following a quarrel over property."

The incidents were found to be true on verification. The shooting took place in 1948. Gopal was born eight years later. Asked by someone where he had spent the eight years between his death and re-birth, Gopal said : I don't know."

Gopal was taken to Mathura by his parents on Sunday last. Though this was his first visit to that city he had no difficulty in locating the shop "owned" by him once and the house in which he lived. He recognized the photographs of himself and other members of the family in an album brought by an old friend and also those hung on the walls.

He recognised Shakti Prasad's widow but refused to greet her because, he said, he had a quarrel with her over money. "The day I was killed I had asked her for Rs. 5,000 but she told me to take the money from the factory. When I went to the factory my brother shot me dead".

Gopal brought with him from Mathura a photograph of Shakti Prasad taken at the time when he got the M.A. degree.

MAN UNDRESSED IN MARKET

(Courtesy : Saint Brieus, Brittany, April 20, 1962)

Police and church officials have begun an investigation into reports of a ghost in two Brittany villages are said to have attacked people's clothing.

A man at Landebia recently found himself practically undressed in the market place after seams in his clothing had given way, the reports said.

Large acid like burns were said to have appeared on the clothes of a family in Henabihen while they were wearing them. The ghost slit all the bed sheets of another family, it was stated.

The Bishop of Saint Brieuc has sent a priest to investigate the happenings while police have begun an inquiry in case the 'ghost' is eventually identified (Reuter).

PREMONITION OR COINCIDENCE

(Courtesy : N.S. Chandramouli)

The recent Caravelle crash in Bombay has brought to light several incidents where relatives of the victims claim to have had a 'forewarning' of the impeding accident. Was this premonition? Or mere coincidence?

Several incidents relating to some of the victims of the Caravelle crash at Santa Cruz airport, In Bombay, on October 12, 1976, defy "scientific' explanation. These incidents were related to me by those who were close to the victims.

One of the victims was a senior executive of a private firm in Madras. According to the horoscope of this young man, he was to meet his end in a plane crash. When he was in his teens, he appeared for the Indian Air Force entrance examination and came first. But his parents, fearful of the astrological forecast, would not even hear of their son joining the air force. Yet in the end, the astrologer's prognostication came true.

The executive's younger brother, who was in Calcutta, had a dream the night before the crash. He dreamt that his friend got killed in an air crash. He woke up weeping to find it was only a bad dream or was it?

The victim's elder brother narrated the most extraordinary experience. A month before the crash, the elder brother also had a dream in which his brother gets killed in an air crash. In his dream be heard a female voice saying. "I told him not to go." He forgot all about the dream soon afterwards.

When he heard that his brother had died in the air crash, he rushed to Bombay. A young woman, who was his brother's friend, came to convey her sympathies to the bereaved family. This girl told the elder brother" I told him no to go. I told him not to go." It seems that this girl had asked his brother not to leave on the day of the crash.

Suddenly the elder brother's memory was revived. The dream which he had a month ago came back to him in a flash. He had not seen this girl before, but he had heard her saying what she was telling him now. Premonition?

Then there is the case of a creative director of a Madras advertising agency who was aboard the ill-fated plane. His wife said she was asleep at her home in Madras when her husband boarded the Caravelle in Bombay. But at 1.40 a.m. the time of the crash, she was woken up by the sound of her bedroom windows rattling. She was startled when she saw the apparition of her husband appear for a moment near the window and disappear.

The frightened woman went to wake up her little daughter. She found that her daughter had already woken up and was weeping. She told her mother that she saw her daddy getting into a plane which crashes and kills him.

On the day prior to the crash, this ad. man told his colleagues in Bombay "Give me two strong pegs of gin. This may be the last time that I may be meeting you." Prescience?

A peculiar incident concerning another passenger, who was staying in Bombay, was narrated by his friend. On the day when this man started to leave his house for the airport, his dog wouldn't allow him to go. It kept on pulling at his clothes. His exasperated wife locked the dog up in a room. Its master left the house, never to return.

The next morning the day of the crash the faithful dog pocked up the newspaper carrying the news about the crash and started whining. It went to where its master's wife was sleeping unaware of the tragedy, and woke her up. The dog then dropped the newspaper in front of the surprised woman. Did the dog have a sixth-sense?

What do these experiences indicate? Apparently, there is much more to life than what it seems at the surface. In his book, "The Roots of Coincidence," Arthur Koestler has made a powerful plea for an open minded approach to the phenomena of parapsychology- extra-sensory perception (ESP), clairvoyance, pre-cognition hypnosis, telepathy, psychokinesis (PK) and so on. Avoiding rigid materialism and superstitious credulity, one should follow the example of C.G. Jung who "refused to commit the fashionable stupidity of regarding everything one cannot explain as a fraud."

Paranormal cognition may consist of a sudden hunch that something has happened an unaccountable impulse which makes a person run out of a house just before it is bombed or undertake a journey to see someone who turns out to be dangerously ill; or a "crisis apparition" when the person "seen" is in danger or dying. Though such events are unrepeatable and uniquely personal, many such phenomena have been verified by standards of evidence acceptable in a court of law.

It is well known that while some people have a photographic memory, others have a selective one, some can recall the names but not the appearances of things. Similarly, extra sensory perception varies vastly from person to person. Often, ESP is not so much an act of cognition or a piece of information that is transferred, but rather a feeling or an emotion. This is why repeatable experiments are so hard to achieve in psychological research.

DREAMS AND REALITY

Sir, I have read Mr. D.K. Chatterji's recent letter on the above subject and join him in requesting any one -- who can -- to throw light on the reality or otherwise of dreams particularly those which indicate coming events. I have a record of very strange dreams foretelling coming events which turned cent per cent true. Here are three of them and my explanation of them. They are of two kinds -- night dreams and day dreams.

One night I dreamed of my eldest brother coming to meet me. He came the same day in the afternoon. I had no prior intimation.

I was about 1000 miles away from my mother. She became seriously ill. Her other sons were present at home. One morning after taking bath, I was reading the Gita Slokas, Suddenly I began to see the face of my mother in between the blank spaces of the letters of the Slokas and it moved as I moved reading the lines further. I closed my eyes and she was there. I saw her face even I was dozing and also in actual position in which she was lying ill in my dreams at night. I continued to be pestered by these images day and night for three or four days till the day she expired.

I was about 60 miles away from my younger brother. He became seriously ill, of which I had no intimation. I saw him in a dream lying ill in a hospital and being attended to by our mother and his wife, both of whom were already dead. I wondered in dream as to why a living person should be attended to by dead persons and considered it an ill omen. He died on the third day.

In all the three cases I had no prior intimation nor do I remember having thought of them. In fact I was the object of their thoughts. I cannot say that when they were thinking about me they could see me in their night dreams or day dreams. But I know that if I deeply thinking subjectively and objectively, both.

But the main question is, who sees the dreams; the mind or the soul of the dreamer or the thinker? Opinions differ on this point. Some say the mind, while others say the soul and hold that both are immortal.

The mind controls the senses and their activities, being their master, At death it goes away with the soul to the next birth with the essence of all the accumulated knowledge good or bad gathered by the senses. It is not only thinking, feeling, seeing, hearing and doing etc. but also searching and delving into the future and can, thus, foretell the coming events in dreams. Everybody knows that the past and the present events are reviewed and revived in dreams. That is easy enough to explain.

The individual soul is part of the cosmic soul who knows all -- past, present and future. But when the soul is tied to a body, these qualities of the cosmic soul are lost. Those qualities can, however, be revived by intense thinking contemplating or meditating. That is to say, by a process of transcendental meditation, enabling the soul to see past, present or future in dreams. I cannot say which view is correct. It is common knowledge that many people foretell coming as well as past and present events in dreams. Let any one who knows better throw more light on the subject.

G.R. Bhatt
2 Malviya Road,
Lachchhman Chowk, Dehradun.

MESSAGE FROM THE DEAD

Rangoon, March I (NA-FEN). Two weeks after her husband had mysteriously disappeared, Ma Ohn Kyine, wife of a one-time police reserved officer, held a séance. At this séance the medium, a woman, spoke in a voice resembling that of the missing man.

"I won kyats 600 at cards at Changone village that day," the voice said. "As I was returning home I was waylaid by five armed men whose faces were masked by scarves near a bridge between Changone and Myagone. They forced me to accompany them to a forest. Then they sruck me down with daggers. Later they severed my head and my torso at the thighs. I lie buried in the forest. Please search for body and give it a religious burial."

This gruesome message from the dead started a search in the forest near Mwehauk village, a head constab'e on the search party found an inch of coloured cloth protruding above ground. He tugged at it to discover it was a longyi (sarong) with dried blood stains. A foul odour came from, the ground.

Digging soon uncovered the mutilated body of Ko Kyi shein, owner of the voice from the dead.

Motive for the murder has not been established. It is not known if the dead man really won at his last card game. No money was found on his body. But the deceased was once notorious for his oppression of villagers as a leader of a peace guerilla force favoured by the politicians then in power. He had made enough enemies to justify suspicion of a revenge killing.

TEN YEAR OLD BOY NARRATES PREVIOUS LIFE STORY

Mathura, July 19 - On getting information that on July 14 about 10,000 people collected at Kosi Kalan to see the boy, named Prakash Varshaneya of Chhata town in this district, who had identified a large number of persons of Kosi Kalan, including his parents in previous life, I at once proceeded to Chhata town and met the boy and his father Sri Brijlal Varshneya, a businessman of the town.

He told me that his son Prakash was telling him when he was only 5 years old his house was at Kosi Kalan. He often insisted on being taken to Kosi Kalan and when his wishes were to complied with, he alone ran towards Kosi Kalan sometimes at a distance to two miles from Chhata towards Kosi Kalan. Once in order to satisfy his whim, he took him to Mathura and told him that it was Kosi Kalan. But as soon as the bus started for Mathura the boy cried that Kosi Kalan was on the opposite side. Then he took him to Kosi Kalan on June 30, 1961. The boy on reaching there immediately recognized his previous father's shop and double storeyed house. But the family members of Sri Bholanath Jain, general merchant Kosi Kalan, has gone to Delhi. But he recognized his neighbours by their names. Then came Sri Jain to Chhata with his eldest daughter Srimati Taradevi. The boy on seeing them began to weep bitterly and Sri Jain and his daughter also wept. They insisted on taking him to Kosi Kalan for a few days to which request he did not agree. He then went to Kosi Kalan on July 14, where the boy recognized every member of the family. Sri Jain offered to educate the boy at his own expense to which Sri Varshneya did not agree.

In this case it is most remarkable that the features of Srimati Taradevi and Prakash resemble so much that no one can say that they are not real brother and sister. The name of the boy in previous life, as was said by the boy and confirmed by every one concerned was Nirmal Jain and that he died of small-pox at the age of 10 year. This fact was also stated by the boy and was confirmed by the parents of his previous life.

REINCARNATION

(Courtesy : V.V. Sundaram)

This topic is of interest to many. Here are two incidents about which I have personal knowledge.

A fairly well-placed American came to know that an old American lady had the capacity to tell one's past life. For no rhyme or reason he got interested and approached the lady. This happened in the US. She told him that in his previous life he had been very attached to each other. On being questioned further, she told him that his younger brother was now living in India, as a Sikh gentleman, that his name began with a G, and that the American would find him as soon as he landed in India.

Things were left at that. A few months later, the American had occasion to go to Manila. During his stay there, he learned that there was an old lady in the outskirts of the city who could tell about one's past and predict the future. He met her. Strangely her version matched exactly the one given by the American lady.

He was now fully convinced that what he had been told by the two women was not just coincidence. So, instead of returning to the State as planned, he changed his course and set out to India. In Delhi, having nothing specific to do, he went to the Tourist Department to hire a car to visit the Taj Mahal and other places. A car was given to him, its driver was a Sikh. On the way he enquired the driver's name. "Gurmeet Singh," was the reply. There was no doubt in the American's mind that he had located his brother. But he kept mum. At the end of the trip, he tipped, the Sardarji lavishly and also jotted down his address. Gurmeet did not attach any special significance to this except feeling happy that after a long time he had got a tourist who was liberal with tips.

Thereafter, correspondence began between the two. For Gurmeet's sister's marriage, the American sent a substantial sum. Later, he disclosed to Gurmeet what he had heard from the two different ladies, and asked him if he would care to come to the States and live with him. He then helped Gurmeet to buy land in the Punjab for the members of this family and arranged for Gurmeet's immigration to the States. Gurmeet (with his wife and children) and the American are now living together happily, with Gurmeet in no way cashing in on the situation but devotedly attached to his elder brother.

Another instance in which a colleague of mine was involved went like this. He and a relative were once passing through the interior of Punjab in a bus. At a particular spot, the relative shouted to the driver to stop the bus, although his destination was far far away. He got down and ran across the field shouting: "they have broken my leg; but I won't spare Man Singh. I will shoot him. Let me get my gun." He ran towards the Police Station. This was the first time that he had set his foot in that area, but he passed through the various roads as though he know exactly the way to the Police Station. On reaching there, he looked here and there and asked the police officials; "Who has changed the set up here; my room used to be here; and where is my gun? I used to hang it here." My colleague, who was following, was flabbergasted, unable to make any thing of it.

On thorough investigation, he came to know from an old man of the locality that, about fifty years or so ago, there had been some very notorious dacoits in the areas; Man Singh was their chief's name. The then SHO of the Police Station, a devoted police officer, had faced them boldly, but the dacoits had cut his leg in two. Despite this he had taken a vow to contain them, but he had died of the injury a few days later.

The names uttered by my friend's relative and the other details matched exactly the story narrated by the old man. My friend strongly feels that his relative was that SHO in a previous birth.

'TRANSMIGRATION OF SOUL' FIVE YEAR OLD BOY RECALLS PAST LIFE

Moradabad, Aug 24, Quite a sensation has been caused here following the arrival here on Aug 15 of a boy Pramod from Bissauli, Badaun district, who revealed the incidents of his previous life which were found accurate to the minutest detail. Thousands of people, including several prominent figures of the city visited him during the two days of his stay here and a clear case of transmigration of soul was established in the end.

The boy, aged five years, said that he was Parma Nand, brother of B. Mohanlal, proprietor of a catering firm, Messrs, Mohan Brothers, having branches in Saharanpur and Moradabad, and he died at Saharanpur on May 9, 1943 following a chronis pain in stomach.

Born at Bisauli on March 15, 1944, just nine months and six days after the death of Parma Nand, as son of Babu Bankey Lal Sharma, M.A., Shastri, a professor in an intermediate college, Bisaun, the boy as early as he could pronounce the words clearly uttered the name of Mohan, Moradabad and Saharanpur, meaning Saharanpur, and later also pronounced the words Mohan Brothers. When ever he saw his relatives purchasing biscuits and butter he said that he had a big biscuit factory in Moradabad. Whenever he saw some big shop in the market he said that his shop in Moradabad was bigger than any other shop. He used to insist, every now and then, that he should be taken to Moradabad. The name of the boy as entered in his Janma Kundali (horoscope) by the Pandits was Parmanand, a strange coincidence, but the name of his elder brother being Varmod, he also began to be called as Pramod. However, the child always insisted that he was Prama Nand, that he had his brothers, son, daughter and wife at Moradabad.

It so happened that early this year, one Lala Raghunandan Lal of Pisauli told one of his relatives living in Moradabad about the boy and his assertions regarding his relationship with Mohan Brothers. Thereupon the relative concerned told the whole story to Mr. Mohan Lal, the proprietor of the firm. Mr. Mohan Lal, together with some of his relatives, visited Bisauli, last July, and met the boy's father. The boy was, however, away in some distant village with some of his relatives and, therefore, could not be seen. Mr. Mohan Lal requested Prof. Bankeylal to bring the boy to Moradabad, and he request was acceded to. It was promised that the professor would bring the boy to Moradabad during the forthcoming Independence Day holidays.

On August 15, on alighting from the train the boy at once recognized his brother and embraced him. On the way from the station to the residence of Mr. Mohan Lal, the boy recognized the Town Hall and told that his shop was now near at hand. When the Tonga was bypassing the shop, as arranged in order to test the boy, the boy at once asked the tonga to be stopped before the shop of Mohan Brothers. Then he stepped towards the house situated in front of the shop and got in the room where the late Parma Nand used to keep his articles of worship and his each box. On entering the room he bowed in salutation.

It was a very pathetic scene when he recognized his wife and to her relatives, and recalled several incidents of his past life which concerned them. All admitted that the incidents were true. The boy could not recognize his eldest son, now 17 years who was only 13 when Parma Nand died. When the boy recalled that all the brothers used to set together and drink lemons, etc. all the brothers present and others began to weep.

The boy then expressed his desire to go to his 'gaddi' and on entering the shop he went to the soda water machine, and explained the process of manufacturing aerated water, a thing which he had never seen in his present life. When the machine did not work he at once said that the water connection had been stopped, as it had really been done to test his memory. The boy then expressed his wish to go to Victory Hotel, cousin of Parma Nand. He led the owned by Mr. Karan Chand, building and to the upper storey and at once pointed out that the rooms at present constructed on the roof were not there before.

Sahu Nandlal Saran the premier citizen of Moradabad took the boy in his car to the Meston Park, and asked him to locate the place where his civil lines branch had once been. He thereupon led the company to the Gujarat Building, owned by Sahu Nandlal Saran, and pointed to the shop where once the branch of Mohan Brothers had been located. On his way to the Meston Park the boy had already recognizes Allahabad Bank, Water Works and the district jail. The boy recognized several other places and persons who used to visit the shop during his past life.

A large public meeting was held on Aug 16 at the Arya Samaj where the boy's father, Prof. Bankey Lal, explained the development of the boy's memory since his childhood.

It was with great difficulty that the boy was taken back from Moradabad. As he was not willing to go away from his old relatives and shop, he was carried away in the early hours of

Aug 17, when asleep.

Neither the boy nor his father had ever visited Moradabad previously. The tone, the unhesitating manner and the correctness of details narrated by him were found to be absolutely fool proof and not even once did he falter.

REINCARNATION CASES

(Courtesy : (PTI), Allahabad)

Though modern scientists will not believe, Dr. Ian Stevenson, alumni Professor of Psychiatry Virginia University, U.S. A. claimed here today that reincarnation was not only possible but definite in certain cases.

Citing instance of definite cases of reincarnation,

Dr. Stevension, who is making a research and study on the subject of reincarnation, said that in Bhind district in Madhya Pradesh an enraged zamindar chopped off the fingers of the right hand of a village Patwari and later murdered him.

The incident occurred years ago. When this Patwari was reborn with his three right hand fingers missing, he remembered his previous life and related the whole incident to his new family members.

Dr. Stevenson, who was making this unbelievable disclosure in a talk on "scientific study of cases suggestive of reincarnation" at the Indian Institute of Parapsychology, said that when he came to know of the case in course of his research tour he verified the fact or chopping off the fingers of the Patwari and his murder from the old postmortem records and found the same to be absolutely correct.

A 23-year old woman college lecturer in Chhatarpur in Madhya Pradesh, Dr. Stevenson disclosed, still now visited her home of previous life and regularly ties "rakhi" to her brother of previous life.

In a case in Burma, a boy with blue eyes was born in a family after Second World War. When he grew up he told his Burmese parents that in his previous life he was a German and had been killed in the war.

Dr. Stevenson cited numerous such cases to prove that reincarnation was possible in cases of murders, shooting, stabbing and suicides. In case of army men, who died in the field, he said many were found reborn and again became military men.

'SATI' THE DIVINE DISPOSITION!

Mathura, Aug 22 - Thousands of people are throngoing the Sripalson village, about 16 kms off here, which had witnessed the 'sati' (self immolation by a woman on August 16 within three days of the death of her husband, reports UNI.

Taking note of the money that has been flooding the village through donations by the visitors, the District Magistrate has formed a committee to maintain account of this sum. A decision on how to utilize the money will be taken later.

According to eye witness account, verified through more than one sources the woman, Hardevi tried to immolate herself with the body of the husband. She was however persuaded against it and she agreed. But she refused to leave the husband's body. The matter was brought to the notice of the district authorities who succeeded in preventing her from her plan to immolate.

The police Circle Officer of Mathura advised her to have a dip in the river Yamuna before immolating herself and she agreed.

It is stated that when the woman had gone about two kilometres away it dawned on her that the body of her husband would be burnt in her absence. She immediately told the accompanying police officer that if this was tried. The upper portion of the body, which she had taken in her lap would not burn.

'Surprisingly this was what actually happened. With the woman away, fire was lit to the body. The four-hour long continuous efforts went in vain as the fire could not consume the upper portion of the body as had been indicated by the woman.

The half burnt body was then immersed into the river.

On August 17, the woman was arrested under Section 309 IPC and hospitalized.

On her discharge from the hospital after thirty six hours on August 19, she took a bath and wore a white sari. 'As she finished with this job, a saint appeared on the scene and talked to her for about two minutes.'

'She sat over the spot where her husband had been cremated and asked for Ganga Jal which was promptly supplied to her. She sipped a few drops of it and sprinkled the rest on her body. And then she folded her hands.

The eye witness account said that "within seconds, she was in flames. Within one and half hours she was reduced to ashes."

She leaves behind five children, the eldest being 12 years old.

SPIRIT OF MOTHER SAVES DAUGHTER

(Courtesy : Sachin Chakravarty)

My brother-in-law and I were sitting in our rented house near College Street in the evening and were talking about the impending danger of my younger sister's life who had been seriously ill in bed for a long time at our residence due to anaemia and congestion of liver after child-birth. Calcutta was then under the threat of imminent Japanese bombing and day to day panicky rumours were being spread and the people living in Calcutta were very much awe-struck. My relatives including my old parents had already gone to my native village in Diamond Harbour (24 Parganas).

We had to sit up many a night jointly and alternately to nurse my sister along with our boy servant who was her constant attendant. Her condition grew worse and worse day by day. We felt anxious. Resulting on God, we were doing our utmost to nurse her according to the attending doctors.

Shadow On The Wall

It was a very hot evening of June 1942. My brother-in-law and I had been both at her bedside. That day we noticed that her condition grew worst ever, during the entire period of her illness. She seemed very feeble, her body was cold and sagging and she was some times gasping. All hope of her survival was completely gone from our minds. Within a matter of moments she would give up her mortal coll. We were only looking at each other for the extreme moment. Light within our room was dimly burning and outside there was dark all over. Those were the days of blackouts. The boy servant was sent for the doctors.

Doctors came and advised us to administer oxygen to the patient. The patient was in a state of coma. We ordered our boy servant to bring the oxygen cylinder which was kept ready there for any emergency as previously advised by the doctors. We administer to oxygen gas to her. As soon as we administered oxygen to her we noticed a shadow on our front wall, a shadow of human being faintly appearing and disappearing just under the very picture of my mother. At first, we could not detect it but whenever a whispering sound was heard from above, we looked up and found the shadow. At times, the shadow was recolling and enlarging. And a very sweet spicy odour filled the air.

Uncanny Fear

We being very much afraid switched on the more powerful electric light of the room and to our astonishment the shadow vanished then and there. After a lapse of time, we put out that powerful light and switched again the dim light. The shadow reappeared again. This time it was more distinct than it had been before. And to our utter surprise, I found the shadow was that of my old mother coming to bless her dear child for her recovery. We were dump founded. My mother was then alive at home and how was it that she came to bless her daughter in the shape of a shadow? My mind misgave me. Uncanny fear and deep-felt anxiety seized me. I was extremely sad at this strange affair.

We passed that terrible night with my sister at her deathbed. Morning came and I went to report the condition of my sister to her attending physicians. No sooner had I returned home than I received an urgent telegram from my father that my mother had left this world at 8.45 in the previous night. The time of my mother's death coincided with that of the first appearance of the shadow at the previous night. I then broke down and all seemed blank to me.

Miraculous Recovery

As usual, doctors came to attend on my sister and declared that her condition was improving. It might be that she could survive this time. For three consecutive nights at the same hour (i.e. at 8.45 p.m.) the shadow of my dear mother appeared. But never again did we notice that shadow after those three nights.

My sister got round. The attending doctors were heard to have expressed surprise at her coming round so quickly though she had been so dangerously ill and she was given up for lost!

We all think that the blessings of the holy spirit of my mother did the miracle of saving the life of my dying sister. Modern science cannot explain this mysterious state of affairs, yet we have to believe this and take it for granted.

GHOST STORY : A BOY GHOST'S UNCANNY VISITS

(Courtesy : S.P. Nag)

I record for my readers what happened to me in Calcutta in 1942 when the city was 'evacuation ridden.' I had a printing press in Gour Mohan Mukherjee Street, Calcutta-6. The place is very near Swami Vivekananda's birth place. There are three buildings within the compound with a common gate. I occupied a ten-roomed building at the extreme end of a small passage. My office was in the first room on the right side of the building. In adjoining room there was a flat bed printing machine. I resided on the first floor with my family. In front of the office there was another door which I used as an entrance for the members of the family only.

One day at about 9 a.m. I was chatting with some of my friends when in a flash I saw a very beautiful boy hurriedly entering through that private entrance. I remembered distinctly that he had curly black hair, a chubby face and a very fair complexion. He was about 11 to 12 years old and wore a khaki pant. I took him to be one of my neighbours and so did not go in and enquire at that moment. But when I went in for my midday meal I enquired of every member of the family as to who the boy was. They said that no such boy had come in. I left that mater there as the idea of a ghost did not occur to me then, neither had I any faith in its existence.

Calcutta began to be bombed and I also had to evacuate my family. I then stayed in the building alone. One night while I was sleeping, I felt a sort of icy creep on my legs. I sat up only to get a dim picture of a small boy with curly hair, quickly vanishing away. Immediately I recalled the experience of months before which I have already recorded. It then flashed upon me that the boy that I saw in broad day light bore a striking resemblance to the one I just now got a dim picture of. I felt uncanny but soon repeated the name of Ram Krishna and controlled my nerves. I spent the rest of the night wide awake.

Strange to say, the same experience was repeated on the following night and, as far as I remember, on two or three nights more. Every time I felt as if two very soft hands were shampooing my legs. This strange experience made me fidgety. What can this be? Why does he come and treat my legs thus? Had I any connection with him in my past cycles of birth? I could not unravel the mystery.

One day an aged Brahmin astrologer who happened to be a scion of our preceptor-family became my guest. We slept in the same bed. At dead of night I was awakened up by a muffled sound. I sat up and found the Brahmin, lying by me, making agonizing yelps. He woke up after a rude shaking by me. I then switched on the light and wanted to know what was all about because he looked quite bewildered. He said that somebody was pressing him by the neck. I ejaculated that it was all a nightmare. But the poor Brahmin was not to be cheered up. He looked about with vacant eyes and did not want to sleep. I then asked him if he could describe that somebody. He gave a vivid description of a boy of 11 to 12 with curly hair, beautiful face and wide eyes. I then understood, but just to remove his fear, put in, "But what on earth did the ghost press you by the neck? He comes daily and shampoos my legs. He hasn't done any mischief so far..." Yet the disconsolate Brahmin lay wide awake throughout the night while I slept soundly.

FAMILY MEMBERS

After this incident several months rolled by and being financially oppressed, I wound up my business and removed. After a year a friend of mine rented for me a house in Nidhiram Majhi Lane, Howrah. It was a two storied house with a big compound but the rent was comparatively low. There I started my press again, helped by the friend. He occupied a room on he first floor. Within a month every one of my family fell ill and I had to ask my parents to come over from Midnapur. People of the locality told me that the house was a hunted one but even at dead of night I saw no apparition. I thought that the boy ghost affair has ended in Calcutta.

One day my father told me to leave the house at once. I asked the reason. He narrated that on the previous night at about 2 O'clock. He had gone to the latrine on the first floor. When he was there somebody pulled at the plaited cloth at his back. He got angry and turning round, found a small boy with curly hair, smilling at a distance.

My father, Sri M.N. Nag, editor, Medinipur Hitaishi, since dead who was an acknowledged authority on mesmerism and hypnotism was well-aware of the mysterious world of ghosts. So, in his own way, he prayed to the spirit to tear off the bonds of matter and not to intimidate any one. The spirit then vanished.

My friends also had a queer experience that night. It was about dawn. He was going downstairs to answer nature's call, when a small boy whisked past him. His description corroborated my father's and I felt sure that the boy ghost of Calcutta had come there too! I then had an uncanny feeling that I would have again to wind up. And in a month I had to. I have been in Calcutta again since 1944 but have not had so long that queer feeling. A tablet in the house where I first saw the ghost prompted me to enquire about the original owners. Local enquiry revealed that all the buildings in the said premises once belonged to a Brahmin barrister. Most of the members of his family died of cholera in quick succession. A small boy of 11 or 12, who was a pet of the locality, also died. He was very beautiful.

I do not know whether the boy ghost I saw was that dead son of the barrister. Moreover I still marvel as to why he behaved so gently towards me although twice his visitations prognosticated changes in my life.

SPIRIT IN LOVE WITH A BOY

(Courtesy : Narendra N. Banerji)

About 20 years ago when my friend Sudarsan Banerjee was working in a zemindary estate at Rajshahi, his wife and his youngest son Bibhu, about 12 years old, were living with him in a rented house, Bibhu was a student of the local school and was exceptionally fair and healthy. His elder son Shamir was a judicial officer in Calcutta.

Bibbu used to sleep in a separate room. One day at about midnight when all were asleep, Bibbhu was suddenly awakened by the sound of silver coins falling on the floor, but he did not take any notice of it an slept again. Early next morning when Sudharsan's wife was sweeping Bibhu's bed room she saw several silver coins (rupees) lying strewn over the floor. She called Sudarsan to Bibhu's room and showed him the coins. Being unable to make out anything he called Bibhu, who was still lying on his bed, and asked him about the scattered coins but he could not say anything except that he heard the sound of coins last night.

From that night the shower of silver coins became almost daily affair, but it was very strange that none of the inmates of the house though they tried their utmost could find out any clue as to how and whence the coins were coming.

Sudarsan kept the matter secret but gradually his neighbours got the information and began to throng his house in a large number. As the crowd of visitors increased day by day the shower of coins became more and more scanty.

Sudarsan wrote a letter to his eldest son, Shamir in Calcutta informing him everything and requested him to come to Rajshahi as early as possible.

WATCH INCIDENT

After a week Shamir came to Rajshahi on a Saturday afternoon. His mother took him to Bibhu's room. Shamir heard everything patiently and laughed and said that he did not believe anything at all. No sooner had he uttered those words than the table on which he kept his watch turned upside down with a loud sound, as if some body angrily pushed it, and the watch was broken into pieces.

They were all dumbfounded. Shamir then got up from his seat and searched all the rooms, the roof and every corner of the house through and through to find out who it was who did the mischief but to no effect. He saw what happened with his own eyes yet he did not fully believe that something unnatural was going on in the house.

That night he slept with his brother in the same room and talked with him till late hours about the shower of coins but his brother could not say anything about it. Of course, coins did not appear that night in his presence, He left for Calcutta the next day.

Nothing happened for about a fortnight Bibhu was generally a late riser but one day he got up very early in the morning and came to his father's room and said " I saw a strange thing last night, father."

"What was it?"

"A very strange thing."

Bibhu hesitated to say anything beyond that and his father was annoyed."

"What a silly boy you are, don't bother me in the morning, go to your own work."

BEAUTIFUL GIRL

Bibhu said "Last night, at what time I cannot say, I saw a beautiful and well dressed girl sitting on my bed and staring at me. At first I got very frightened but she did not harm and did not utter a single work as long as I saw her."

Sudarsan thought that his boy must have seen the girl in his dream, so he did not take any notice. But from that day Bibhu complained of the appearance of the same girl in the same dress in his bedroom every night.

After a few days it was noticed by his parents that Bibhu was getting emaciated and pale day by day, though he did not complain of any disease. They became very worried and consulted a physician. The doctor thoroughly examined the boy but could not find out any disease. He however, prescribed a medicine. The boy used the medicine regularly for a month but his health continued to deteriorate. The boy was then placed under the treatment of an experienced Kaviraj. For five weeks, Bibhu strictly followed his prescription but to no purpose. He was reduced to a skeleton.

When all manner of medicine failed to cure the boy, Sudarsan became hopeless and did not know what to do.

At this stage his wife one day suggested that the boy was not suffering from any disease but some malignant spirit was giving him so much trouble and it was beyond the power of any physician to bring him round. She pressed him to consult an astrologer without delay.

UNDER FIRM CLUTCH

Sudarsan had very little faith in astrology. However he went to an old well-known astrologer of that place and told him the full history of the case. The old man after hearing it said, "The girl of exquisite beauty who comes to your son every night is a female spirit called fairy. Your boy being extraordinarily handsome, she has fallen in love with him. She could not fulfil her desire and therefore, wants to satisfy her by taking his life. I have treated several cases of this nature but your son's case had taken a very serious turn. You have wasted a very long time : for that negligence the boy has fallen under the firm clutches of the girl and it is now very difficult to extricate him. You should have come to me long before this. Anyway do not be hopeless, I will try my utmost to save your boy's life."

He proposed that he would come to the house next Saturday morning when after performing some Pujas and Homa he would give the boy a talisman to wear on his right arm with red thread.

From that night, Bibhu complained that the girl remained in his room for a longer time that before and wept silently.

UNWILING TO LEAVE

On the appointed day the astrologer came to Sudarsan's house early in the morning and asked the boy to bathe in the river. He then performed Pujas and Homa for a long time. No one was allowed to stay in that room except Bibhu. Then the astrologer came out of the room and said "Now I have heard everything from the fairy about the incident. On full moon night the boy being well dressed was walking with his father under the plum tree in the compound of your house. The moon light fell on your boy's face and he looked exceedingly charming. The fairy sitting on the plum tree saw him and fell in love. She is now unwilling to leave your boy's company. However, I will try once more.

Sudarsan believed that the astrologer's statement was correct. He remembered that on that full moon night he had an invitation to join a bridal party and it was arranged that the party would pick him and his boy up from his house on their way, but for some unforeseen circumstances those people were late and he and his boy had to spend the time walking to and fro in the yard of his house.

Again the Pujas and chanting of incantations went on as before for more than an hour after which the astrologer came out of the room and said At last I have been able to please the girl. She has agreed to leave the company of your boy, on condition that he must never set his foot under the plum tree of your yard."

Bibhu and his parents agreed. The astrologer tied a talisman in Bibhu's right arm. After that the boy did not complain of the reappearance of the girl. He gradually regained his former health and became as healthy and handsome as before. Of course he never set his foot under the forbidden plum tree again.

A HAUNTED HIGHWAY

(Courtesy : Emile Gomez)

A headless ghost believed to be the ghost of a British soldier who committed suicide by hanging himself has been seen by residents of Meerut for the past three decades or so. Always dressed in khaki shorts and a white banyan, the ghost is reported to cause accidents at a particular spot on the Meerut-Roorkee highway. Nine out of every ten of its victims have died.

The apparition always appears at a crossing on the Meerut - Roorkee highway on moonlit nights. On the left of the highway before the crossing, runs the boundary wall of Gandhi Park and on the right are a few residential houses. The wall of the park turns to the left at the crossing and runs parallel to a Methodist church and a cinema house. The residential houses have a boundary wall which turns to the right at the crossing. This road leads to the Remount Veterinary Centre (RVC). Even the most courageous rickshaw pullers fight shy of passengers heading for this areas after dusk.

A teacher in St. Marry's Academy in Meerut, Miss Jalusha, narrates a frightening incident: "One morning in March, a few years ago, we were jolted out of our sleep by a loud thud followed screams of women and children. We sprang off our beds and rushed to see what the matter was. We saw a bullock-cart which was carrying women and children, lying on its side near the church. Almost embracing the boundary wall of Gandhi Park was a truck. The bullock-cart, we learnt, was moving towards Roorkee and the truck was coming towards Meerut. The truck driver reportedly said that as he came towards the crossing he saw a headless man in khaki shorts and a white banyan signal to him to pass from the left of him. The driver had failed to see the bullock-cart approaching from the opposite direction. He swerved to the right and rammed into the bullock-cart. One of the bullocks died, the other freed itself and ran towards Kankarkhera, about 5 km away. When the villagers saw the bullock return alone they sensed something had gone wrong and some men soon reached the spot. It was a heart rending sight. This is just one of the many accidents", concluded Miss Jalusha.

Another resident of Meerut Mr. Bharat Bhushan claims to have actually seen the headless ghost. He was sleeping in the courtyard, and his dog was sleeping under his charpoy. An insurance agent, Mr. Bharat Bhushan said that at midnight he awoke to the vociferous barking of his dog, and saw the spectre in khaki shorts and a white banyan walk towards the gate. His dog sprang upon the ghost, landed on the ground and sprang again; but seemed to be leaping in mid-air. The ghost moved on unmindful of the ferocious dog close behind and went past the gate onto the road.

Mr. Anand Singh of Begum Bhag, Meerut also claims to have seen the ghost. One evening at about 8.45 p.m. last September while Mr. Singh was walking past the Methodist church, he saw the apparition. Mr. Singh was unnerved as he was the only passer-by on the road at the time. The cinema house being close by, Mr. Singh pulled himself together and quickened his pace towards the theatre.

Another person who claims to have seen the headless ghost at almost the same place is Mr. Naresh Chandn of Muzaffarnagar. It was on a moonlight night that he happened to see the apparition. He was in Meerut then and had gone with a friend to the evening show at the cinema house nearby. Mr. Naresh Chand was walking along with his friend outside the church when he saw the headless ghost.

Another resident of the area, Miss Urvashi Kapoor, said that a young man was nearing the accident-prone crossing on his scooter when suddenly he lost control of the vehicle and fell. When asked what had happened, the young man disclosed that he had seen a very strange type of man. A man who had no head, but was moving all the same!"

A businessman of Meerut, Mr. Jagdish Kumar Chandna, said that about two years ago, he was going to Sardhana, 18 Km from Meerut. The road to Sardhana is just off the Roorkee road. Mr. Chandna was on a scooter with a friend on the pillion. It as 8.30 p.m. on a moonlit night when the two reached the deserted crossing. It was here that Mr. Chandna saw the headless ghost.

I was seized with inexplicable fear, so much so, that I had almost lost control of the sooter. My hands shook violently, but

I managed to speed away," recalls Mr. Chandna!

Mr. Surender Raj Kapoor, a finance manager, whose home is on the Roorkee Road (near the crossing) disclosed that the headless ghost had wanted to shake hands with him.

According to Mr. Kapoor, " I went to an evening show at the cinema house nearby. The picture finished at ten past nine. The distance to the cinema house is about 200 yards from my home. With my hands in my coat pocked. I walked at a quick pace. As I approached the RVC road, my eyes caught sight of the ghost. To my horror I realised he was coming towards me!

"The ghost followed me to the gate of my house and stood there as if he was the chowkidar ! How was I to enter the gate? Beads of cold sweat appeared on my forehead as I picked up courage to go past the gate. When I reached the gate, the ghost extended its right hand in what appeared to be a friendly gesture! I ran as fast as my legs could carry me. It was a horrible experience. Since then, I have been very particular about returning home by 6.30 p.m."

Mr. Kapoor had another chilling story to tell. He has reasons to believe that the headless ghost had claimed his father's life.

In an open space in front of Mr. Kapoor's house, there was a small drum containing water, which the servant used for washing the utensils. The distance between the water drum and the threshold of the Kapoor's drawing room is about 15 ft. One morning, his father, Mr. Barkat Raj Kapoor, said that he had seen the headless ghost near the water drum the previous night. He had reiterated that it was no fantasy born of panic. He had seen the ghost alright, in khaki shorts and a white banyan.

It was not long after he had seen the ghost that Mr. Barkat Raj Kapoor fell ill, and was soon bedridden. A doctor examined Mr. Kapoor and diagnosed his condition as blood cancer. Gradually his condition started deteriorating. A month later, the spectre was seen again this time two feet from the water drum. A few weeks alter, the headless ghost appeared again, this time still nearer. The ghost seemed to advance by two feed each time and each time he advanced, the ailing Mr. Kapoor's condition took a turn for worse.

While the headless ghost was stealthily drawing nearer and nearer towards our threshold, my father's condition showed a conspicuous deterioration," recalled Surender Kapoor.

"The headless ghost continued drawing nearer and nearer until eventually my father died," continued Mr. Kapoor. Ten days after the death of my father, the ghost appeared again with my dead father in his arms! This happened in November 1976.

GHOST LEFT A BANGLE

(Courtesy : S.M.)

Ever heard of Ghosts?" asked my fellow traveller as he lowered his newspaper and leered at me from his corner seat in the compartment. His question almost startled me, for it was midnight when he opened this topic. We had a compartment all to ourselves. It was pitch dark outside and the train was speeding through a tunnel. Above all, the stranger looked like a ghost himself! He might be forty years or thereabout, but he had a shiny bald head with not a stubble of hair on it! And right in the centre of his pate was a big bump suggesting as though he had two heads!

"No!" I said. "I never heard of ghosts. I am a student of science, you know......"

"If science has not cared to know anything about ghosts, it is the fault of science, not of the ghosts," he retorted.

His reply was so refreshing and original that I became interested, I sat up.

"So you know ?" I asked him, eagerly.

"Don't I ?" he laughed derisively rubbing his bald pate again, "Well it was just ten years ago. I remember it all as though it happened only yesterday. I was residing in a bungalow in San Thome facing the sea.

"Among my best friends and neighbours was Krishna Kant, a very handsome young man. He was living in the bungalow next to mine - a very rich fellow with refined manners. He was in love with Bimla Bai a distant cousin of his, a remarkably pretty girl, soft and slim like a creeper.

"Bimla, too, loved him and declared to her parents that she would marry none else. Being business man in the city, Krishna Kant invited the bride's people to go over to Madras and arrange the wedding since his hands were too full with his own business affairs. They were only too obliging and complied with his wish.

"The marriage was to have come off on a Sunday, but just three days previously Krishna Kant received shocking news from his Ceylon branch. The manager in charge there had reportedly swindled, and his business was collapsing. He feared, naturally, that his reputation was at stake. So he had a straight talk with his future father-in-law and stressed the urgent necessity of a visit to Colombo to set matters right. He asked him to postpone the wedding by just a week. The girl's father agreed that Krishna Kant must go at once to Ceylon and assured him he would not mind the delay at all.

"But Krishna Kant didn't turn up on the following Friday, as he had promised. There was no news from him. One of the worst of cyclones that ever visited our eastern coast was raging then. Whether any ship could venture across the seas was a matter for grave doubt.

"On Sunday, however, the storm had abated. Everybody had turned up for the wedding but the bridegroom! The bride was in tears almost on the verge of distraction.

"It might be 10 a.m. then. A clerk from Krishna Kant's Madras Office dashed in among the party and was saying excitedly that they had just received news from their Colombo branch.

"What became of Krishna Kant's? snapped the bride's father in his impatience.

"He committed suicide replied the young fellow. Suicide my God shouted everybody.

The guests were all aghast. Grief choked the girl's father. And as for the bride herself who heard this news, what do you think happen to her? She yelled aloud in her grief and dropped down dead- stone- dead!

"The tragedy was too deep for tears. But more stupefied than anyone at this turn of events was that foolish clerk himself who realized that he had unwittingly killed the bride himself!

"How was that? I asked my fellow traveler.

"How? Because the man who had committed suicide in disgrace in Colombo was Krishna Kant, the manager of the branch, and not Krishna

Kant, the proprietor and bridge-groom to be! Strange isn't it that a mere coincidence in names should have been responsible for this stark tragedy?

"Well the funeral took place in the afternoon and by six o'clock in the evening everybody had left madras. There was not a soul in the bungalow when Krishana Kant dashed up home in a taxi.

"It was I who broke the news to him. He heard it, quietly, went in and bolted the door. From that hour he became a changed man. He, of course attended to his business in the day, but he would return to his bungalow at sunset and wouldn't stir out before dawn. He allowed none into his house.

"But he had some unusual regard for me. So one night when I knocked at his door, he came out took me in and chatted with me for an hour. I wanted him to give a job to my young nephew. As I was talking with him my eyes couldn't help straying about.

"The hall in which we were sitting opened into a small room, most remarkable furnished. I saw a cot with too big a bed for one man. Next to it was a small round table with two chairs placed opposite. And on the table were placed the most dainty dishes two cups of milk and a basket of fruit.

"I became very curious and was about to ask him about it when the clock struck ten. Krishna Kant looked startled and there was a strange glitter in his eyes. It is time for my wife to come now. Then he seemed to remember my presence and bit his tongue. You'd better clear out now this minute he shouted at me and most unceremoniously pushed me out of the hall.

"I forgot his insult but what I saw and heard roused my curiosity to the highest pitch. I didn't go home. I crawled on 'all fours' towards the small room and hid myself behind a big flowerpot outside the window. I could see what was going on in the small room. Although all the lights in the bungalow had been extinguished a small crescent moon enable me to distinguish clearly every little object before me.

"Krishna Kant and a dazzlingly beautiful woman were sitting opposite eating their meal. Darling I heard Krishna Kant say you only provide the sweetest moments of my life. But how long are we to keep apart like this? Why not let me join you?

"Wail a little dearest! We don't know the nature of divine dispensation as yet. I pray that the day is not far off, she replied.

"I echo your hope Bimla, "So it was Bimla the ghost bridge of Krishna Kant. My heart was in my mouth. I had a good peep at her to assure myself that it was the same girl. Yes, she was looking dignified and graceful. Everything about her had an eerie touch something that was not of the earth. I have never seen any other woman smile like her and when she spoke she compelled your attention. Even Krishna Kant seemed nervous and afraid in her presence.

"All of a sudden she rose and flared up. 'Darling! I smell someone about here watching us!' she fitted out of the room, with Krishna Kant pathetically calling her back in vain. His shouts rent the very air. As he ran here and there to get hold of his sweetheart I heard the table getting upset, the crockery falling down with terrific noise. Where silence brooded an hour ago nothing but confusion reigned supreme how.

"I was interestedly watching this scene when someone form behind came up and administered a hard rap on my head. I was agile and caught hold of a shapely hand. But before I could turn round to see who was the owner of it, the beautiful hand had wrenched itself away from my grasp and I saw no one but this!

"The fellow traveler took out his long purse from his coat pocket and produced from it a nice gold bangle. This was what slipped from her hand as it was wrenched away. See the name carved upon it? He asked as he handed it to me.

"With a trembling hand, I took the bangle and examined it very closely. 'Bimla Bai' was the name I read gasping with amazement. The fellow traveler nodded his hand.

"Oh we are nearing Bombay! But I haven't much to say by ways of conclusion...Then I shipped back home quickly after securing that bangle. But when my wife opened the door she yelled in horror at my sight and swooned on the spot. I put her to bed and before she recovered consciousness, I looked in the mirror accidentally and recoiled in fright at my own reflection. There was not a single hair left on my head! When I went to see Krishna Kant that night I hag a big bun of hair on the hear, but the ghost turned it bald.

"And the bump? I asked him with a laugh.

"Oh, that? he said as he felt the knob with his hand. That was the result of the rapping!

"And what became of Krishna Kant? I queried.

"He hanged himself that very night in the same room, in the same place, where Bimla had died. Sometimes I pinch myself and ask myself if it was all true. But how else can you explain away the bald head and the bangle?"

SHE RECALLS HER DEATH

(Courtesy : Sarswathi)

Mrs. Mridula Sharma is an accomplished house wife who has taken a master's degree in two subjects and in two "lifetimes."

She first did her M.A. in Hindi from Banaras University and subsequently in Political Science from Meerut University. Between these two degrees, however, is the gap of a lifetime. Mridula believes she is a reincarnation of her former self.

First born in Dehra Dun, her death is recorded in 1945, at the age of 24. She believes she was born again in 1949, this time in Nasik. During her first birth she was a Bania, now she is a Brahmin.

One can dismiss the Mridula case as fantasy. What lends it some credence is the fact that a Virginia (US) University professor has confirmed it as a case of rebirth. Dr. Ian Stevenson, Professor of Parapsychology was in Bangalor in March 18 and 19 this year to investigate Mridula's case. He returned home convinced that there was no other explanation but rebirth in her case.

The Mridula case assumes importance because of the personalities involved. Her first mother Sethani Satyavathi, was a prominent social worker who rubbed shoulders with the leading figures of her time.

Both Sethani Satyavathi and Mrs. Shanta Shastri, Mridula's present mother, are alive, and each dotes on her daughter.

It all started when Mridula (Munnu in her previous birth) was hardly two. The offering of a plate of leechies triggered her recollections. She remembered her past life in her Dehra Dun house which had boasted of the finest quality of the fruit.

Amused, her parents encouraged her to go on. Slowly their banter dissolved into curiosity and a desire to learn the truth. They started investigation.

They went to Dehra Dun. Mridula led them to a place where a meeting was in progress. Recognising an old lady she entered and sat in her lap. The old lady patted her affectionately responding to the child's gesture. She was not aware that this was her own daughter in a new identity. The child then turned towards another woman seated next to the old lady. "You are my younger sister," she said with an air of confidence.

"However that be?" the woman replied. "I am big and you are just a child".

"I am your elder sister, Munnu."

The younder sister (as it later turned out) was stunned. Nevertheless, she questioned her closely to make sure it was not a hoax. Mirdula's replies strengthened her belief that she was, indeed, her elder sister.

But her mother was not convinced. She believed that the child was indulging in innocent prattle. To prove this, young Mridula was taken round the house. She recognized every room, including the one that was hers in the previous life. Then noticing a ceiling fan, she said "it wasn't there before." Her father who was all agog, admitted that the fan had been shifted to the room.

"This portion looks new," she remarked seeing another wing of the house. She was right again. That part of the house had been renovated.

Mridula was taken outside to see if she could recognise old faces. "Don't take anything from this sweetmeat vendor. He had snatched my purse," she said, pointed towards an old man. The vendor admitted the truth. When she saw Mr. Kushalchand (now Anandswamy) the founder of Milap, an Urdu daily, she exclaimed "Swamiji since when have you started wearing a saffron robe? Previously you used to wear white clothers". Mr. Kushalchand was astounded.

Her father, who had been watching this drama, incognito, finally said to the girl: " Baby, you have recognized everybody except your poor servant." "You are not a servant. You are my daddy," she said, embracing the old man.

Her mother was overjoyed to see that her daughter had returned to life. She has been showering her affection and generously on the girl since. Her wedding gift to Mridula was a posh bungalow, Rs. 10,000 in cash, besided jewellery.

"Apart from your memory, what other evidence do you have to prove that you were reborn?" I asked Mridula in Bangalore.

"I don't know. Dr. Stevension says I am a full-fledged case of rebirth. He is now working on my birthmark. According to him, a birthmark is retained in all cases of reincarnation."

Mridula's photographic memory of her past life, and particularly of the golden chain she had been presented with by her previous mother, is additional evidence of a possible rebirth. The chain has some sentimental value for her. She had been wearing it at the time of her death.

It is amusing to her Mridula refer, to her former self as she" I am a different personality now," she adds.

Do you remember how you died?

"Yes, it appeared as though somebody was trying to wrench my legs. I was in great pain which started from the bottom upwards. Them I had a severe headache. Soon I flew away.

Can you describe your experience after death?

"When I left the body I seemed to be flying. Of course, I now have only a faint recollection. But it was vivid when I was two as my mother has affirmed.

"I was floating in space," she continued. I went to the stars and returned.

What did you wear?

"Nothing that I can remember."

And what did you eat."

"Nothing."

Do you think your nature and mannerisms are different from what they wear in your past life?

"It is difficult to remember. But my previous mother says that she (her previous self) was a good girl."

Mridula is one the many cases of apparent rebirth listed by Dr. Stevenson who is doing research on the subject. He narrates the case of an American couple who happened to visit Bombay on a holiday, Though they were there for the first time, they seemed to be familiar with every nook and corner of the city. The buildings, the roads, everything seemed to be familier. Investigations revealed that they had been born in Bombay in their previous life.

The case of Shanti Devi, a north Indian housewife, is also interesting. She was familiar with dialects spoken in Muttra, 135 km from Delhi. Her previous name, it appears was Lugdi and that she was born in 1902. A Choban by caste, she had married a cloth merchant named Kedarnath Chaubey. She had died ten days after giving birth to a son.

In 1926 she was 'reborn' in Delhi. She began to recall her former life, three years later. As Shanti Devi continued to make strange statements, her family tried to verify her claims. A letter was sent to Mr. Chaubey who wrote back confirming the girl's statements. Soon after, he dispatches a relative to her home in Delhi and followed it up with a personal visit. Shanti Devi indentified both the visitors,

In 1936, a committee was set up to study her claim to rebirth in Muttra which she had never visited during her Delhi existence. At the Muttra railway station she identified another relative of Chaubey picking him out from a large crowd that had turned up to see her. She recognized the streets and also Chaubey's house which had since been repaired. As Shanti Devi was surveying the scene and recalling past events, an old man emerged from the crowd. She identified him as Chaubey's father. She also recognized other family inmates.

Shanti Devi claimed to have hidden some money in another house which belonged to Kedarnath Chaubey's parents. When the particular spot was dug up, it was found to be empty. Yet Shanti Devi insisted that she had deposited the money there. The riddle was solved when Chaubey admitted that he had ferreted out the money soon after his wife's death.

Scientists are baffled by the phenomenon of rebirth. While they have not accepted the concept they do not entirely reject it. Empirical evidence suggests that reincarnation is not confined only to Hindus, Muslims and Christans, Buddists and Jains have at one time or other, recounted experiences of apparent rebirth. Of the 14 such cases detected among Muslims, there were a few in which the subject were either Thakurs or Brahmins in their previous birth.

"We don't know how to explain these cases which are apparently genuine," says an eminent psychologist.

FACT OR FANTASY?

A recent editorial in The Times of India (Serpent or Rope? September 13) stated that there was no proof for reincarnation. This is not true. With the large number of rebirth cases reported and scientifically investigated, it is not proof that is lacking but hard facts about certain aspects of the phenomenon.

Independence investigations have confirmed that several persons' recollection of events before their birth could not have been acquired by normal sensory means.

Dr. Ian Stevenson's two papers, titled "Evidence for survival from claimed memories of former incarnations" (Journal of the American Society for Psychical Research), discuss some well attested cases of rebirth. The recollections of Mrs. Mridula Sharma (in the accompanying article) and of Miss Uttera Huddar (She lives two lives." The Times of India Sunday Magazine, May 9) are strongly suggestive of reincarnation.

The main reason for skepticism about reincarnation seems to be that few investigators have tried to explain how the recollection of previous life occurs. The conscious mode of perception is not the only one available to us. Perception is also possible through that realm of the psyche which Jung calls the unconscious.

This realm is not subject to the laws of time and space, which are concepts of the conscious mind. Thus, the unconscious can perceive events which to the conscious mind would appear to be in the past or future, near or far. Jung says, "....we are finally compelled to assume that there is in the unconscious a priori knowledge or immediate presence of events which lack any causal basis.

Recollection of past life, prediction by various divination arts, premonitory dreams and visions are perceptions through the unconscious mind, which is normally concentrated on the present, happens to relax and the rational process are in suspension. Jung has recorded in his autobiography many premonitory visions he experienced when in a "dreamy condition."

One reason why very few people recollect their previous lives may be that this paranormal ability, like say musical talent, is not universal or perhaps it is held in abeyance as a biological safeguard, for memories of previous lives might make the present life too complex to bear.

Another hypothesis is that all of us have paranormal abilities but they have atrophied or are inhibited owing to excessive dependence on the rational mode of thanking. For example, in the extra-sensory perception experiments conducted by J. B. Rhine, whenever the subject tried to reason out a solution or felt bored with a test, the results tended to be negative, while with the freshening of interest the results became positive.

Some scientists hold that man is still in the evolutionary process and that the paranormal abilities now seen in a few node of perception which may one day become common in all human beings.

It is interesting to note that a person who remembers his previous life feels certain that he was an active participant in the events recalled: there is an identity between him and the dead person he claims he was in his previous birth. In contrast, a clairvoyant for instance has no such feeling of identity: he is only a witness.

This sense of identity suggests that there is some factor which survives physical death and is embodied again. It has been suggested that this factor may account for the rather rare phenomenon of a person in deep coma "seeing" in detail activity going on around him. Dissenters put forward an alternative that hypothesis that the sympathetic nervous system may be taking over some of the functions of the cerebral cortex, the seat of consciousness which does not work in a coma.

In any case, we have no certain knowledge of the factor which survives death, how it persists and how it is embodied again. Perhaps, we have been trying to understand the phenomenon by a mode of perception - conscious mind - which is ill-suited for the purpose. This mode is limited by the sense organs which as experiments have shown are designed to receive only such information as is absolutely necessary for individual biological survival. If they were not data-reduction systems we would be overwhelmed by various kinds of energy forms such as X-rays, ultrasonics and so on.

It seems, then, that the surviving factor can be known only through another mode of perception - the unconscious. Jung writes towards the end of his life he had a series of dreams which seemed to describe the process of reincarnation. He did not want to construct a theory of reincarnation as he had not come across such dreams in others and therefore had no basis for comparison.

Again, we do not know for certain whether reincarnation has any purpose. But if a causal connection can be deciphered between the events recalled by a person and his present life, we shall have confirmation of the doctrine of karma, according to which rebirth provides, a chance to wipe away the "sins" of a previous existence.

EXORCISTS IN KERALA

(Courtesy : Sohaila Kapur and T.R. Arun Kumar)

Shankara Menon, 80, was rudely awakened one night by something heavy falling on his stomach. He was horrified to see a black, rotund, jelly like creature with long matted hair perched on him.

The creature held his throat with one hand, while with the elbow of the other prodded and threatened him. In a sudden surge of strength brought on by fright, he pushed the creature off. It fell with a sickening "plop" and disappeared.

The creature, according to Shankara, was Kuttichathan- the mischievous spirit feared and worshipped in Kerala. The local people believe that unless regular pujas are conducted for kuttichathan, he can drive them up the wall with his pranks.

We met a family that claimed to have had a harrowing experience with the spirit not long ago. Strange occurrences took place in the house furniture was turned and moved from one end of the room to the other hair and human excreta were flung into the food, strands of women's hair got singed and fell off mysteriously and sections of the house burst into flames every now and then. In desperation and on the advice of a pujari they made an offering to Kuttichathan and their trouble disappeared just as suddenly.

A fowl's neck is wrung and its blood drunk by the officiating preist (a non-Brahmin) accompanized by weird dance during the pujas conducted to propitiate Kuttichathan at a stone altar. (Kuttichathan that are trapped during exorcism are used by black magicians for witch craft.

We visited the Chathan Sewa Samaj, near Trichur run by a family which claims hereditary powers of ridding harassed people of

Kuttichathan. Their impressive bungalow in the midst of thatched juts, deep in the Kerala countryside, is an indication of the thriving business that they make out of exorcism. They were however not willing to show us whatever mysterious puja they conducted within closed doors for propitiating their deity, Vishnumaya, said to be the son of Shiva and the Lord of the Chathans.

Sleepless nights, nightmares fever and very odd behaviour like talking nonsense, urinating uncontrollably and going into fits are said to be signs of "possession -the presence of a spirit in the body. When this happens, people in Kerala resort to one of the four alternatives-go to temples (especially the Chottanikara temple, the deities of which are said to have the power to exorcise) seek the help of a pujari go to the witch-doctor or visit the medical practioner.

Vaguely Chinese in structure with its curving roof, the Chottanikara temple on the outskirts of Ernakulam town has an unostentatious interior with a dark and damp inner sanctum. We were in time to watch the evening puja being performed. Rows of lighted lamps threw flickering shadows on the contorted faces of a group of young women, chanting the name of the benevolent Devi with a sense of urgency.

Narayana Menon a high school teacher and our escort to the temple told us that the women were "possessed" and were pleading to the deity for their release. There were surprisingly no "possessed" man. The puja began with the beating of the chendas or drums and cymbals.

The woman began swaying drunkenly to the rhythm of the beat. The tempo of their dancing increased with that of the drums till it reached a deafening crescendo. Gyrating frenziedly with their long hair swishing the women started shouting in Tamil and Telugu languages we were told later that were not generally known to them when in a normal state.

Mr. Menon informed us that if was the spirit in them that spoke out at this stage because it was fronted and threatened by the superior might of the Devi. He translated the squeals shrieks and guttural sounds to mean, "I won't come." Don't touch me. Take me away or I will kill her!" As we watched fascinated some of the women fell on the floor tearing at their hair and going into impossible contortions. The evil spirit, Mr. Menon told us gravely, is struggling against the Devi." The fever abated with the end of the Puja, which lasted for half an hour. The women were then carried, half dead with exhaustion to the lower temple, with Kali as its deity. The Puja conducted at this temple is known as the Gurdi because of the red liquid (made of lime and turmeric) representing blood that is used as an offering. This is a special puja done to keep evil spirits and influences away.

The ritual is similar to the one in the upper temple, with the exception that the tempo of the drum beats is much faster. The "possessed" women gain exceptional strength and it takes a human cordon to fence them off the idol of Kali towards which they keep dashing. At the end of the Gurdi they slip into unconsciousness, they remember nothing of what had transpired.

The spirit is said to take anything from fourteen days to a couple of years to leave a human body. The spirit informs the Devi, during one of the conversations as to when it would leave. On that day the possessed person drives a nail into a tree, usually with the forehead, thereby nailing the spirit.

We visited the temple a number of times, mainly to follow up on Vasantha, a young girl of 14. Her father told us that she had got scared at a Devi's temple and ever since had been behaving strangely. Vasantha was there at every puja, constantly going into fits and swoons. As we watched her during one of her fits, a terrifying expression gripped her face: she rolled her eyes, struck out her tongue several inches and made strange noise them had a severe convulsion and became unconscious.

The Kallur family is perhaps the most well known for performing tantric pujas to exorcise evil spirits and to bring prosperity to people. When Parsurama Rishi is said to have created Kerala. He bestowed upon six families the right to perform tantric pujas. The kallur family is one of them. We met Kallur Narayanan Nambudripad, a member of the family, in Bombay. He comes twice a year to Bombay to perform pujas. We watched him perform an exorcism, through a tantric puja which involves a muttering of mantras with tantric actions over several lamps representing the various goddess.

We travelled miles from Alwaye into the wilderness to meet a 'witch- doctor' who, like the Nambudri performs exorcism though his method differs. He is a very poor Harijan and lives in a thatched mud house. It was dark and eerie inside with a few lamps lit before grotesque images of Kali. Filled with curiosity we watched him draw a very weird circular design with bright, contrasting colours. He lit a lamp and placed it in the middle of the design. He put on a strange head dress reminiscent of an African witch-doctor's hat.

He took two large glistening knives and made weaving motions with them. He chanted a few mantras to one of the knives. He then pushed the knife down his throat. He picked up a piece of log and hammered the knife down his throat he was pushing the Devi into his body.

He took the other knife and placed it across his forehead. With a sickening thud he hit the knife with the log. A two inch cut appeared on his forehead and he began bleeding -Kali had been offered blood. With blood flowing down his face and his body shivering he told us he was ready to perform and exorcism with the help of mantras and the Devi.

We were surprised to meet Dr. Somsundarm a clinical psychologist at the Chottanikara temple. He had come to supervise a gurdi puja being done for his brother though he himself had no faith in the powers of the temple. He dismissed all the cases at the temple as 'hysteria' due to a 'suggestion' affecting weak minds or repressed desires generally sexual in nature specially in the case of young women.

He was perhaps right in that we come across a few women who were obviously putting on a show. One of them went to the extent of striking various suggestive poses for the benefit of the camera.

But he avoided an answer when asked about the phenomenon of the 'possessed' speaking many languages - he said he had not witnessed it. He however agreed that cures were possible at the temple or by an exorcist attributing them to psychological causes rather than any 'supernatural power.' He felt that 'wrong diagnosis' was the culprit in cases where patients failed to be cured by doctors but found a cure in the 'supernatural.'

From all that we saw, heard and experienced we believe Dr. Somsundaram is partially right but a lot remains unexplained. How can one explain the strange phenomena of Kuttichathan where not only one person is affected but many and not all could possibly be suffering from a mental disorder of the same kind at the same time? How can a person speak languages that he/she has no idea about? There are many theories that purport to explain these strange happenings every theory has a point to make but is not complete. Science will have to expand further to clear the fog that covers many apparently unusual happenings around us.

A DEAD MOTHER GUIDES SON

(Courtesy A.S. Bhatnagar)

It was 10 a.m. of July 12, 1947 at 9 Yudhishtra Road, Krishangarh, Lahore. Piare Lal Sharma, 38, was at his breakfast table. He was planning to rush to the University and submit his thesis for the doctorate. Suddenly he saw his (dead) mother floating in the air. He was greatly puzzled. She spoke in her usual commanding voice, "Piare I have discarded my body and am, therefore, in the world beyond. Go sharp to the village and perform my last rites".

Piare Lal Sharma was fairly upset. All his plans of the day had to be dropped. Mother spoke again and warned her son "No chance for your thesis now, my son. The whole of Lahore is to be overtaken by communal riots. The town will be reduced to shackles. Hindus will be badly massacred. You must, therefore, swiftly shift along with your family to the village else you will be in troubled waters. Don't bother about the property."

Piare Lal complied with the instructions of his mother from the other world and left for Manali, his village in district Ropar. Mother was, indeed lying dead. Pandit Dwarkadas, his father had died leaving behind his widow and Piare as a few days old baby. The widow mother had brought up Piare and, therefore, had an unusually intense love for her son. It's, therefore, this intensity of love which helped the mothers' soul to materialize herself to be nearer her son to constantly guide him throughout his life. This mother-love, being one of the holiest and most unselfish of human feelings, is also one of the most persistent on higher planes.

Materialisation of the soul's astral body in order to held and guide a near one is a rare phenomenon. At the same time, the instances are not lacking where the departed souls do materialize themselves to communicate with a dear one.

On 16th March, 1967 at 3.35 a.m. Prabhuashritji Maharaj appeared in the doors of his disciple Acharya Vishnu Sahai Sadhak of Malviyanagar, in Delhi. As the latter bent down to touch his Gurus' feet the Guru just disappeared. At 10 a.m. a telegram was received informing him the death of Parabhuashritji Maharj at Rohtak in his asharam. The Guru had obviously visited his dearest disciple after leaving his physical abode.

Similarly, Saraswati Devi Sharma of Krishan Nagar, Delhi, used to be visited by her dead brother after her first delivery. The brother used to hold the child for fondling him and then used to disappear. One day Saraswati Devi seized her brother by his Kurta and declared that she would not leave him. Why should he quite like this every day?

Do not bother the materialized, soul replied. I will now be with you forever. " Later he was born to her as her next son. So perfectly the child resembled this brother's face that everyone in the family remarked this fact. This second son is now grown up boy. He is now a lecturer in engineering deptt. of BHU.

Some people have a faculty to see the departed souls in the astral world. Vishnu Dayal Verma of Itwari Hills (MP) can see the spirits but cannot hear their voice when they answer his questions.

Piare Lal's mother Praja Devi appears before her son in a materialized from even 40 years after her death and advises him through ups and down of his life. Piare Lal Sharma found it hard enough to run a family of seven children and was always under pressure of his tight family budget. He once consulted his mother in her materialized form Why don't you write a Hindi novel. This will bring you some money? Piare Lal had not even read a good novel, not to say of writing one. He, however, strategy writing of fiction. His pen ran through pages after pages. Soon enough a voluminous novel was ready, entitled "walking walks". However, no publisher was willing to publish it. Mother appeared again and gave out the name of a publisher of Daryaganj, Delhi. The fiction was published. It was picked up by the Punjab University and prescribed for studies.

There is a series of events when Piare Lal received help and guidance from his so called dead mother. On 9th July 1983 mother appeared before her son as suddenly as ever and warned that at 2 in the night your elder son Shashi will open fire on Ravi." In spite of his struggle to sit up awake through the night Piare Lal dozed off in to his bed. The heated battle of arguments between two boys Shashi and Ravi over the claims for ownership of a house reached its climax. Exactly at 2 a.m. Piare Lal was startled up at the fire shot of Shashi's pistol. In this family squabble Piare Lal was badly involved. He was accused of a criminal assault. A complaint was lodged with the police against him. What appears to be unbelievable is that the mother gave him a typed counter complaint. This completely neutralized the pending charge of a criminal offence against him. Again when once Piare Lal was seriously ill his mother placed a few pills in his hands. Thus material things like a typed document and drug pills can also be produced from the astral plane.

Equally surprising and strange is a case reincarnation. A deceased son was in a constant communication with his father and subsequently reincarnated in the same family.

It was a dull and suffocating Sunday morning on the 6th Feb., 1983. The telephone in the house of Dr. Balbir in Hauz Khas urban village of Delhi shrieked in a sad loud tone at 8.15 a.m. A friend from the other end broken a tragic news. His young son Ram Pratap, 24, had died of a truck accident on way to Khalaria Haat Coal Mine, Meghalaya. He had taken up the steering wheel himself as the driver had fallen deep asleep and failed to be woken up. It was urgent for Ram Pratap to rush up to the mine site to disbursed wages to the labour. The young boy lost control of the vehicle which slipped down into a sideway ditch. After completion of funeral rites on 8th Feb. the grieved father of the young deceased boy decided to establishe contact with his son's soul. He first operated the planchette but after close cross- checking and ensuring the identity of the contacted soul he shifted to the method of mediumship by completely surrendering himself as a vehicle for him. Now the son was speaking through his father's vocal chord. All the members of the family will sit together closeted in a small room, put questions and record answers in a notebook. They were ascetics in the beginning as to the identity of the contacted soul but the answer were so convincing that they had ultimately to believe that they were in communication with the soul of their dear one.

The continued mediumship of self by Dr. Balbir Singh for allowing his departed son Ram Pratap the use of his vocal chord caused him considerable weakness. Ram Pratap realized this and advised his father to instead, continue the use of planchette. In the countries where the mediumship of this kind is more frequently in practice cases are on record in which his weight has been considerably decreased while manifestation of this character were taking place.

Ram Pratap's soul requested his father to continue the sitting of collective prayer for him as this gives him a great solace. Prayers and good wishes for the departed soul of a person give him a great comfort and strength. This has been indicated by several studies on the subject. Arthur Ford, while writing the book the World Beyond through the mediumship of the noted journalist of USA Ruth Motegomary by automatic writing on an electronic typewriter wrote about the support Kennedys got after their death from prayers... the power of prayer is as important on this side as on your side of veil that man calls death... Those prayers for the souls of depart dear ones which are spoken in living kindness by souls they knew in the earth plane comfort and nurture them and make no mistake about it, God hears them all. The Kennedy brothers are a striking example of the power of prayer. Such a tumultous, spontaneous wave of prayers poured forth when the President was slain that he really never lost consciousness. The custom amongst Hindus to regularly pray for 13 days for the departed soul is, therefore, very significant and rational.

On a scanee sitting in August 1983 the coin was moving on the drawing board with a speed touching the alphabets for formation of words and sentences. A suo-moto significant message emerged. It said, "I am very-very happy today. It has now been decided that I am to be reincarnated as my elder brother Krishna Mohan Singh's son on 10th January 1984. The scheduled was indeed strictly kept up. This writer has seen this little boy of three years. He does give indications of his being his own uncle Ram Pratap. As he starts speaking he may perhaps give more and more evidence of his reincarnation of Ram Pratap. His name has, of course, not been changed for this life as well on his own request. On his another request his clothes of previous life have not been disposed of. He has perhaps, an attachment with these clothes as he said, "I will wear them myself after growing up to that age."

Ram Pratap's soul was consulted sometimes in family matters. His sister was engaged with a boy for her marriage. On being consulted about his approval and suitability of match the brother's soul recorded a categorical disapproval of this engagement which was, of course, then broken off.

Dr. Balbir Singh, a professor of philosophy in Hindu College, Delhi by profession is very investigative and rational by temperament. He will not accept a fact without scrutiny and weighty rationale behind it. So far as this case of reincarnation is concerned he will convince his listener with his vibrant arguments and dramatic description of the series of conversation he had with the soul of his deceased son.

This para-normal event concerning his own family has evoked in him a great interest in the physical phenomena and a deep searching study of the same.

He has narrated this reincarnation story in the lecture meets of the Delhi Physical Research Society which he heads as its President. Many cases come to him of grief ridden people for communication with a deceased dear one. Recently a young man from Chandigarh along with his mother approached him with a peculiar problem. His first wife had committed suicide. The second one proved to be a tyrants for her husband as well as her mother-in-law. The deceased wife was haunting this youngman in his dreams almost regularly. Dr. Balbir Singh had a revealing conversation with him and his mother. As they stood up on their feet to leave, the mother suddenly fell down and got in to a trance. Possessed by the former deceased wife she spoke of her agony to see this trouble making second wife in the house. This soul also revealed that the suicide was not committed by her of her ownself but was under an evil spirit effect. This is now a regular feature the dead wife speaks through the vocal chord of her mother-in-law.

A MYSTERY THAT IS YET UNSOLVED

(Courtesy : T.S. Luther)

Certain events origin with never- staling memories. The time factor has no effect on them. One may grow old but the memories, sweet or bitter remain young and fresh in some unknown corner of a weary heart. I too cherish a memory of this sort.

It was the end of September 1947. The repercussions of the partition had not yet fully subsided when Ferozepore, a border city in East Punjab where we lived in those days experienced another disaster. The water of the rivers Sutlej and Bias crossed the previous flood levels and straight gushed into the city making it impossible or the authorities to control it. They did whatever they could and in the end ordered the residents to abandon the city. They in their turn did whatever they could and in the end abandoned the city. Only three or perhaps four very obstinate families did not move and our family was one of them.

With a few belongings and eatables we moved upto the roof. For complete three days the water kept on rising till the maximum level of the water in the city measured seven feet. On the second day our house gave way. On the fourth day our bellies refused to keep pace with our patience so I had to descend from our "Invincible Castle" in a frantic search of eatables.

POWER OF SENSES

(Courtesy : K.M. Talgeri)

Men who have the sixth, seventh or eighth sense are sometimes called supermen. But their mysterious power of extrasensory perception (E.S.P.) comes within the scientific field of para-psychology.

Pschological phenomena are under subjective experiences or physical effects. Subjective experiences are grouped under E.S.P. This is the awareness of something outside of one's self acquired without the use of the senses Clairvoyance, precognition and telepathy belong to this category.

Clairvoyance is the extrasensory perception of an object or objective event. To illustrate there is the case of the late Miss Raihana Tyabji, a devoted friend of Mahatma Gandhi. When the Mahatma was imprisoned at the Aga Khan palace in Poona, Raihana was in Nasik. "I could very clearly see from my residence at Nasik everything that happened to Bapu in far-off Poona. Manu was beside me and I used to record all that was revealed to me. When I met Bapu and Ba later, I showed them my diary. Ba was astonished when she read what I had written, but Bapu not seem to be much impressed and he laughed the mater away.

Precognition or precognitive E.S.P. is the foreknowing of future occurrences. I knew Mr. Amar Gaga Singh, the well-known Nepal-born clairvoyant who died some years ago in Adelaide Australia at the age of 117. The chief astronomer of the Adelaide observatory, Dr. George Frederick Dodwell, investigated had his case.

Dr. Dodwell wrote to me : "Amar Gaga Singh was my guest for three months and I was greatly impressed by his unusual gifts or insight and foresight...He spoke to me beforehand of the great comet which would shortly become visible and when it was seen a fortnight later, he said : "What did I tell you? He had also predicted a large display of sunspots at Christmas and later on an aurora and stormy winds and a tidal wave which occurred at Adelaide and on our seacost of a man of science.

When I asked Mr. Amar Gaga Singh how he predicted future events he relied: "I don't know. All my prophesies come to me during my waking hours, usually when I am walking in a meditative mood or when I am lying on my bed absolutely relaxed. Once I suddenly saw in my mind's eye a great comet and all at once I became aware of the exact day it would appear to the inhabitants of this earth. Six weeks later, on the exact day I had forecast the great comet made its appearance to the amazement of scientists. I had also predicted the length of its tail and its exact distance from the sun and the earth without conscious thinking or reasoning.

Mr. Amar Gaga Singh had made too many predictions to be mentioned here but among the astounding ones were the Russian earthquake in which 5000 people perished the volcanic eruption in Congo, which is not known for any volcanic activity and the death of Mahatma Gandhi three weeks before the assassination.

Telepathy, or awareness of the thought or mental state of another person, is another E.S.P. phenomenon. Who is not familiar with that common occurrence of an identical thought passing through the minds of two persons at the same time? "I just thought of the same thing," says one to the other in surprise. Some have an inborn faculty of reading others thoughts.

Mrs. A. David Neel, author of With Mystics and Magicians in Tibet, describes many experiences she had with lames having strange E.S.P. abilities. Mr. Upton Sinclair, in this book Mental Radio, discusses the endless experiments he made with his wife in thought transmission. Mr. Charles T. Seymour who investigated the telepathic phenomenon says that 300 kilometres is a fair distance to sent out thoughts without the help of a physical link.

Besides, these subjective experiences of E.S.P. there are the physical effects known as psychokinesis. Some individuals can produce a physical effect upon some object in his environment without the use of their motor systems. Thus, psychokinesis is the direct action of the mind on matter.

Swami Rama of the Menninger foundation Topeka Kansas, U.S.A. whom I met during the world congress on yoga in Delhi in 1970, could shatter a glass tumbler kept at a safe distance by merely concentrating his gaze upon it. And then there is the well known case of Yuri Geller who could cut a ring into two by staring at it and who once looked at a row of speeding cars on a Munich road and froze them into immobility.

Yoga literature is replete with parapsychological experiences and contains techniques for acquiring these powers. Autobiography Of A Yogi by Paramahansa Yogananda and Search In Secret India by Paul Brunton describe the wealth of parapsychological material in our country. On the other hand, Dr. J.B. Rhine's New Frontiers Of The Mind deals with modern research in parapsychology.

Most parapsychologists say that one out of every five individuals has extrasensory perception. It is staggering to known that we are standing at the threshold of a huge unknown world.

TALES OF THE PARANORMAL AND LIFE BEYOND

(Courtesy : M.A. Azam)

More than a couple of years ago this gruesome incident was reported in the column of leading daily newspaper.

One evening in a bamboo hut a farmer sat down to take his dinner. Earlier his wife had announced that she had prepared a delicious dish of meat and the farmer was happy over the prospects of a heavy meal. As usual he squatted on the floor and took a heap of rice on his plate. Just as he was about to taste the meat a snake no longer than a yard stick dropped from the ceiling right in front of him.

Naturally, he was scared. To his horror he watched the snake slither into a bamboo basket. Since the basket was loosely covered with a lid, the snake could easily slide inside. He called his wife and told her. She immediately screamed in fright and this brought neighbours in. They armed themselves with sticks to kill the snake.

By means of a pole one of them cautiously lifted the cover. But there was no sign of the snake. It might have slid away through some hole in the side of the basket which lay against the bamboo of the house. The basket was then examined closely. To his amazement the farmer discovered a skull.

As was later disclosed, it was the skull of his two year old son. It was also disclosed that the child's step mother the farmer's wife by his second marriage had killed the child. This demon of a woman who hated the boy bitterly had butchered him, cooked his tender meat and was about to feed the child's father with the meal. Perhaps the unsuspecting parent would have eaten the tender meat of his son, but a messenger in the form of a snake came as it were to save him from that dreadful deed, in the nick of time. This timely messenger was thereby responsible for leading to the discovery of a crime and to the arrest and punishment of a vicious criminal.

The Punjab Story

Another recent snake story, originating from the Punjab was given ever wider circulation and corroboration from many authentic sources.

Unfortunately, this also refers to a woman who after her death was taken to be buried. As the coffin was being lowered into the grave it was found that a large snake lay coiled on the ground below. Since this was considered an evil omen for the departed soul, the grave was abandoned and new one was dug not far from the first. But there too strangely enough another snake was waiting. Some Moulvis (or Muslim divines) were consulted and they counseled that no more graves should be tried. The woman should be buried in the second grave. If the snake could not be scared away. It should be allowed to stay and should not be molted.

The corpse was then laid in the grave, but as the shroud was removed from the face of the dead woman to allow her relations a last glimpse of the face the snake slowly raised its head and sharply bit the woman in the moueh. The tip of the dead woman's tongue was held tightly between the fangs of the snake. To the horror and dismay of the observers the snake even pulled the tongue out of her mouth. The snake then disappeared through a hole in the ground.

On enquiry it was revealed by the husband that the woman was his second wife. She had been exceedingly harsh and cruel to his children by the first wife, who had died a few years back. On the slightest provocation, the step-mother used to scold and abuse the timid little souls. The husband was helpless as he had often to live away from home.

A Lady's Hospitality

Apart from these fact finding tales of the paranormal there have been others which are less startling but perhaps more significant in asmuch as they have some interesting bearing on the life after death, rebirth or transmigration of the soul.

I have been directly concerned with one such incident which happened in 1937, when I was holding a small job with the Government of Bengal. I was given a special assignment to a village where, on behalf of the

Government, we were holding an exposition of cottage industries. I had just finished saying my evening prayer, when one of my assistants brought me the message that a respectable lady wanted to meet me. She was going round the stalls and wanted to see me for I happened to be the officer-in-charge.

My visitor -- Mrs. Mazumdar -- was an elderly Hindu lady in her mid forties. Her husband was the Headmaster of the local High School. She asked me a few questions about our exhibits, their source, prices, etc. Before leaving she invited me and a couple of my Hindu assistants to have breakfast next morning at their residence which was in the neighborhood. I was, however, a little surprised, for, as a Muslim I did not except this hospitality from a Hindu family especially since I had not acquaintance with them before, I was of course, very pleased and promised to be in time for breakfast.

My Own Son

We were seated on the porch and our hostess treated us to a hearty breakfast. As we were about to take leave of her I was requested to wait. After my companions had left I was led into the inner apartments of the house and shown round the different rooms, including the sacred place of worship. Both the male and female inmates of the house, including children were exceptionally cordial and I could hardly make out the reason. For my part I was very grateful, reverent, and courteous. After a couple of hours I was back to my camp and to my work.

In the evening I was summoned thing appeared strange. The adults greeted me more warmly, the children more joyfully as if I had been known and loved for ages. Mrs. Mazumdar then placed a plate of sweets before me and said :

My Child you must be wondering what have brought us close to you. You may find it difficult to believe, but it is nevertheless true that the moment I saw you for the first time in my Life I had no doubt that you had been my own son in a previous birth. The lady has since loved me as her own child and she has been a mother to me.

This incident was cited in an article by the author published in the Asia Magazine, USA June 1944 under the caption "My Brother's Face" and reprinted in Amrita Bazar Patrika.

Mother & the Child

And now there is a story of a mother who died years ago, but appeared in flesh and blood at the death bed of her only child. It was in 1925 and concerned the brilliant son of Mr. Mukherjee, Headmaster of the local government High School.

Young Mukherjee was at that time 17 years old and was exceedingly well behaved and gentle, but a little moody. He had lost his mother when he was a child. His father a deeply religious man never took a second wife. The boy became very sick shortly after he passed his high school examination with distinction.

On the night of his sad demise, Mr. Mukherjee was sitting by his besides along with a few of his students who used to nurse the patient and help the father since there was no female member in the family. As the clock struck eight a lady dressed in an ochre coloured sari entered the room. She wore a necklace of rosary beads and carried in her hand and iron rod of a Sannyasi (Mendicant) Mr. Mukherjee along with other attendants stood up in silence out of respect for her, but everyone appeared to be struck dumb. Not a single work came form the lips of nay of them as long as the lady stayed there. Mr. Mukherjee recongnised at once that she was the mother of the boy. She sat beside her ailing son touched his forehead and then departed. The whole thing lasted for a couple of minutes. As everybody came out of their stupor they found the boy had expired. His soul or spirit went out to follow his mother who came as it were to escort him to the abode of eternal rest.

But has any one from the life beyond ever come here to stay except in the form of a flickering apparition as in the case of Chester Hayworth who was visited by his father about 4 hours after the latter's death at 8.30 on the same night. More than 12 years ago, a Brahmin from Bengal aged about 50 who had settled in Banaras, UP one night dreamt a strange dream. The dream was repeated twice in the same week.

BRAHMMA DAITYAI FAMILY GUARDIAN

(Courtesy : S.N. Dawn)

This is a fact which has been related to me by my father and other members of my family, who have seen everything of it with their own eyes. It is so real to them and so closely connected with the day-to-day life of our family that I have hesitate for sometime to term it as a ghost story.

Not very long ago in the heart of the city of Calcutta, at Joy Mitter Street, stood our ancestral house the two hundred and fifty year old massive building of the Dawn Family of Darjipara. The house had two mahals. The outer apartment had a beautiful marble hall to worship deities where Dol Durga pujah and other ceremonies were performed all the year round. In the yard of the inner apartment there stood and old Bel three the foot of which was covered by a cemented platform. Near that Bel tree, my father along with other members of my family used to see every evening a majestic figure of a human being an embodiment of heatlh and beauty moving in a pensive mood. Even they saw him on the roof of the pujah room engaged in deep meditatiorr with folded hands. That beautiful heavenly figure was about eight feet tall with his limbs proportionately developed. He wore a spotless white Dhoti and an equally white Chadar which covered his left shoulder beneath that bunch of sacred threads were clearly visible laid across his broad chest. This superhuman being was known to every one of our family as Brahmman Daitya. He was greatly feared and equally loved with reverence. It was a custom of our family and still it is not to blow conch shells in the evening which it was feared might disturb him in his meditation.

The later under the Bel tree was always kept clean and washed with

Ganges water. One day a naughty boy of a neighbour ran away from his home and somehow managed to hide behind the tree where he committed nuisance and no sooner had he done so than was he caught by Brahmma Daitya. Attracted by the loud cry of the boy household members ran to the spot and saw the boy was caught in the neck by some invisible one and was being dashed against the ground over and over again. Knowing what had happened they cleaned the place with Ganges water and prayed for mercy. Them the boy got relief from his clutch. Once our drawn threw unclean water on the spot and was punished and rescued in the same way.

In their school days, my father along with my uncles had to study their lesions under their provoke tutor. Annanda Babu. Every day after their study the majestic figure of Brahmma Daitya was visible on their passage with a ray of sweet smile o penetrating his lips. Annanda Babu with folded hands did pray to him "Baba boys are afraid please give us passage" The figure vanished within a winkle of an eye. Boys used to run towards the inner apartment in breathless speed, accompanied by a servant. There was a separate kitchen in the house for boiling milk which was kept under the personal supervision of my grandmother where the cook was not allowed to enter. Sometimes in her preoccupation with other family matters grand mother was late in attending the boiling milk. On several such occasions she heard the tone of the Brahmma Daitya Mother ! The milk is fully boiled. At this he hurried to the spot to see to her utter astonishment that the bowl containing milk was taken down from the oven and kept at its proper place. With folded hands she down her head.

Although my family members became much acquainted with Brahmma Daitya and it was good that they were no longer much afraid of him. Yet the house was kept perfectly clean so that he might not feel uneasy.

After the daily pujah of Narayansila our family deity a separate and fresh arrangement for pujah was kept ready and just at midnight Brahmma Daitya was kept ready and just at midnight Brahmma Daitya used to go to the pujah room. The sound of his wooden slipper was audible even from a distance. He took his seat and performed pujah behind closed doors. In the morning any one could see the signs of pujah inside the room and till then the charming fragrance of dhoop and dhoona emitted from the room. All these happened for years together. One day the spirit appeared before my grandmother to say that he had lived in the family with perfect peace but as his time was over he was going to leave the family soon. After the death of my grandfather the spirit was seen no more.

The Brhmma Daitya left our family for ever, but all does not end here. I have something more significant to say. Our family had reputation in the business field and in numnerous charities for generations but with the appearance of the spirit during my grandfather's young age, his business flourished in any field he entered. He earned name and fame in an inordinate measusre. But within a very short period of the disappearance of the spirit misfortune had a grip over our family. A feud arose which ruined everything. One question still baffles many a mind whether the appearance and the disappearance of the Brahmma Daitya in and from our family had anything to do with its rise to the pinnacle of glory and its subsequent sudden downfall or not.

UNRAVELLING THE REBIRTH RIDDLE

Jasbir, the three-and-a-half years old son of Girdhari Lal Jat of Rasulpur village in Muzaffarnagar, was thought to have died of small pox. As it was late it was decided to cremate the body in the morning.

A few hours later young Jasbir began to stir, and gradually revived. But it was a few days before he could speak again. When he did there was a complete transformation of behaviour.

Jasbir now said he was the son of Shankar of nearby Vehedi village and a high caste Brahmin. He would eat no food cooked in his former lower caste farming home and wanted to go back to vehedi. A kindly Brahmin neighbour agreed to cook for him and did so far one-and-a-half-years.

Meanwhile talking of his previous life, Jasbir alleged he had been fed poisoned sweets during a wedding by a man he had lent money. He had become giddy, fallen off his carriage, suffered a head injury and died.

Later, a Brahmin lady originally from Rasulpur now married in Vehedi came visiting. Jasbir immediately recognized her as his previous wife. The details of his previous wife that the three-and-a-half year old narrated corresponded with the life and death of 22 years old Sobha Ram, son of Shankar Lal Tyagi of Vehedi. Shoba Ram had died exactly in the manner Jasbir described.

Although it still cannot be proved that reincarnation exists more and more evidence is coming to support the existence of this phenomenon, Dr. Jamuna Prasad one of India's top two researchers in the field told me at this Allahabad home recently. The evidence collected so far certainly emphasises the need for more serious research.

Dr. Jamuna Prasad is the former Director of the Bureau of Psychology, Allahabad and a Deputy Director in the Directorate of Education. Now retired, he has actively worked in the fields of parapsychology, since 1947. For nine years he also collaborated with Dr. Ian Stevenson of the University of Virginia Medical School who has done significant in reincarnation.

In our books on philosophy, our religious scriptures, and in our mythological stories, we find suggestions about the continuity of life," Dr. Jamuna Prasad explained. According to Plato's Theory of Reminiscence, our present knowledge is a recollection of what was learnt or known by the soul in a previous state.

"Today efforts are being made to investigate the problem scientifically on the basis of empirical evidence instead of philosophical logic and reasoning," he continued. "If pre-existence should happen to be a fact it is obvious that the only possible empirical evidence of it would consist of verifiable recollections of that existence.

Findings of research now underway in one of India's top scientific institutes could also prove that many of us had a previous life. So far at least 45 possible reincarnation cases have already been ferreted out -- challenging traditional human belief.

Behind the extraordinary research is Dr. Satwant Pasricha, a 39-year old woman psychologist at the prestigious National Institute of Mental and Neuro Sciences (NIMHANS) Bangalore, and formerly a research associate at the University of Virginia, Charlottesville.

Dr Pasricha was sceptical about finding a single reincarnation case when she started her work in 1973. But after many miles and months of driving through bandit-infested areas, and wading through flooded roads, she reached towns and remote villages where 60 cases mostly children came to light.

Fifteen were eliminated because of insufficient or unreliable information. Thereafter she conducted over 400 interviews often several with each source over many months to catch any difference in account and probed numerous municipal and hospital records.

For those who wish to believe in reincarnation the evidence is fairly strong. She said quietly but firmly in an interview that there is enough data now.

Using Dr. Stevenson's scientific techniques Dr. Pasricha has established some very interesting common features, also reported from other cultures. Firstly the child starts talking about a previous life between the age of two and four. It stops talking about it between seven and eight. There is a high incidence of violent death. And all the kids can describe the way they died.

"Research in the field of reincarnation can be grouped into two categories, Dr. Jamuna Prasad pointed out. The primary one aims to prove the existence of this phenomenon. The secondary one the why and how of it. Secondary research should also try and find explanations for the various findings from primary research."

Six years old Ashok Kumar was brutally murdered with a knife by a neighbouring relative. The relative's only motive seemed to remove obstacles for inheritance of the property of the boy's barber father, Sri Jageshwar Prasad of Chipatti, Kannauj.

A few years later word reached Sri Jageshwar Prasad that a boy born six months after his son's death in another part of Kannauj and was claiming to be his murdered son. He was also giving details of his murder the murderers' names, and other details of Ashok Kumar's life and death.

When Jageshwar Prasad went to see the reincarnated child, the boy recognized him. He also narrated details of his previous life which were perfectly accurate. The boy carried a linear mark on this neck which closely resembled a knife wound.

Many explanations are sometimes offered for such memories in children who remember their previous lives, Dr. Prasad pointed out. For instance, fraud, genetic memory extra-sensory perception or possession. But there are a few unique cases in which no other explanation seems to be plausible, except the existence of the phenomenon of reincarnation. For example when children have unusual behavioural features, special likes and dislikes, special skills like some unlearned language, dance or boxing and finally birth marks.

He explained that in several cases of reincarnation there were birth marks which corresponded to injuries sustained in their previous lives causing their deaths. In quite a few cases the places and kinds of injuries indicated by the reincarnated person's birth marks tallied with the autopsy reports of the previous life person.(Dr. Stevenson has studied many cases in Turkey where the places of injury as indicated by the birth marks have been corroborated by the autopsy reports.)

In some cases emotions and feelings for some particular persons may also be carried over and be revived with the same intensity on meeting that person," the 72-years old soft spoken parapsychologist said. "But only in very few cases is there a change of sex. In such cases, the children show unusual forms of behaviour.

"A female relative of mine claims to have been a male in her previous life," he added. "She is still more masculine than feminine, and dominating and authoritarian in her general behavior. She uses the masculine gender for herself. Her tone and style is always that of an elderly male in authority, even though she is now a grown up woman."

Sushma Srivastava was two-and-a-half years when a relative in Banaras died. Her Allahabad based father asked the family to go and condole. They did not know the location of the house. The driver parked the car on the road and was asked to find out where the relatives lived.

Sushma suddenly remarked, "What is the need to ask people the location of their house. I know where it is!"

The family was stunned and questioned her how she knew. She said just follow me, and went on ahead. She led the family straight to the right house, inside it and to the kitchen. The dead relative's widow was cooking and was started to see all of them. They were asked to sit in a room.

At the back was another room with lots of plants. When two-and-a-half years old Sushma peeped into this room, she got very angry and shouted "Why have you kept plants in this room. I had this built as a servants quarter?

After that people were curious to know who this child was? Slowly the mystery began to unravel.

Sushma's family discovered that she was the dead person's father in her former incarnation. Her previous name was Raghunandan Prasad who was a lawyer. He had two sons and a daughter.

Sushma's behavior with her present brothers and sisters was very abrupt and off hand. She did not encourage affection or friendliness, or even play with them. "Go and do your own thing' she would say.

Dr. Jamuna Prasad's wife said, "Sushma was my paternal grandfather in her previous birth. She has been visiting us regularly ever since she recogonised our house in Benaras as a child."

"My own father, after a lot of investigation, was completely convinced that the little girl was his own father in her previous birth," she continued." He gave Sushma a lot of respect. He would always wait for her to sit before sitting himself"

There are certain questions which arise from all this and need to be researched, Dr Jamuna Prasad pointed out. Why do only a few children remember their previous lives, and why should they mostly have met with violent deaths? Why don't all of the latter have birth marks indicating their death? Why is it that in some cases the period between death and rebirth is small, and in other instances several years? What happens in the interim? Why are some children reborn in the same family, neighbourhood or town, and others thousands of miles away?

It is the answers to these critical questions related to reincarnation that serious researchers in the field are addressing their efforts to.

SHE LEADS TWO LIVES

On every ashtami, the eigth day of lunar fortnight, Ms. Uttera Hudar, a 34-years-old former college lecturer, gets "transformed" for a day into a 19th century Bengali woman.

In her new personality of a coy housewife, she calls herself Sharda, puts vermillion in the parting of her hair and wears the sari in the Bengali style. She completely forgets her mother tongue, Marathi, and speaks a higly Sanskritised version of Bengali which was in vague during the 1850s. Following the purdah custom of those days, she refuses to come before strangers.

Motor cars, cooking stoves, fans and similar modern appliances surprise her. The entire day is spent in singing or writing Bengali devotional songs in praise of goddess Durga. As the evening approaches, she calls her parents to perform arti and promptly reverts to her personality of Uttera, totally forgetting what she had said or done as Sharda during the day.

During these spells, which began about a year ago in February 1975, she has revealed that she is Sharda, daughter of Brajmath Chattopadhyaya who lives opposite a Kali temple in Burdwan. Her masi (mother's sister) was very fond of her and had arranged her marriage with Biswanath, a nephew of her meso (masi's husband). Her father-in-law, Nandkishore Mukhopadhyaya, who was a resident of Shivpur in Khulna district, had disliked the alliance.

Her husband was a Kabiraj (ayurvedic doctor) and had to travel to many places. Sometimes he would not be able to turn home for days together. Sharda had two miscarriages. She was carrying her third child when she was bitten by a snake at her masi's house while pluking flowers. Shoe does not recall anything after that. By a strange coincidence, Uttera's mother, whicle she carrying her, often dreamt of a cobra about to bite her right toe; she would kick it away and wake up shrieking. These nightmares stopped completely after Uttera was born.

Uttera has done her M.A. in philosophy and is interested in literature and was for some time a lecturer in college. She is modern in her outlook and supports women's liberation. She has no links with Bengal or Bengali, except for her liking for Sarat Chandra's novel which she has read in Marathi.

Uttera's father, Mr. Balasaheb Huddar had fought in Spanish civil war and was imprisoned there for six months. Although a member of Communist Party of India till 1952, when he lost his card for opposing the railway strike he is not an atheist. Uttera learnt religious slokas from him at the age of eight and later took to worshipping Durga. Uttera's mother also is deeply religious.

Besides her fortnightly "spells", another uncommon trait in Uttera is that she is still unmarried at the age of 34. Mr Huddar told us that a boy had once promised to marry Uttera but had later backed out. Since then she has refused a number of marriage proposals. When asked, Uttera said: "Marriage is no problem to me. If I want to marry anyone, I can always tell my father, who is more of a friend to me, and the marriage can be arranged. But I myself don't feel the need for marriage."

This, then, is the "story" of Uttera. It has triggered off a lively controversy between parapsychologists, who say that it is a case of rebirth where Uttera is reliving her previous birth, and psychiatrists who maintain that Uttera is a schizophrenic and can be cured with modern treatment.

Dr. N.K. Sinha, a homoeopathy and parapsychologist of Indore, who has studied the case, went to Bengal and verified the place mentioned by Sharda and confirmed her genealogy. A similar investigative tour was undertaken by Prof. P. Pal, a retired head of the philosophy department of Chinsura university who is now working in the field of parapsychology in collaboration with an American, Dr. Stevenson. But neither Dr. Sinha nor Prof. Pal took Uttera to Bengal with them.

Prof. Pal believes that Sharda must have died 116 years ago. With Uttera being 34 now, this leaves a gap of 82 years between the two "lives", Prof. Pal also rules out Uttera's being possessed by an "evil spirit." As Sharda, Uttera believes that her husband and 'masi' are alive, and any mention of their being dead makes her weep. Prof. Pal contends that a "spirit" does not mourn the death of a relative nor can it worship a goddess as Uttera does in the role of Sharda. With the existence of a "spirit" ruled out, the only explanation left is that of a rebirth, according to him.

On the other hand, Dr. C.A. Tiwari, a psychiatrist at the Nagpur government mental hospital, who has examined Uttera, believes that she must have undergone traumatic experiences, perhaps sexual, from which she wants to escape, and the role of Sharda provides that escape. Medically this is known as dissociation - from the present to a different personality. The role of Sharda brings order to her disordered life and acts as a safety valve. If she could not have escaped into the role of Sharda she would have had a nervous breakdown.

Dr. Tiwari says that he would advise treating Uttera's dissociation so that she does not have to resort to the Sharda role. The treatment would help evoke pleasant memories along with those of her unpleasant experiences through hypnosis or even conscious association. Dr. Y.W. Kelkar, superintendent of the mental hospital, concurs: "It is a case of schizophrenia and can definitely be cured within the means available in psychiatry."

And what does Uttera think of the whole thing? "I want to get rid of her (Sharda)," she said. "It has disturbed my normal life, constricted my movements and interfered with my work. That is why I had to give up my lecturer's job. Moreover, when I become Sharda, my overworked mother has to shoulder an additional burden and my father is also unduly worried."

Uttera wants to go to the Pondichery ashram to get rid of Sharda and acquire peace of mind.

THE HAUNTED MEADOW

A Strange feeling ran through me at this unusual and unexpected sight. Was I afraid, not exactly, may be the very beginning of it. Uncle's first lecture was reiterating itself at that very moment, every word fresh, clear and distinct as it had been a fortnight back. Were these apparitions or realities that I saw so clearly on that full moon night.

Holidays had an additional charm for me, not because I was funk of school or loved skulking. That was the time when I was the sole boss of myself. I could carry out the behests of the inner-self and satisfy the instincts of selfassertion and leadership. As a reward of good work in school parental indulgence allowed me a free expression of these natural instincts, which never took an objectionable turn.

Uncle invite us to spend our summer holidays in the hills. It was an additional charm. The journey was long and boring, whenever the train stopped it was not our destination, we were told. After twenty-four hours' restlessness we came to the end of our train journey. The next part, Dehradun to Mussoorie, was delightful journey taken in two stages, first part in tontgas and from Rajpura in 'dandies' and on horse-back right up to our house in Mussoorie. Time simply flew, we could hardly believe that we had been on the move for about eight hours.

"Hills are entirely different from your plains" remarked uncle. The difference was obvious, I did not see the need for this introduction. "Don't be frightened of anything, there are no wild animals here. Those terrible looking black-faced monkeys are most innocent and harmless. There are no dangerous people here. The dirty-looking 'perharis' are very honest and helpful. Have a good time, go anywhere and at any hour of the day or night and you are safe. Beware of two things only, do not step into a water fall and do not run down a trackless valley". It was fine encouragement uncle would back our adventures I was sure so we could have a real good time.

At some distance from our house we found a lovely huge lawn, as big as two football fields put together. It was a mutual discovery of all four of us, myself, my sister and two cousins. Although it was only about 40 yards from the main road, there was a valley separating us from this table-land covered with thick grass. It had the appearance of a freshly mowed lawn. It was a very pretty shade of green. The like of which I had never seen before in the plains. At first we took it for an artificially leveled ground intended for some sort of European game in the hills. We acted a contingent of Himalayan explorer and discovered a lovely broad foot-path leading to it some two furlongs away from the main road. This 'walk' was not very well maintained like the other roads but good enough for hiking we went up to it and hovered round the out skirts as we were not sure whether we could play on the lawn.

We made a detailed survey of the whole place during the afternoon. The lawn was neatly devoid of strewn stones and no trees on it. Obviously it was maintained by some club, the turf felt like a huge Persian Carpet. Observing from close quarters we noticed the green was not all of the same shade. There were ever so many shades of green most artistically blended. Actually one could sit there and admire it for hours on end. For the first time we had seen such superb natural beauty, in fact we were in love with that spot. There was a well marked boundary all round. Outside the boundary there were plenty of stones and boulders, with a couple of groves of stately hill trees. There were lovely picnic spots and enough room to lay hide and seek or other little games. We spent a couple of hours as we reckoned, during that time we saw no 'Mali' or 'Chaukidar' to frighten us away. Nearby there was a small spring with lovely cool and refreshing water, which gently and noiselessly flowed down the deep valley at some distance. It was not a dangerous waterfall of which uncle had warned us.

With the declining sun our first day's adventure was over and we returned home beaming with joy. The next problem for investigation was who used it, and when did they use it, besides was there any one keeping watch over there? This was undertaken with the object of finding out the safest hours for us to make full use of this charming spot.

I was the second eldest in the group and the only boy, so spying business was allotted to me. I could go out at any time and make the necessary observations. It took me only ten minutes to get to the nearest observation spot. From there the lawn was about 40 to 50 yards straight crow-flight, besides the elevation of my observation post and the slope of the meadow gave me a very clear view of the whole place. On pretext of an early morning walk I made regular observation from 6 O'clock to 8 O' clock in the morning, and returned punctually at 8.30 a.m. for breakfast. The nearby Church clock chimes were a great aid to my punctually. The morning observations did not solve our problem. During a whole week's observation I saw no one use it during those hours, besides no 'Mali' or 'Chaukidar' popped in. our regular picnics between breakfast and lunch were absolutely uninterrupted. Besides, between lunch and afternoon tea we were the sole occupants of the place. It was surprisingly strange that no casual visitors ever came there sight-seeing, in spite of its natural charms. There were no evening visitors as well. All keen and vigilant and watch from sun-rise to sun-set failed to solve the mystery.

Now we racked our brains and got a real brain wave, it was surely an open air dance-lawn. We thought we had made a great hit. I could safely be out till 10 p.m., people would start coming in before that if our guess was right. I would have some report to submit regarding this important missing and a top ranking secret of us, kids. Nearly a whole week was spent without any success. "Never give in" was the motto I had learnt in school and was determined to put it to practice.

At last came the eventful night the last day of the week and a full moon night. The cool silvery rays added charm and romance to the whole scene. That night I made up my mind to stick on till after 11 p.m. Soon after 10 p.m. I saw a few shadows moving over the meadow. For some time I only saw the moving shadows without the figures of those who cast the shadows. I had a creepy feeling running through me at this strange scene. I was not sure whether to walk home immediately or to wait and see a few more acts to this novel drama. There was one more important consideration which made me stick to my post.

Each day's successful adventure made us more and more bold. All our games were being played on the meadow itself. During that Saturday afternoon we build a few play houses with the ample supply of well hewn stones lying on the outskirts. Now came the final and the most interesting part, we had not only used the meadow but utilized it for purpose most interesting to us.

Soon after the shadows came strange figures in a considerable number. They apparently searched the meadow for something. Soon they came to the corner we had monopolized, and the stones comprising our play houses started flying out and falling a yard or two beyond the boundary. It was an astonishing sight, the stones as if by magic, rose in the air and flew in the desires direction. I thanked my stars for not being too near the spot. The stones went flying like bits of paper. The fierce and angry group of figures stood at the spot till it was rid of every stone and pebble. Soon after this followed a large number of figures male and female, fairly well discernible in the clear silvery light of the full moon. They were all of unusual stature, yet some of them seemed head over shoulder taller than the others. The taller figures were dressed differently than the shorter figures. It looked more like a ghost show, and I felt it was not safe to linger on. At this thought I got up ready to go back, but not without the last lingering look. I saw them moving about in mighty haste, very busy with something invisible. This last look sent through me and I rushed on the shorter foot-path which was densely shaded by large trees. Being in the shade I could not be seen so I stole another glance and to my horror I saw huge skeletons moving about. Then I rushed on without looking back and within a few minutes I was safe in my bed in the front verandah, pretending to snore while wide awake just to avoid any questions regarding my late outing.

Next morning I put some pointed questions to uncle regarding the beautiful meadow. He said it was haunted meadow and there were many stories about it. Of course one thing was very obvious, no one had ever been able to build anything there. Every construction started on it had its walls pulled down and the building material thrown out of the meadow. This statement corresponded with my experience.

GHOSTS AND THE TOWER OF LONDON

Some 900 years ago William of Normandy successfully invaded and occupied England. One of his first acts was to start the building of the grim fortress on a site on the east of the city.

Along one side flowed the Thames; on two other flanks were grey crumbling town walls which constructed the relic of an earlier set of invaders, the Romans.

The Tower is not a museum; it is a palace, a military strong point a repository the Crown jewels are kept there and, in theory at least, a State prison.

Today excavations by archaeologists are going on prior to the building of a new Jewel House, and these diggings have thrown further light on William the Conqueror's plans for dominating his newly-gained capital.

Some people who have made a study of the Tower claim it is the most haunted place on earth. There is certainly ample and rich material out of which ghost stories can be fashioned.

Here, in buildings which serve as a vivid and dramatic container in stone of English history going back to 1067, several persons who committed treason or incurred the displeasure of the monarch, were beheaded or in other ways put to death. Here, too some of the most famous state prisoners suffered anxious days and nights in their cells.

Jail for spies

As recently as the first World War, after some years of peace, the Tower suddenly became jail to which spies were sent and shot.

In 1964, with admission charges bringing in a revenue of lb100,000 visitors, as they are conducted through ancient apartments and shown deep dungeons, can speculate to their hearts content on supernatural happenings.

Inevitably they will hear the story of the Tower's most famous "ghost"-Anne Boleyn, (1507-36) one of the wives of Henry VIII who lost her head on Tower Green, 428 years ago.

Continuing generations of warders swear they have seen the spectre of Anne at various times. Many say that she make an appearance frequently. Here is one story of her appearance on the eve of an execution which occurred 50 years ago.

It was 1914 and a group of German espionage agents were in the Tower, waiting to go before a firing squad. An Army sergeant in charge of the guard saw a women in a rustling silk dress of a kind worn in a dim and distant past approach his men. And she came closer the air chilled and an even colder breeze sprung up.

The sergent and his solders gaped and they rubbed their eyes in utter disbelief as the woman swept by them to walk through a wall six feet thick.

Other stories

Other stories of Anne's visits include one by a soldier on duty in the middle of the 19th century. Midnight struck and he suddenly saw the figure of a woman dressed in white come gliding towards him from Tower Green.

He challenged and received no reply. Frightened he lunged forward with his bayonet but the weapon met nothing more solid than air.

He fainted. Later he was accused of being drunk, but other sentries gave independent testimony that they too had seen the apparition. The charge was dropped.

Supreme of the tales circulating about the unhappy Anne was told by a captain of the guard many years ago. Accompanied by an escorting soldier he was on his rounds one night when he saw a light in the tower chapel.

The place should have been in darkness. The captain clambered up to one of the high windows and balancing himself rather precariously on ledge gazed in. What he saw nearly caused him to lose his balance. The chapel was illumined by a ghastly blue white light which had no apparent source and coming down the centre aisle was a procession of men and women in the costumes worn in the days of King Henry VIII.

At the head of the procession, richly costumed, was a woman whose face seemed strangely familiar. The captain recalled that only a few days earlier he had been gazing at a portrait in oils of poor Anne.

Eerie Light

As he watched the eerie light faded and the blackness of the night engulfed the ghostly company.

Some accepted the captain's story; others scoffed, but one man whole accepts it whole heartedly in Guardsman Johns. Seven years ago he was on a sentry duty at the Salty Tower.

Something clattered on to the roof of his sentry box. He looked up and 40 feet above him saw what he described as 'a shapeless white ghost.'

He yelled and the guard commander and other on duty came running out. They searched and found nothing.

It was on Feb. 12, 1954 that another Tower victim ended her days with the executiones axe severing her head. She was Lady Jane Seymour, a helpless victim of the intrigues of those desperate times.

THE GHOST THAT KICKED

Granny knew all about the 'nasty kick' incident, but she kept me blissfully ignorant of them. Naturally I could not see eye to eye why she insisted on my taking shorter road in preference to the lovely road through the extension colony. For me both were equally safe, only one took a few minutes more than the other to take me to my destination, and perhaps to a misleading square.

The decision was momentous, but not safe when I turned away from the directed short road to uncle Elwin's place. Being my first visit to him in his new quarters, granny gave me detailed instructions with sketches and important signboards along the road. Besides I had positive instructions not to take the broad road through the extension colony. The misleading square at the end of the road was emphasized the most, but the ghastly experience linked with the square was carefully withheld. She had treated me like a child of five, carefully avoiding the decade I had added on to it.

The last train steamed out only about ten minutes back, yet there was hardly a soul to be seen in that huge space in front of the station. It used to be full of coolies, vehicles of all kinds, as well as many stray passengers. As I strolled out of the railway premises and stood at the bifurcation wondering which road to take, a coolie rushing home remarked that there would no train for about four hours, and no likelihood of finding a conveyance there for some time. I was not worried about a lift. I could easily carry the light suitcase up to uncle's place. The full moon shining in a cloudless sky gave a silvery touch to those marble white blocks neatly standing one after the other. Sure enough, I was not going to miss the lovely moon light view of the extension colony. Little did I know that I was heading for a blood curdling experience, if not a nasty kick.

Granny's prophecy came true, I missed the first turning on the right, walked straight on admiring the blocks till I reached the contusing square. I got the least expected shock, it was 10.30 p.m. by my time. Undoubtedly I had missed the way else I should have reached home some 20 minutes back. If I had taken the first narrow street on my right, I walked along the left of the broad road and no street opened on that side. I was anxious to get home before 11 p.m., otherwise a search party of servants would be looking for me all over the place. I did not want to create a scene. As luck would have it, an empty tonga came towards me. I engaged it and directed the man as best as I could, with fragments of granny's instructions still fresh in my mind. He seemed to know the place inside out, so I let him take the shortest route.

He stopped at the next crossing and looked for some thing in the way. I grumbled at him for wasting time, he came out with a shocking confession, he had missed the way so he returned to the same square. That was the most likely place to meet somebody who could direct him to my place.

After a few seconds he got a brain wave, jumped out of the tonga and ran to the first block on the right, just opposite to where we stood. There was hardly ten yards frontage separating it from road. There were no lights in the ground floor as well as in the first floor. Besides there was not a soul to be seen in the compound. I wondered from whom was he going to enquire. He ran up to the staircase leading to the first floor, stopped there for a minute to confirm his first observation and returned with a broad idiotic smile. "Sahib" he said " while I looked for a candle under the hay I saw a hazy figure moving in the verandah of the first floor." This was a quite possible. The adjoining white block reflected enough of the moon light to make things dimply visible. "So I went up to the staircase and lieard a sahib walking there, up and down with measured steps, like a sergeant Sahib on duty. May be he is waiting for the 'call boy'. Let us get the directions before he goes on duty. I wonder if he knows enough Hindustani to explain it to me, you ask him in English and he will tell you the easiest way to get to your place."

It was not a bad idea, a providential relief I thought, so we both walked up to the staircase landing. A strong urge from within stopped me from going up. I distinctly heard the heavy measured steps with which he paced the verandah. The gentleman was not visible from where we stood, so I moved a couple of steps back till I could see the shadowy figure in his non-stop up and down march. I stood in bright moon light and any one in the verandah could easily see me. I thought that would attract his attention for my enquire. I stood there for some time but he took no note of me. Then I advised the tongawala pretty loudly to go up and tell the sahib that I wanted to speak to him. I thought that would be a better way of drawing his attention but there was no luck, he remained as indifferent as ever. As he walked very close to the wall, I could only see him from the shoulders to the knees. The dark heavy shadow from the blocked arches of the verandah reached up to his shoulders, this made it impossible for me to see his head.

As I failed to draw his attention for the pressing enquiry I sent the tongaman up to him, of course with the instructions to remain in the staircase. He stood there with his bust showing up, and said. "Hazur. The sahib down below wants to speak to you." Saying this he waited for the reply. While he was speaking, the gentleman happened to be at the other end of the verandah opposite to the staircase. He walked straight on towards the tongawala without a word. While the gentleman had walked half way through the verandah, this fellow ran down terribly scared and ran up to me quite out of breath. "The Sahib up there is walking without a head." He stammered. This made my hair stand on edge, for I too had not been able to locate his head. I masked my feeling and explained in a pretended calm voice, that it was the heavy shadow of the blocked arches which made the head well high invisible in that semi dark verandah. Frightened out of his wits, he half accepted my explanation and was ready to go up again, if accompanied him to the staircase, just for moral support, I agreed to it. This time he just popped his head above the verandah level.

He stared at the approaching figure for a while, and the beckoned me to come up and stand by him. I held my breath when I saw the headless from coming towards us. The tongawala repeated his request when the figure was about 10 feet from him. He was afraid to look at the form so he fixed his eyes on me to make sure that I did not slip down on tip toes. I stood like a statue grapping at the figure and thinking of granny and the misleading square. We seemed glued to the place awaiting the inevitable kick. He walked up to the staircase landing without a word and kicked the tongawala straight in the face. He dropped on the rung with hands out-stretched to ward off the kick. It caught him straight on the left palm and left a red mark which I later examined under the tonga light. His hands dropped and he almost reeled into my arms.

This incident gave me a very close view of the figure. Unmistakably, it was a headless form. I walked back to the tonga supporting the fellow, without exchanging a word or a look for it had given me the shock of my life. We sat there too funked to speak, our hearts thumped keeping time with his measured steps

As luck would have it, the 'call boy' turned up a few seconds after we got in the tonga. He got a free lift for showing us the way. He told us all about the headless sahib who parades from 10.30 p.m. till midnight, and mentioned about a dozen names of the people who had been kicked by this ghost. He was surprised at our ignorance, for it was a well-known incident. Now it dawned on me, why granny insisted on my avoiding that way.

PART–IV

Epilogue

EPILOGUE

In the Geeta, Chapter II, Verse 20, Lord Krishna says

Meaning : The Atma is never born in any period of time, nor ever dies. Nor it will be ever procreated. It is unborn, everlasting, eternal. It never ceases to exist even if the body is destroyed.

Those who have been bred up in Hindu traditions can have no two opinions regarding this matter. It is a tenet with them that the soul does not die with the body. The soul adopts a new body, or, at least prepares to do so. The same thing is made still clearer in Verse 22:

Meaning : Just as man gives up old clothes and puts on new ones, so the soul relinquishes the old body and takes on a new one.

Reincarnation and transmigration of the soul is such an eternal truth that one day the world will have to accept it - such is the overwhelming evidence of instances in support of the principle.

But the above verse does not mean that the soul adopts a new body immediately after leaving the old one. The intervening period may be a month or two, a year or two, even, as long as a century or two. On the contrary, some souls take on a new body immediately after leaving the old one. On the other hand, some souls have to pass years in suspense. This interval the soul passes the form of a spirit.

An important question concerning this is : Every day, about 30,000 people leave this world. Why do all of them not become spirits? The reason is that every soul gets a span of spiritual life, depending upon his deeds and misdeeds of his previous lives. And the principle of Karma (Action and retribution) is not as simple as 'Two and two make four.' Had it been as simple as that, everybody could calculate and find out the answer to the query as to how long he would have to pass in the form of a spirit. Chess players know that every cell is under the influence of several chessmen : knight, queen, pawns etc. How much influence each of the chessmen is exerting even accomplished players cannot tell with exactitude. If the matter were subject to mathematical calculations there would be no such thing as victory and defeat in the game of chess.

Astrologers too base their calculations on the position of planets vis-a-vis the house they occupy. And they spend all their mental faculties in the matter. Even then their conclusions are very often wrong. There will be hardly a single astrologer all of whose predictions come out to be true.

If we accede the existence of ghost-life, the next question is, 'What kind of life is it?' Do they have pleasure and pain as we do? Do they ever feel hungry or thirsty as we do? Do they have desires and ambitions like us? These questions cannot be answered unequivocally.

But this much is certain: An inhabitant of that world is not free from desires. It is clear from the evidence recorded in the preceding pages that some of the spirits have saved the lives of the ones they loved. Also, a few of them have fulfilled their promises. On the contrary, some of them have instigated, and even abetted, human beings to commit crimes of a heinous character. Sometimes they have blackmailed them, and even put them to death.

An obvious conclusion follows that when a person leaves this world he does not relinquish all his desires and wishes. He carries some of them with himself. Possibly he leaves the unimportant ones here and carries the more momentous ones with himself. And such desires and ambitions he fulfills either in the ghost-life, or the next incarnation.

This much is without doubt, that our time and space limitations do not bind them. The letter of Dr. Rajindra Prasad is enough to testify that our three-dimensional world does not delimit them. And now about our time. The limits of that too do not seem to bind them. Many instances given in this book indicate that the spirit can cross thousands of kilometers in seconds.

But even these things do not conclusively prove that there are absolutely no limitations of time and space upon the spirits. All that we have said above is that 'The limitations of our time and space do not bind them.' It is not unlikely that they have their own scales of Time and Space. We know that one day of Braham is equivalent to 1000 chaturyugs, and one chaturyug consists of 1200 years. Thus,

1 day of Brahma = 1000 x 1200 x 365 days
= about 450000000 days

Now, time, length and weight are measured in the same scale in the universe of Brahma. So, one pice in the universe of Brahma is equivalent to 450 millions of our pice and the metre of that universe is equivalent to 450 millions of metres in our scale.

There is an episode in the Puranas : A certain man asked Brahma, 'You have immeasurable wealth in your coffers. Can't you give me one pice therefrom. He thought he would be able to bamboozle Brahma by playing upon words, as a pice for Brahma would mean crores of rupees for the man. But Brahma was equal to the occasion. He said to the man, 'Wait a minute.'

So, the man had to wait for crores of years.

Of the episodes of the Yog Vashishtha, the longest and the most talked is perhaps that of Leela. We are giving it here in brief. Once a very able king Padm reigned over the earth. His devoted wife was Leela, a deeply religious lady. She asked Goddess Saraswati, of a boon 'If my husband dies before me, his soul should remain in my room.' Saraswati agreed, and said, 'I will come to you whenever you invoke me.'

When time came, king padm kicked the bucket. Leela was extremely grieved. And immediately she received a message by telepathy: 'Grieve no more. The soul of your husband is still in your room.' Leela preserved the corpse of her husband and invoked Goddess Saraswati. When the latter manifested herself, Leela said to her, 'Where is my Lord at this moment. Saraswati replied, 'He is still in your own room, but in a universe different from yours.' That universe is more subtle than this and is totally assimilated therein.

Saraswati told Leela that there is a system of universes, one contain in the other, and so on. And this order goes on till infinity. Or dinarily the inhabitants of one universe are no existent for an other universe. But, by penance and devotion, one can acquire the capability to enter into another universe and witness the activities going on therein.

Leela was very anxious to see her husband in his new environments. Then Saraswati and Leela entered the universe in which her husband was living in his new life. Hardly a few minutes had lapsed since Padm entered the new world, but according to the scale of his new universe, he had already reigned over it for full 16 years, and, for years he had been the head of a vast empire. His name was now Vidurath. Leela was flabbergasted at the sight. She could not understand how so many years could have elapsed during the short span of a few minutes. Nor could she make any head and tail of the information that a vast empire was accommodated in so small room as hers.

Saraswati told Leela that the two universes had entirely different scales of measurement. One moment of one universe could incorporate several years of another universe. Sometimes lying on bed one can peruse over events that have taken years to happen. There have been cases when a person taking a bath in a river has, in a single dive witnessed all the happenings of his entire life.

Saraswati said to Leela, 'If you do not believe all this, I will show you something equally miraculous. Before coming into your life in the form of -Padm, your husband was a Brahman of the name Vashishtha. He used to live in a hutment. Not even a week has elapsed since he died, and his kinsmen are still bemoaning his death. Leela was anxious to see the hutment.

Saraswati took her to the hutment where Vashistha used to live with his wife Arundhati.

Saraswati told Leela that one day Vashishtha saw a procession of king going on with all his pageantry. Vashishtha aspired to go in a similar procession some day. The same day half the world. Arundhati had asked for a boon that she should not be separated from her husband even after his death. So, the soul of Vashishtha too was confined to the room. Arundhati performed Sati (burnt herself on the pyre of her husband).

Saraswati told Leela that Vashishtha became Padm and Arundhati entered the world in the form of Leela in the third life. Now, the two entered the universe in which Vidurath was reigning. And, to their amazement they found that Vidurath, whom they had left as a boy of 16, had grown up into an old man of 70. Leela and Saraswati appeared before Vidurath. After hearing the entire story, Vidurath said he would like to become Padm again.

Some days later, a battle raged in which Vidurath was killed. His soul again entered the body of Padm. Padm was rejuvenate and he had another spell of several years of kingdom.

It is here that the brain begins to reel and almost ceases to function. After the life of Vashishtha, the entire life of Padm was finished within a week, and after the death of Padm, a period of years passed almost in the twinkling of an eye.

This much about element of time. Now, let us come to Space. In the hutment of Vashishtha was accommodated an entire universe and the palace of Padm occupied a very small part thereof. And a tiny portion of a room of that palace could encompass the entire kingdom of Vidurath. What a wonder!

The body of ghosts is not physical. It is ethereal. We have seen that the entry of a ghost did not break even a single wire of a thin gauze. However thin the gauze may be, the body of a spirit can pass through it. And the gauze will be none the worse for it. Not only that. From the body of a spirit emanate beams of light (or, whatever be the substance of which they are made) which even our ordinary camera cannot catch.

Our scriptures tell us that there are seven. Loks (universe) in our cosmos:

I. Bhoo Lok (Earth) 2. Bhuvah Lok 3. Swah Lok 4. Mah Lok 5. Jan Lok 6. Tap Lok 7. Satya Lok (True Lok, The final Summum. Bonum).

The body of only our Bhoo Lok (Earth) is physical. The body of the inhabitants of all the other universes is ethereal.

Our scientists have established the fact that no other planet contains air or water. Even if there is a semblance of these elements, it is so little that it cannot sustain human life. But why should the scientists suppose that the only form of life that can exist, is the physical form? Why should they not believe that life can exist on other planets which is of some form other than physical? Why should we take it for granted that no kind of life can exist without air and water? Is it not equally feasible to imagine the existence of a kind of life which does not require air and water for its sustenance?

And the planets are only nine in number. What is the status of our entire solar system in the cosmos? The universe contains millions of solar system each containing nobody knows how many planets. It would be far too egoistic a view to assert that, out of billions of planets, satellites, stars and nebulae, God endowed life to just one of them - our own earth! It would be nothing short of vain glory and false pride!

Science is yet to find out many of the secrets of nature!

We have hinted at some characters of ghost life in the previous pages. Perhaps they know more of past and future events than we. But it would be fallacious to suppose that they are omniscient. Many of their prophesies have turned out to be false. Also, we shall have to concede that some spirits are good by their nature; other are bad like human beings. Some turn out to be true; others are liars. Some of them, as seekers of Virtue, improve in every life, and pass on to the next higher universe, and in the end, reach the Eternal Truth! Others, who commit evil deeds, are demoted to the next lower plane, and sometimes have to descend to the earth once again, after ascending a few steps higher. We are basing our conjecture on observed facts. A good deal of research is required in this direction. Rigorous proof is far from us like the child's horizon.

□□

A WORD ABOUT THE AUTHOR

Born on the 11th of April, 1908, at Moradabad, Dr. Brij Mohan put in 34 years of service at the Banaras Hindu University, firstly as a Lecturer, then as a Reader and in the end as Professor and Head of the Department of Maths. He was a Ph.D. from the Liverpool University of England. For eight years (1960-68), he served as the Principal of the Central Hindu College of the Banaras Hindu University. In between, he served at the Humboldt State College (now a University) of California (U.S.A.) as a visiting Professor for one year.

Though he was a Professor of Mathematics, Dr. Brij Mohan had an intense love for Hindi bordering on a passion. He wrote 46 books-10 in English and 36 in Hindi and some of his renowned books are—

1. English-Hindi Dictionary	:	Meenakshi Prakashan, Meerut
2. Hindi-English Dictionary	:	Meenakshi Prakashan, Meerut
3. History of Mathematics in Hindi	:	Hindi Samiti, Govt. of U.P.
4. Mathematical Dictionary (English-Hindi)	:	Chaukhambha Sanskrit Series, Banaras
5. Manak Hindi (Standard Hindi)	:	Macmillan, New Delhi and also Vanee Prakashan, New Delhi
6. Shabd Charcha (Discussions on Synonyms)	:	Raj Kamal Prakashan, New Delhi
7. Nagri Lipi–Roop Aur Sudhar (Nagri Script–Form & Reforms)	:	Teen Murti Publications, New Delhi
8. Arth Vigyan–Hindi Semantics	:	Raj Kamal Prakashan, New Delhi
9. Bindi Yukt Akshar	:	Shabd Lok Prakashan, Varanasi
10. Visheshan Prayog (Usage of Adjectives)	:	Raj Kamal Prakashan and also Vanee Prakashan, New Delhi
11. Bhasha Aur Vyavhar	:	Vanee Prakashan, New Delhi

12. Hindi Angrezee Kahawat Kosh : Vanee Prakashan, New Delhi

These books have been highly talked of in the Hindi World. Some of his books which are in course of publication are—

(A) Urdu-Hindi Dictionary
(B) Muhavra Kosh (Dictionary of Hindi Idioms)
(C) Phonetics
(D) History of Mathematics (in English)
(E) Chinh Vigyan (Semiology)

Throughout his career, Dr. Brij Mohan had been of the view that all scientific and technical subjects should be taught through the medium of one's mother tongue. For this purpose, a great number of books have to be written on these subjects in Indian Languages. Also, if necessary, some books written in foreign languages should be translated into Hindi and other Indian Languages. With this end in view, Dr. Brij Mohan began writing books on such subjects in Hindi. He also translated Hardy's Pure Maths into Hindi, named as Shudh Ganit Ki Pathcharya. It was published in 1970 and has been highly talked of in the Hindi and Mathematical Worlds.

So far Hindi has been lacking in scientific terminology. The Government of India established a Scientific Terminology Commission for the preparation of technical terminologies in subjects like Physics, Chemistry, Mathematics etc. Dr. Brij Mohan served as a Member of the Mathematics Committee of the said Commission for about 15 years and his contributions in the field were highly appreciated. The Government of India has adopted hundreds of the Mathematical terms given in his Mathematical Dictionary.

The Hindi Language has been lacking in accurate scientific expressions. Besides, the Nagri Alphabet is not as suitable for printing and typewriting as the roman alphabet. With a view to removing these defects, Dr. Brij Mohan began writing actively on related topics in Hindi. He has contributed 22 articles on the Hindi Language and 33 on the Nagri Script.

In recognition of the services he was honoured on a number of occasions. In 1954, he was awarded by the Hindi Samiti, Government of Uttar Pradesh for his book "Ganitiya Kosh" (Mathematical Dictionary). In 1969, he was awarded again, by the Hindi Samiti,

Uttar Pradesh Government for his book "Nagri Lipi–Roop Aur Sudhar."

In 1989, he was given the Prime Minister's Award for production and propagation of scientific and technological literature in Hindi called the Atma Ram Puraskar which comprised of a cash prize of Rs. 10,000/- with a citation and a shawl.

Dr. Brij Mohan passed away to his heavenly abode on 31.08.1990.

Contact address :
C/o Sh. Krishna Mohan,
729, Sector-8B,
Chandigarh–160 008

OTHER WORKS/ACHIEVEMENTS OF THE AUTHOR

1. ACADEMIC QUALIFICATIONS

a) 1923 : S.L.C. Class-I, Distinction in Mathematics.
b) 1925 : Intermediate Class-I, Distinction in Mathematics and Logic, Ist in the Province.
c) 1927 : B.A. Class-I, IInd in Province, First in Province in Mathematics; Won the Cox. Medal.
d) 1929 : M.A. Class-I, Ist in Agra University, Won the Krishna Kumari Gold Medal.
e) 1933 : Ph.D. (Liverpool University, England).

2. PUBLICATIONS

i) 46 books (10 in English, 36 in Hindi).
ii) 22 articles on Hindi, the National Language of India.
iii) 33 articles on Nagri, the National Script of India.
iv) 116 research papers and articles on Advanced Maths., History of Maths., Math Terminology etc.
v) 37 articles on miscellaneous topics.
vi) 2 review articles.

3. 35 YEARS TEACHING EXPERIENCE

i) 1929-30 : Lecturer at D.S. Intermediate College, Aligarh.
ii) 1934-45 : Lecturer at Maths., Banaras Hindu University.
iii) 1945-60 : Reader in Maths., Banaras Hindu University.

iv) 1960-68 : Professor and Head, Department of Maths., Banaras Hindu University.

v) 1962-68 : Principal, Central Hindu College, Banaras Hindu University.

vi) 1966-67 : Visiting Prof. of Maths., Humbolt State College (Now Humbolt State University), Arcata, California, U.S.A.

4. ADDITIONAL REMARKS

a) His research work has been incorporated by the late Prof.E.C.Titchmarsh F.R.S:, in his treatise on "THE THEORY OF THE FOURIER INTEGRAL". Nine of his original papers have been incorporated in the work.

b) His research papers have appeared in leading international journals of Maths.

c) 20 of the pupils who worked with him on Transform Calculus, have been awarded the Ph.D. Degree by the Banaras Hindu University.

5. CONTRIBUTION IN THE FIELD OF HINDI AND NAGRI

(A) (i) At present an ordinary press of Hindi has to keep about 600 kinds of types while English Printing requires only about 150. Dr. Brij Mohan has suggested certain reforms in the Nagri script. If they are accepted, only 167 kinds of types will be required for Hindi printing.

(ii) At present, there are no signs in Nagri for certain sounds of some Indian Languages. His suggestions have accommodated all such signs also.

(B) Dr. Brij Mohan has proposed a modified keyboard for the Hindi typewriter. Its special features are—

(i) It accommodates most of the compound consonants of the Hindi Language.

(ii) The signs of the four arithmetical operations have been provided for.

(iii) Certain special signs have also been accommodated.

(iv) Besides the standard keyboard, there are several specialised keyboards for the English typewriter like the Mathematical Keyboard, the Chemical Keyboard, the Linguistic Keyboard etc. No such keyboards exist for the Hindi typewriter at present. In his reforms, Dr.Brij Mohan has made room for several such keyboards therefor.

6. SPECIAL AWARDS

i) 1954 : Award by the Hindi Samiti, U.P. Government for the book Ganitiya Kosh (Maths. Dictionary).

ii) 1969 : Award by the Hindi Samiti, U.P. Government for the book, "Nagri Lipi-Roop aur Sudhar".

iii) 1979 : Award for prolonged service of Hindi by the Hindi Sansthan, U.P. Government–A cash prize of Rs. 15,000/- with a citation on a copper plaque and a silk scarf.

iv) 1983 : Award for "Service of Science through the medium of Hindi" by the Vigyan Parishad, Allahabad–copper plaque of Natraj and a citation.

v) 1985 : Award by the Maths. Association of India–a silver plated tray with two cups and a citation.

vi) 1989 : Prime Minister's Award for production and propagation of scientific and technological literature in Hindi–called the Atma Ram Puraskar–a cash prize of Rs. 10,000/- with a citation on a copper plaque and a silk scarf.